the Cimarron Bride

GRETCHEN LEE RIX

Gretchen Lee Rix

The Cimarron Bride
Copyright © 2018 by Gretchen Rix All rights reserved.
First Print Edition: 2018

Published by Rix Cafe Texican
Cover and Formatting: Streetlight Graphics

No part of this book may be reproduced, scanned, or distributed in any printed or electronic form without permission. Please do not participate in or encourage piracy of copyrighted materials in violation of the author's rights. Thank you for respecting the hard work of this author.

This is a work of fiction. Names, characters, places, and incidents either are the product of the author's imagination or are used fictitiously, and any resemblance to locales, events, business establishments, or actual persons—living or dead—is entirely coincidental.

DEDICATION

Thank you, Tam Francis, Rebecca Ballard, Megan Creel, Phil McBride, Wayne Walther, Todd Blomerth, and Roxanne Rix. A better group of critique partners would be hard to find.

Cimarron—a Spanish word meaning wild or untamed.

PROLOGUE
Getting To Know You

At the end of the prologue, it's late April, 1895, and the time of the last big land run in the Oklahoma Territory.

JUNYUR WILDE, THE YOUNGEST OF the illustrious Wilde brothers from the north Texas-Oklahoma border (and the most stunning—curly blond hair, seductive blue eyes, dimpled chin), had one overwhelming bad habit. He fell in love at the drop of a hat. Stetson, derby, straw, or black silk topper. Didn't matter. Same with the women. Pretty, plain, smart, bold, or shy. He fell in love with all of them.

And not the puppy-love variety, either.

Not for him, the dramatically deep sighs, the fervent hypnotic stares, and the writing of exquisitely bad poetry. All down the line, he went straight for the jugular. Wedding proposal on his lips, engagement ring in his pocket, and the most romantically enticing kisses this side of ruin. Everything guaranteed to make even the most vigilant of virgins spread their thighs.

Junyur's life was one long smorgasbord of self-indulgent revelry, carnal gluttony, and lascivious tutorship.

But that came later.

At age six, he made his first recorded conquest, chaste as it was.

His Sunday School teacher, Mrs. Collins, a handsome middle-aged woman of thirty-five, had taken his declarations of love quite seriously. A somber person herself, she let the little boy have his say, then gently turned him down. She kept the diamond-studded ring.

Her husband, less understanding, threw that first of Junyur's many engagement rings out into their corral where the horses trampled it. Then he moved himself and the missus as far from the Wilde brothers as they could get. It was safer that way. Even at age six, Junyur Wilde was immensely persuasive.

At age ten, it was Becky Miller. At fifteen, Maria Gonzales. And at sixteen, when he'd finally bedded a couple of his romantic companions, his older brothers abruptly put an end to it. They cut his allowance to a pittance, took back any and all rings in his possession, and then spread the news far and wide that any girl caught accepting Junyur's wedding proposal would soon find herself shackled to the poorest of the Wilde clan.

If Junyur married before age twenty-two, he lost all claim to the richest ranch in the north of Texas.

None of that stopped Junyur from falling in love, however. One woman right after another. A never-ending procession of women to love, to cherish, and to have his wicked way with. By then he'd realized that with some women he didn't need to dangle the carrot of marriage in front of their noses. His unmitigated and well-honed sexual prowess alone would do the trick.

All that ended when his oldest brother's wife died. Junyur saw first-hand the devastation that resulted, and it changed everything.

A full year passed, and still the children cried inconsolably onto their uncle's shoulder, and their father, Marcus, had let his grief fossilize him into a surly old man. At age twenty-nine.

Junyur finally couldn't stand it anymore. He lived for the passion of a new conquest. Figured deep down, all men were like that. Obviously, Marcus needed to find another wife. And if Marcus was going to hole up in his sprawling ranch house and brood instead, Junyur would be a good brother and do all the preliminary work for him.

He took the bit between his teeth, spied relentlessly on his oldest brother for any breach in his defenses, and came up with a splendid solution so obvious that it shocked even him.

A mail-order bride. From China. Where all the women were beautiful. Where all the women were sweet-natured and subservient. And where all women could be bought, if you could afford it.

Junyur got the idea from the Sears catalog that he'd found on the long kitchen table at his brother's home. You could get anything out of that catalog, if you had the money. Livestock, clothing, food, even a kit to build a house out of. But no wives.

In the back of a penny-dreadful, he found the advertisement he'd been waiting for. And purchased one Miss May Ling.

A living China doll whose photograph stunned him into incoherence and stole his breath away. Whose subsequent flirtatious, bantering missives from across the sea made his heart leap in his chest (and sent him flipping through the dictionary for the first time in his life).

He was scheduled to collect her in Guthrie, Oklahoma, the very week before his birthday, and without his brother Marcus knowing a damned thing about it.

Of *course,* he'd fallen in love.

Junyur Wilde, a whole year closer to passing his twenty-second birthday, and the curse of being cut out of the family business for his romantic entanglements, had fallen in love with the woman meant for his brother. Without ever seeing her in the flesh. Deeply, madly, permanently in love. With a photo and a series of letters.

With a mysterious woman who had since vanished. She hadn't made it as far as Guthrie, Oklahoma. Somewhere between New York and Texas, she'd fallen off the face of the earth.

Then, exactly a year and a day past the time she was supposed to have met him in Guthrie, they finally faced one another.

Junyur Wilde never fell in love again. He no longer needed to.

Miss May Ling held him captive as no other woman could, or ever would. Truly, deeply, madly.

Only one problem. Or maybe two.

May Ling was supposed to have married his brother.

And by the time Junyur caught up to her, May Ling had become a whore. Complete with a whorehouse under her control.

What Junyur needed to figure out, was how to come to terms with the hand life had just dealt him. Could he really be in love with a prostitute? (He figured the brother problem was now moot.)

And what the hell had happened in that missing year?

It wasn't going to matter.

Miss May Ling was about to teach him what true love was. And capture his heart all over again.

1
Junyur's big mistake, leaving May Ling behind

SITTING UNCOMFORTABLY IN THE DRAFTY train compartment, Junyur Wilde watched the soot from the steam engine destroy his camel-colored cowboy hat lying innocently in the opposite seat. The normally hot-blooded twenty-two-year-old just didn't give a damn. He'd buy another hat. And when he could coax the clearly distraught young woman practically in his lap to let go of his arm, he'd leave the seat to stretch his legs. That would relieve the cramp that had finally escalated from irritating to painful.

She hadn't let go, however. Junyur couldn't repress his too-loud sigh. The girl had become a big problem.

He studied Jai Li from under hooded eyes and tried flexing his leg. It didn't help. May Ling—

Damn her, he couldn't even think her name without getting aroused—

May Ling had told him this girl was sixteen years old. But Jai Li acted as if she were much younger, terrified by almost everything that crossed her path. Like his brother's children during thunderstorms.

Clutching at him, screaming uncontrollably when the train hit a bump on the tracks, all of it drawing unwanted attention to the two of them.

Maybe taking Jai Li away from the whorehouse wasn't as good an idea as it had seemed at the time. Junyur didn't think Marcus was going to like this girl. Even at eighteen, she'd be a little too young for Marcus to marry. He'd just crossed into his thirties. Junyur had begun to worry that this flat-chested, black-haired little beauty named Jai Li might only be thirteen or so.

May Ling should have been on this train with him. Not the girl.

But all the arguments, the shouting, the barely concealed contempt they'd shown one another for the few days they'd shared living space in Guthrie had proved May Ling's point beyond any doubt. May Ling did not belong with Marcus Wilde.

Junyur didn't figure his oldest brother would cotton to marrying a whore, anyhow. No matter how beautiful, how desirable, or how damned smart the vixen was.

Junyur was totally surprised to realize that *he* would. Marry her. If the chance arose.

May Ling would have none of him right now, however. Junyur had at last realized nothing he could say or do would make her give up the whorehouse she'd ended up running in Guthrie, Oklahoma. Her one concession was the girl, Jai Li. She'd persuaded Junyur that the girl was still virginal, and that having her stay in May Ling's establishment would prove detrimental in the long run.

Together they concocted the plan to pass Jai Li off as the mail-order bride Junyur had purchased for Marcus. The bride was supposed to be May Ling. But May Ling the whore could not, would not ever be Mrs. Marcus Wilde. She'd coerced Junyur into thinking that Jai Li would make a fine wife.

Right now, he didn't believe a word of it.

All he wanted was to deposit this crybaby somewhere safe and go back into central Oklahoma so he wouldn't miss the great land race. It was his dream. His only chance at independence, and he was going to take it. Even if he had to leave Jai Li with the authorities at the next train station. He'd been fighting himself all morning about what to do with the girl. Texas was really too far away. He'd miss the land race if he took her all the way to the ranch.

Junyur shrugged the girl's head off his chest, suddenly ashamed of himself. May Ling trusted him to protect her ward. And he knew Jai Li absolutely trusted his honorable intent. Glancing down at her uncovered head, the young man thought of the kitten of his niece's that loved to cuddle in his lap. He barely caught himself in time He'd come this close to petting Jai Li's hair.

She might make a good wife for Marcus at that. He needed someone other than his children to care for. Their other brother Timothy would soon move out on his own. Junyur planned to be long gone sometime in the next few weeks. When the last great land race started, he would be on the front lines. A ranch of his own, far away from Texas (and the reach of his oldest brother), that was Junyur's plan. His dream.

He let Jai Li slip a little more down his chest while trying to ease the pain in his legs. May Ling had been right about him. He wouldn't just leave this girl to the mercies of the next station master, or the local sheriff. He'd see her safely to Marcus on the Texas-Oklahoma border then make his way back to one of the towns housing the race participants. There was just enough time. Maybe.

As long as nothing else happened to throw them off schedule.

Junyur fell asleep to the rocking of the steam train traveling over the Oklahoma prairie, May Ling heavy on his mind instead of the girl resting in his arms.

Nothing about his first face-to-face meeting with May Ling had gone well. Starting with his disparaging comments about the name of her thriving business: Miss Adelaide's Club For Discerning Men. He knew a whorehouse when he saw one. Told her to call a whorehouse a whorehouse.

Standing toe-to-toe with him, the young Chinese beauty had informed him point blank that she *managed* this establishment. In his book, that made her a whore, whether she bedded down by the hour or not.

Pity that she had such a beautiful face. And an unexpectedly voluptuous body. And that he'd been in love with her for the whole of the last year.

Junyur had groaned softly, mightily embarrassed that May Ling understood his distress. He couldn't fool himself. He loved her. Couldn't fool her, either. Despite May Ling's circumstances, he wanted her more than anything. Except for the Oklahoma land race.

He should never have agreed to that meeting.

Their second fight began when he asked for his money back.

An agitated May Ling had stomped her way through the exotically decorated sitting room of her whorehouse, tossing silk-embroidered pillows to the floor, overturning delicate flower vases, and even throwing a teacup against a pastel-painted wall. When she finally picked up a hand fan from a collection on the table, she caught Junyur unprepared. Before he could protect himself, she'd smacked him in the face with it twice.

He caught her ascending hand on the third strike. Unwanted lust spread in his loins at her aggression. *His* subconscious took the violence as foreplay, but one clear look at May Ling's distraught face corrected that notion. Still, Junyur twisted May Ling's arm behind her back, drew her close, and deliberately bent to taste her desperately tight lips.

The pistol she pressed against his belly made him disengage.

He backed away with a big smirk of satisfaction on his face. May Ling tasted of honey. She kept the pistol trained on him.

"Not whore," she said.

Junyur shrugged. *Whatever.* "I can't take you home with me," he told her. "Marcus expects a wife, not a working gal."

May Ling shrugged. *Who gives a damn* clear in her mocking eyes. Junyur grew incensed.

"I still want our money back."

"No money," she replied. Then when he took a step toward her, she added, "All invested."

Junyur responded with a sigh of resignation. She probably really had used what was left of his money fixing up this place. He wasn't going to let her think she'd gotten the better of him, though.

As he began to demand the money one more time, she stopped him with the flick of that damned fan. If he saw that fan in her dainty hands ever again, he'd snatch and shred it right before her exotic eyes. She misunderstood his vexation.

"You want understand?" she asked, ignoring his rage, her cool tone of voice somehow soothing his indignation and anger.

She didn't wait for his answer, but began to talk softly, facing away from him. Staring at the wall she'd disfigured with the thrown teacup. After a moment, she walked past him to sit in her chair.

"Taken from dock when boat landed," she said.

Junyur leaned forward to better hear her as she hesitated.

"Kept prisoner. Room with many girls. Many girls," she repeated.

"Men came. Men left. More men came."

Junyur blanched at the pictures she painted. She'd clearly been raped. But what had happened to the escort he'd paid to get her safely from New York to Guthrie, Oklahoma? He opened his mouth to ask her, then shut it. The escort had been the first to betray her. Or maybe the second, if you counted her father selling her.

"They paid," she continued. "When new girls came, let me go. I followed your letter."

An unexpected ache distracted Junyur from her words. He felt great pity for the woman, he realized. Even responsibility. After all, it was he who'd brought her here. But nothing changed the fact that she was not the woman for his brother. No matter how she'd become one, she was a whore now.

"Like what see?" May Ling asked, rising from the chair and then presenting him with a graceful bow. Her yellow dressing gown covered with flower designs swirled around her like the train to a wedding dress.

Hell, yes, he liked what he saw. The voluptuous curves, the small stature, the straight black hair cut into some sort of fringe around her delicate, heart-shaped face. But most of all it was her eyes that captivated him. Her eyes were like no woman's he'd ever seen before.

And still he'd let her send him away with Jai Li in his care, and only the barest idea how to get the girl to safety. He never should have left May Ling behind.

Junyur pulled his thoughts back from May Ling and her problems. Hell! He'd bitten off a hell of mess, and he knew it. There was no way he'd make the race deadline now. And he'd left the woman he loved in a whorehouse. Of course, it was what she'd asked of him. Didn't mean he had to follow her orders, though.

With one last shove at the sleeping girl on his shoulder, Junyur resigned himself to making Jai Li his prime responsibility.

He'd get her to his home in north Texas, get her safely settled, and then see what he could do about the rest of it.

2
A relative problem and an unmasking

TIME PASSED, RATHER LIKE THE clouds collecting over the prairie had slowly inched their way across the bright blue sky.

Junyur and Jai Li had begun drinking tea together, already several times that day, which drew a couple of the passengers to them. With an audience, Junyur had to pretend the smoky taste of *Lapsang souchong* was inferior to good old American coffee, although all the coffee he'd ever drunk had come from Columbia. No real cowboy worth his salt would ever admit to liking tea.

Was there even an American coffee? Junyur had no idea.

When the man they'd attracted quickly grew bored in their company, Junyur relaxed. Went back to the tea. The older woman who'd accompanied the stranger wouldn't return to her own seat, however. Instead, she'd insinuated herself across the aisle from Jai Li, where she stared fixedly at the girl as if she held the key to an important puzzle.

To Junyur's utter shock, when the older woman grew tired of ogling his charge, she began accusing her of the most outrageous things.

"Where's my goddaughter, young lady?" she demanded, her voice strident with outrage. "I know who and what you are, even if this yokel doesn't. Stop pretending you don't know English and tell me what happened to May Ling."

Despite himself, Junyur glanced at the girl sitting beside him. Just as he suspected, the older woman, Miss Berrigan, he thought she'd introduced herself as, was scaring the wits out of her. Jai Li shivered as if in a cold breeze.

"Now just a minute, ma'am. You've got my charge confused with someone else." Junyur rose half off the seat before recognizing the name she'd thrown out as an accusation. *May Ling*. She'd said *May Ling*.

How had this harridan known anything about May Ling? And what had she said? Her goddaughter? Junyur plopped back down in place, not paying attention as Jai Li moved away from him to avoid being crushed.

Before he could think of anything else to say, Miss Berrigan had pulled her carpetbag from under her seat and was busy rummaging in it for something. Presently, a crumpled photograph emerged from the bag's interior. Despite himself, Junyur craned forward for a look.

Two dozen young women stood in rows, their white dresses, white gloves, and white ribbons standing out in sharp contrast to their tanned and sallow-toned skin. They were all Chinese. In the middle stood a younger version of May Ling. On her right, Jai Li, openly laughing into the lens.

"Look," Miss Berrigan ordered him. She pointed at the figure of Jai Li at the right. "You can just see the beginnings of her tattoo. A lotus blossom."

Junyur squinted at the picture. There *was* something marring Jai Li's skin at the neckline. He could see that clearly enough. If the girl at his side had a tattoo on her shoulders, did that mean Miss Berrigan was right?

Jai Li tensed as if she knew what he was thinking and didn't like it. Without planning to, Junyur took hold of the girl's arm to keep her in her place. As she began to squirm, he made a decision.

"Jai Li," he said softly, completely unsure how she'd react to his request. "I need to see your naked shoulder. Do you have a tattoo?"

Whatever he'd thought she'd do, what she did next was about as far from it as possible. He stared in shock as she not only abruptly bared her shoulders for his inspection, but also lowered the entire top of her jacket to expose her breasts.

He heard an abrupt squeal from Miss Berrigan. From behind him, he felt the men and women in the adjoining seats stir, probably leaning in so they could see better.

Junyur tried and failed to keep his eyes on the tattoos that marred her shoulders. He had never seen a lotus blossom, but he'd take Miss Berrigan's word that these were them. Not only did she have a tattoo, she had an expansive series of tattoos going right across her shoulder blades.

Her breasts would impress no one. Small as tiny apples, they barely distinguished her as a woman instead of a boy.

As Junyur sat stunned, Miss Berrigan moved in. "Lotus blossoms," she said in a satisfied tone of voice. "That's enough, Jai Li. You may cover yourself up now."

Junyur modified his assessment of Jai Li as bit by bit the expression on her face solidified into one of scorn. And not just any scorn, he realized, but the distaste he'd often seen on a rich man's face when confronted by one of his servant's lapses in education. Jai Li had just that look on her face. She clearly wasn't who he'd thought she was. If she stopped the playacting, would she also speak Oxford-educated English?

Miss Berrigan stood up and began shooing the curious away, even though Jai Li continued brazenly exposing herself.

"Get back to your own seat, little man!" Miss Berrigan ordered. "You should be ashamed of yourselves. The girl is deranged. She doesn't know what she's doing. Get on back so we can take care of her."

Miss Berrigan's strident and commanding voice did more than move the men from their carriage back into their own seats. Junyur noticed a change in Jai Li's demeanor as well. Back was the timid and shy girl who knew very little English. Gone was the arrogance, and with it the power of self-confidence.

If he hadn't seen her reaction, if he hadn't seen that alarming tattoo, she'd still have him fooled.

But after one more look at her downturned face, Junyur wasn't so sure she was trying to fool anyone. It had been like turning off a light switch and then turning it back on again. Surely, she had to be one or the other. Shy or brazen. Unless she was one superb actress.

When Junyur had gotten that far in his ruminations, Miss Berrigan finished re-dressing his charge. The intruding spinster had one more surprise in store for him, however, and he immediately wished she'd never shared it.

"This is the girl all the rest of them called Princess Jai Li," she said.

Junyur heard her all right, throwing up his hands in exasperation. "Who are you people?" he cried. Then he grabbed up the photo and shoved it at Miss Berrigan. She took it from him and carefully folded it out.

"This is my goddaughter," she said, pointing gently with her fingers to the central girl in the picture. "At Oxford University."

Oh, yeah, he told himself. Just had to be the whore. This woman's Oxford-educated ward of sorts just had to be the woman he'd bought and transported to America to marry his brother, and that he'd left to run a whorehouse instead.

After foisting a princess on him and his family.

God only knew how much trouble he was in.

"Young man!" Miss Berrigan's voice abruptly interrupted his internal dialogue with himself. "You've obviously got some news of my goddaughter May Ling. Come on. Spit it out."

Oh, how he wanted to just throw it at her. Tell her that her relative had embraced the worst of her womanhood and would forever remain a pariah to decent society.

He opened his mouth to say just that very thing, infuriated to be caught in this totally unnecessary mess. The stern worried look on the spinster's face stopped him. She seemed genuinely worried about May Ling. He didn't know how long Miss Berrigan could be kept from the truth, but now wasn't the time to bludgeon her with it.

His face set in grim lines as he tried to control his struggle. "May Ling refused to come with me when I arrived to take her to our home. Where my brother Marcus awaits her as his bride." He paused. "She sent this girl in her stead," he told her, hoping no more explanation would be necessary.

The rocking of the train momentarily threw him and the others off balance. He steadied both women without even thinking, but quickly jerked his hands away from Miss Berrigan when she squeezed his hand in response.

"May Ling would do that," she told him. "She always fought for the underdog," the woman continued, nodding her head at the skinny princess sitting between them. At his bewildered expression, she added, "Even princesses sometimes need rescuing. If I remember what they said, Jai Li was being educated to be sent to Hawaii to marry into one of the prosperous families there."

Then she leaned forward and whispered so that he had to bend into her. "Some scandal in her past, I think."

Junyur couldn't help himself. His eyes abruptly fixed on the young woman's face. What sort of scandal could possibly have marred Jai Li's reputation to the point that her family would willingly ship her halfway across the world to marry a stranger? He abruptly thought of May Ling. Did every Chinese family sell off its girl children this way?

Jai Li seemed to read his mind. "I not disgraced," she announced coldly, including both Junyur and Miss Berrigan in her explanation. "Sent to safety," she explained.

Miss Berrigan ignored her, bending toward Junyur and whispering into his ear again. "I heard that rumor, too," she said. "May Ling intimated the girl had offended the empress dowager and was facing death over it. I don't believe it, though," she commented.

Before Junyur could respond, Jai Li drew herself up to sit

straight in her seat. "That is why May Ling and I eschewed throwing ourselves at your mercy, madam. We were better off on our own." Then she turned her head to face the window, clearly done with talking.

Junyur puffed out his cheeks in shock. Complete sentences, and in an English accent, no less. He wondered what *eschewed* meant, but caught the drift of her defiance without it. Jai Li looked away from them, not meeting Miss Berrigan's eyes or his. Sort of what his other brother Timothy did when he was angry.

3
Running the whorehouse

IN THE THREE HOURS SINCE Junyur Wilde had ridden off with the princess safely in his care, May Ling had done a lot of soul-searching. She'd locked herself up in her office and brushed off every attempt to get her attention. To her consternation, she found herself thinking *I love you, I love you, I love you* over and over again. These thoughts were hard to stop, especially when they produced such a delicious, if bittersweet, warmth somewhere near her heart.

Occasionally, her daydreams of Mr. Wilde engendered a different reaction entirely. Something like a kick to the gut that left her feeling bereft. That was when she pictured him with someone other than herself. Jai Li, for instance.

May Ling's working girls tapping hesitantly on her door had backed off immediately at her low-pitched growl, intuitively understanding her moodiness. The bodyguards persisted in annoying her with their indecisiveness, but it was mostly their continuous pounding on her obviously closed office door that made May Ling fiercely grit her teeth. Was she going to have to put out a *Do Not Disturb* sign?

Everyone in her establishment owed her. They knew that. She knew that. That was why they needed to leave her alone. May Ling would mourn her lost opportunity without an audience, thank you very much. She only wanted to remember Junyur's face one more time before getting back to work.

But there it came again. *I love you, I love you, I love you.* May Ling sighed like a forlorn suitor, which in truth, she was.

With one ear tuned to the racket at her door, May Ling continued brooding. She was going to have to find a way to control these feelings. She thought of Junyur Wilde in everything she did. How he'd react. What he'd say. How he'd look.

Never before had she found Caucasian males particularly attractive. So why was she so taken with this one? Especially since he consistently insisted on calling her a whore. And really, they'd only just met.

In her heart, she knew the answer. It had been the letters May Ling and Junyur had shared across the vast ocean that kindled her romantic feelings. The ones where he'd called her *My Beauty* and she'd chosen the more formal *Dear Sir*.

When a letter hadn't arrived when she expected it, her spirits dropped into a depth of despair all out of proportion to its cause. When a letter finally arrived, May Ling soared to manic heights at even the most prosaic of sentences such as *How are you?*

Their imaginary kisses scrawled with XXX's and OOO's at the end of the cursive sent her senses reeling. And the grainy photographs they exchanged of each other—she devoured him with her eyes. Wondered if he found her likeness as delectable as she did his.

And all the lies she'd spun for him—it had taken the full measure of her ingenuity to fashion something reasonably authentic-sounding. Once he learned the truth, he'd never forgive her. She was no mail-order bride like he thought she was. Nor had her family sold her away. May Ling was a bodyguard to royalty. With all the fearsome attributes that came with the job.

For the first time, May Ling wondered if Junyur Wilde had lied to her as well.

No matter now. He was gone. She needed to forget him.

Except she couldn't.

I love you, I love you, I love you.

Her eyes closed as she gently stroked the inside of her bottom lip with her tongue, the way he had when he'd kissed her. May Ling regretted staying behind at the whorehouse, though she had no choice but to remain.

A sharp stab of jealousy intruded at the thought of the lissome Jai Li in such close proximity to Junyur Wilde. May Ling unconsciously put her hands over her belly to massage the pain away. She wouldn't put it past the younger woman to seduce her protector. Jai Li had certainly done so before, up to a point.

With a violent pang, May Ling realized she'd probably never know the end of either of their stories. Not Mr. Wilde's. Not Jai Li's. They were gone.

She remained behind at the whorehouse.

What had happened, had happened. Junyur would either stay true to her (sure, he would) or he wouldn't. May Ling was never going to see him again. She must let him go. Banish all thoughts of him and his honey-sweet kisses.

With a tired shrug, she tried putting all thought of this unexpected knight in shining armor behind her. And his bluer than blue eyes. And his curly blond hair. And strong shoulders. And how she'd felt in his arms.

And what they'd almost done together in the privacy of her bedroom. But hadn't.

Bless the gods, he'd been so tall!

Business had suffered during her retreat from day-to-day work on his behalf. May Ling let another long sigh escape her lips as she attacked the accounting report for the third time that afternoon. Dreaming about Junyur Wilde would do her no good at all. She was here for a reason. She'd stay until the job was done. No American cowboy was going to distract her from her purpose. Especially not the one that had gone away and left her alone.

Though she was hardly alone.

And she'd ordered him to go.

May Ling looked up from her paperwork an hour later to find her two Anglo bodyguards, Big Jim and Richard, staring down at her in concern. They'd found a way to slip the lock and had snuck up on her without her noticing. Not a good thing at all! Had she dozed without knowing it? May Ling narrowed her eyes in irritation. With these two, she was safe. But it could just as easily have been one of Valentin's men. Or the blackguard Valentin himself. She shivered.

"You think Jai Li has dropped the helpless orphan act by now?" Big Jim asked, leaning toward her, his big hands on the desktop. "You think that baby cowboy is man enough to keep his promises once he finds out what a witch he has on his hands?" Jim towered over everybody in town, but it wasn't why he was called big. His girth from shoulder to hip kept him from sitting in most chairs anywhere.

"Jai Li no witch," May Ling absently commented while continuing to sort through the accounting sheets. "Fell into bad company. Acts mean to save face."

Big Jim snorted. Richard chuckled, softly at first, but then broke into full-blown laughter at the idea of Princess Jai Li playing nice, for any reason at all. "That gal don't know the first thing about honor," Richard said. "Has no patience, either. I bet she doesn't make it past day one with that sweet little girl masquerade." Richard, almost as tall as Big Jim, was a freckled redheaded man who thought everything was funny. Most of the time May Ling didn't appreciate his humor. This was one of those times.

"Then the cowboy probably threw her over already," Big Jim added. "Or he's bringing her back here."

May Ling stopped pretending to do the accounts. She was aghast. Neither of those two possibilities had crossed her mind. Junyur abandoning Jai Li or alternatively, returning her to the whorehouse. In the story unfolding in May Ling's head, Jai Li had already met the cowboy's older brother, and was well on her way to captivating him with her subtle beauty. Before long they'd be married. May Ling knew it was too soon for any of that to have transpired, but it was what she'd been thinking. In between bouts of jealousy.

But what if Richard's conjecture was true? What if Mr. Wilde the younger had thrown Jai Li off the train instead?

No, he wouldn't have done that. Dealing with the princess took a lot of patience, that was true. But he'd made a promise. Nothing was more sacred to these American cowboy types than a promise. Every penny-dreadful May Ling had read, every newspaper account she'd seen said so. Even her broken heart told her that. Of course, Junyur didn't know that Jai Li was a princess.

Princess or peon, it shouldn't make any difference, she told herself. Junyur wouldn't abandon a woman out in the middle of nowhere!

With an effort, she kept herself from falling back on her new, painful habit of repeating to herself *I love you, I love you, I love you*. Both her men were looking at her strangely. Had she said any of that out loud?

No, Junyur wouldn't abandon his charge, but he might bring the princess back. He conceivably might return Jai Li to her care. May Ling realized with a start that she hadn't explained the danger of that clearly enough to prevent him.

She shivered in apprehension. Her shawl slipped from her shoulders and puddled on the floor behind her office chair. Nothing would be more dangerous to Jai Li than returning to May Ling's establishment. Or more dangerous to the other girls May Ling had given sanctuary to.

She abruptly pounded the palm of her hand hard on her desk. It was past time to face down the villain Valentin. She needed to let go of her dreams and gather her resources. Meeting Junyur Wilde in the flesh, so to speak, had made her weak. But he was gone. And with the Princess Jai Li well out of danger, May Ling no longer carried the onerous obligation of the girl's safety. She'd passed it to the man she loved.

One last thought, she promised herself. Then she'd put

all her worries for Junyur Wilde out of her mind. Along with thoughts of Jai Li. That near seduction in her bedroom would have to do. For her last indulgence.

Big Jim and Richard coughed in embarrassment, as if they'd read her thoughts, but May Ling pursued her memory of the Wilde boy. How she'd almost stripped him bare as he'd slept in her bed, totally unaware she'd kept vigil by his side through the long night when he'd first arrived.

His hair had escaped from her fingers as she'd caressed the nape of his neck. The dry, spice-laden aroma of his naked skin had invaded her nostrils as she bent over him to check his heartbeat. And when she'd found herself involuntarily tugging his jeans from his hips and down to his thighs to get a better look at the rest of him—here May Ling cut short her fantasizing. Under her breath, she scolded herself. She'd done no such thing, she asserted.

But she'd certainly wanted to.

May Ling allowed herself one last small smile.

With incuriously bold eyes, she turned her thoughts away from what she *couldn't* have to what she *could*. Richard and Big Jim had colored as if they knew exactly what she'd been thinking. May Ling smiled more broadly. They might have an idea what had happened between her and the cowboy the other day, but they didn't really know.

"How many guns?" she asked Big Jim, wiping the smirk off her face so he'd know she meant business. "How many guns we need?"

"Now you're talking!"

Big Jim threw back his head and howled loudly at the ceiling. "Some action at last!"

Richard showed no such exuberance. "It's not so much the guns, Miss May Ling. It's the manpower," he told her. "I know you thought you needed to get that problem girl away from here, but you made a mistake letting that cowboy go."

May Ling chewed carefully on her lower lip. Six solid months of working with these two and they still didn't take her seriously as their boss. To them, manpower meant men. To her, it meant anyone capable of fighting. Which meant the six girls in her care, Richard, Big Jim, herself, and her secret weapon, Squash Blossom.

She repeated her question. "How many guns we need?"

Richard threw up his hands in defeat. "None. Nada. Not any. You can't fight a villain like Valentin. He's got the whole town behind him, with firearms."

It was pretty much as she'd figured. Someone was going to have to approach Valentin through stealth and misdirection. Poison him? Cut his throat, maybe? Set fire to the bastard? She could see all sorts of possibilities. There were endless ways to kill someone.

As long as you were willing to die yourself.

4
Wanted posters

So, not a gunfight.

Valentin had to be dealt with, though. As did the horrifying problem of the girls he had in the cage out behind Miss Adelaide's alley. The girls he'd made available for sex to anyone with an extra fifty cents to spare.

May Ling had finally achieved her first victory over the villain, and the minions he'd attracted to Guthrie—Jai Li had been rescued from the cage and spirited to safety. But it had taken the unexpected help of an outside force to effect. *I love you, I love you, I love you.* For a second, May Ling let her senses run away with her. Junyur Wilde had proved to be an enormous asset.

Unfortunately, he wasn't here anymore. She doubted he'd have been able to save the rest of the girls, anyhow. Especially now. Security had tripled, customers had doubled, May Ling's timeline had halved. Before long the weather would turn deadly with tornadoes. She had to make her move long ahead of the first storms.

Big Jim and Richard understood the way her mind worked. They'd left her to do her own thinking. Hunkered down in the easy chairs the girls had designed especially for the two, they gave every impression of good old boys drowsing blissfully in their favorite whorehouse.

May Ling understood the way *their* minds worked. She basked briefly in the certainty that between the three of them they'd figure something out. Before long, the men would have two very different but feasible solutions to May Ling's predicament. And she would have another. It was how they had rescued the princess from being molested out in the cage.

But it had taken Junyur Wilde to whisk Jai Li away from here and out of danger. May Ling lingered over the memory of her last sight of the man. He was so tall. So handsome. And so not here.

Of all the men May Ling knew in this town called Guthrie where she resided, only two came to mind as possible saviors. Not counting Big Jim and Richard. And discounting Junyur as well. The sheriff, and the sheriff's deputy.

She pushed all thoughts of her lost lover aside, but couldn't tamp down her need to repeat *I love you, I love you, I love you.*

May Ling focused her thoughts on the sheriff and his deputy. Who were father and son, oddly enough. And very much under Valentin's thumb. Might they be motivated by money? Lots and lots of money?

And who had more money than anyone in the whole world had a right to, than the empress dowager of China? Who happened to be the one who'd put that ridiculous bounty on Jai Li's head in the first place. If May Ling could get the word out about the bounty...

She snorted, already far ahead of the game, and prematurely savoring the deliciousness of having the empress dowager paying to save the very irritating, impossibly troublesome Princess Jai Li she hated so much. Out of her own treasury!

"Get sheriff. Get deputy, too. Talk in here. Now."

But as May Ling cheerfully chortled to herself, she realized her plan would only work once. Or maybe twice. Because although no one but she and her immediate companions knew which of the girls was Jai Li, there were only so many girls she could spirit out of this dreadful town by pretending they were the princess. A couple more than one might be forgiven as mistaken identities, but not all of them.

In anguish over her shortsightedness, May Ling wrung her hands. She wouldn't let herself think of what the empress dowager might do to the girls once she had them, either. Even death was preferable to what they were experiencing right now. May Ling would do her best to see that none of the Princess Jai Li impersonators got caught in the lie. That was what Squash Blossom was being held in reserve for. Covering up her tracks. Tidying up the details.

Big Jim and Richard returned much earlier than she'd expected, and without the lawmen she'd demanded. May Ling settled into her desk chair to await their report. With an effort, she stilled her restless hands.

Her bodyguards had better have a good explanation for why the sheriff and his deputy weren't standing respectfully in front of her, instead of themselves. If she had to traipse from her business down to the muddy, horseshit-pocked excuse for a town street and then cross it to the sheriff's office, she was going to be mighty put out.

With a flash of her eyes, she encouraged Big Jim to explain himself.

"Miss May Ling, they already had a wanted poster up about the princess. Had a photograph of her on it. Your plan about sneaking some of the girls out of here pretending to be Jai Li won't work. None of them really look so ... so ..."

"Princess-like?"

Richard snorted. "I think the word he's looking for is crafty. Or maybe sneaky." May Ling wondered if he'd ever forgive the princess for biting him.

May Ling sat forward and stared straight at the two bodyguards. This was bad news. Her plan wouldn't work after all.

Very bad. It was the only thing she'd been able to come up with.

She assessed the men she saw as her last hope. They'd

always had such inventive schemes for her to reject. As things were now, she doubted she'd reject any plan, even one as bizarre as shooting the girls to the moon in a rocket ship, which had briefly crossed her mind.

Richard interrupted her thoughts. "The sheriff has already contacted the empress's representatives about the princess."

"Does Sheriff know she gone?"

Richard looked at Big Jim for confirmation. "We don't think so, ma'am," Big Jim replied. "They don't seem worried."

May Ling fluttered her hand fan in front of her face. "Sheriffs not know what awaits them," she said. "Empress send swordsmen."

Big Jim shuffled back and forth. Richard distanced himself, as if he feared the other big man might topple onto him. May Ling raised an eyebrow, fascinated.

Finally, when neither man volunteered more information, she asked, "You afraid swords, Big Jim?"

He stopped swaying. Stood straight and looked her in the eyes. "No, not the weapons. It's the girls. They're going to die, aren't they?"

May Ling stood up, gesturing the men to keep still and silent. Then she slowly slid back into her desk chair. She would not tell them this, but yes, the girls in the cage would die. And probably before the empress's lackeys had time to converge on this damned town. Unless ... unless she took action herself.

May Ling stifled a sob. It would mean her death. And she didn't want to die. Probably would, though, since she only had these two men and Squash Blossom to back her up. She couldn't ask her inside ladies for help. A third of them only held onto their sanity by a thread. The routine of Miss Adelaide's was all that kept them stable.

May Ling stifled an inappropriate smile, only now realizing that the routine of Miss Adelaide's was all that kept *her* stable. Had it taken her a whole six months to realize that? She had no choice now but to bring out her last option.

"Get Squash Blossom down here."

With some satisfaction, May Ling saw each of her bodyguards blanch at her whispered command. To their credit, however, neither hesitated. Within a minute, she heard the heavy tread of their steps ascending the staircase that led to Squash Blossom's rooms.

Her secret weapon would be down in a trice. May Ling patted her hair into some semblance of tidiness, and composed her face as best she could. Using someone like Squash Blossom was akin to tossing a stick of dynamite into a herd of cattle.

She wished she didn't have to resort to this, but she could no longer tolerate that hateful cage and sleep the sleep of the righteous.

Time to make a change.

With a wry pursing of her lips, May Ling realized she hadn't had a single thought about Junyur Wilde in the last five minutes. Maybe. But it had been at least four minutes.

A single tear slid down her face.

I love you.

Squash Blossom arrived before May Ling had time to wipe her cheek dry, floating in a cloud of silk. Although the younger woman swayed gracefully up to May Ling's desk in much the same manner as May Ling would have done, this recent layering of new garments, delicate and pretty though they were, could not conceal the lingering trace of steely menace in Squash Blossom's posture.

As Squash Blossom bowed, she also hissed the warning, "I love you, too, mistress."

For the first time, May Ling had proof she'd begun expressing her distress out loud.

5
Jumping off the train

IT TOOK A WHILE, AND it tasked both Miss Berrigan's and Junyur's patience getting the princess decently covered up again, but they finally got her dressed. Thank God the young woman's icy glare repelled any and all of the other passengers curious enough to come over and take a look. Did everyone think he and his two female companions in their bench seats near the front of the train compartment were a circus act?

The steam train chugged onward, rocking back and forth in a pattern Junyur was finally learning to lean in and out of. Jai Li kept herself perfectly still and seemed to be listing with every jerk of the train wheels. Miss Berrigan had seemingly tried to emulate the princess, but she kept getting thrown off balance. For the tenth time, at least, he reached over the aisle and steadied the middle-aged woman.

Junyur Wilde had much to contemplate. He wished he could ponder Miss May Ling's lush and curvy body instead of this problem child at his side. He blushed bright red at the memory, for he had indeed seen May Ling naked. In his experience, respectable women didn't take their clothes off in public. Hell, most respectable women never took all their clothes off no matter what! May Ling had stayed in Guthrie; Jai Li had come away with Junyur. Junyur cursed inwardly, wishing quite the opposite. Yes, he had much to contemplate.

Still reeling from Jai Li's modest breasts thrust into his face, he forced himself instead to consider her manner of speech. No mere peasant girl talked like an Oxford-trained scholar. And he'd heard several such academics in his checkered past. Some of his ladies had forced him to attend lectures with them. That *was* a British accent. That it was an Oxford accent he took on faith. The photograph Miss Berrigan had showed around was stamped Oxford University on its back. Even he could put two and two together and not get five.

Jai Li repeated a variation of her dismissive statement from a few moments before. "We had a fine plan, ma'am, until you showed up. And we had a fine plan when we arrived in New York, as well. Didn't need anyone's help. Valentin ... Valentin promised ..." Jai Li's voice trailed off.

Junyur expected the prim and proper Miss Berrigan to puff up and berate the girl, but she surprised him.

"I know a lot more than you do about the promises of men," Miss Berrigan said quietly. "Especially men of Alain Valentin's ilk. I could have kept you safe in New York."

At that, Jai Li snorted.

"You don't believe me, but it's true," the older woman objected. "Now here I am, again. Whatever it is you're doing with this cowboy, it's time you give it up. You hear me?"

Bristling at Miss Berrigan's commanding tone, Jai Li scrunched down in the seat as Junyur watched in dismay. Could all of May Ling's misfortunes since arriving in New York been avoided if the girls had only waited there for Miss Berrigan's help? Maybe Junyur should have traveled to the East Coast and met May Ling right off the ship. At the very least she would have escaped the attack on her that had led her into whoredom.

There was that word again! Whore. He just couldn't get around it.

Miss Berrigan shocked him right out of his senses next.

"When are we going to go back to Guthrie and rescue my goddaughter?" she said.

Suddenly the train lurched into a long screeching

slowdown leading into a full stop. Even Jai Li scowled at the piercing squeal of metal on metal. The nerve-grating noise was something even she couldn't ignore. It lasted several minutes, and Junyur wasn't the only passenger worriedly peering out the windows to see what the problem was. From his vantage point on this side of the train, he saw only prairie.

"Stay right where you are," he told Miss Berrigan and Jai Li. Then he pushed his way into the central aisle and joined the passengers staring out the other side of the train.

At first Junyur couldn't see over the bruised cowboy hat worn by the little man whose seat he and the others had invaded. But when the fat woman facing from the other bench suddenly lurched to her feet, she crowded Junyur's face flat against the glass. He was too busy trying to breathe to take in the sights. Especially when she pounded on his back in excitement.

"There they are! There they are!"

The fat woman yelled into Junyur's ear with a little bounce that knocked the other sitting passenger's hat right off his head. Junyur gingerly opened his eyes.

Dust rose from a line of carriages and wagons slowly approaching from what he assumed was Oklahoma City, since the conductor had been yelling that destination as he'd passed up and down the aisles several times already.

The conductor called out to them from the front of the car. "Resume your seats, ladies and gentlemen."

"There he is!" the fat woman cried. "There he is!"

Junyur ignored the conductor and ducked his head to follow the woman's pointing finger. A huge wagon drawn by draft horses had peeled away from the line and headed straight for the train.

This hadn't been the first time the train had stopped out in the middle of nowhere to either pick up a special passenger or let one off. Junyur and his brothers often took the same advantage traveling from their ranch in north Texas down to Dallas.

Before Junyur had time to process their change of circumstances, Miss Berrigan pushed herself into the space that had opened between him and the yelling fat woman. Junyur jerked as he felt her breath on his neck, but kept himself from wheeling around. He didn't want Miss Berrigan's breasts in his face. The fat woman's assault had been bad enough. As it was, he felt like a piece of meat in a human sandwich.

No one had yet asked why they'd stopped or where they were when Jai Li commented from her seat across the aisle. In a voice that carried through the entire car, she said, "This is where it begins. They're converging here for the land race. Sooners."

Ahhh.

The sound had come from everywhere. Evidently, Jai Li had answered the universal question that had been on everyone's minds. Even Junyur perked up. This was where he wanted to be. How strange that the unplanned rescue of Princess Jai Li had led him right where he desired. At the starting line of the Oklahoma land race he saw as his salvation.

Or almost. All he had to do was step off the train and walk into town. It was destiny.

Junyur moved Miss Berrigan off him and returned to his seat. Across the aisle, the fat lady continued to shriek and hop around. For a second, Junyur worried about the little man in the big cowboy hat still seated, but Miss Berrigan was finally pulling the guy out of the excited woman's orbit.

Junyur masked his naked desire for the race, but Miss Berrigan had read his mind. "Did you plan to participate in this travesty, young man? I thought you said your brothers already owned a farm."

"Ranch," he said, correcting her. "They have a ranch, I'm just the third brother. And just what makes this a travest ..., whatever it was you said?"

The fat woman across the aisle who was making all the ruckus yelled over everyone before Miss Berrigan could answer. "It's brother Michael come to take us to the land race office like he always said he would!" she yelled at the top of her voice. "Come on, y'all! Let's go down and greet him proper."

Then she looked straight at Junyur Wilde in his dirty clothes, looked at the Chinese princess masquerading as a distraught traveler, and gave Miss Berrigan only a passing glance. She then looked down her nose and announced, "The travesty part is that just anyone can participate."

Miss Berrigan caught Junyur's arm and held him tight. He'd wanted to shove the excited fat woman down so badly he wasn't thinking straight. She'd just insulted all three of them. As if they had cooties or something.

"You can't join the race anyhow," Miss Berrigan told him as some of their fellow passengers crowded toward the exit. "We're taking this girl back to Guthrie, and we're going to get May Ling rescued."

As far as Junyur was concerned, his job was to get Jai Li to his brother as fast as possible and then join everyone else in getting to one of the staging areas before it was too late for the race. This would be the very last one. For a moment, May Ling resurfaced in his thoughts and he shuddered. She would just have to wait until he had his land.

A little more than three days until the race! That was plenty of time to get home and back, but only if Miss Berrigan didn't interfere. May Ling would just have to take care of herself. She'd freely chosen to stay behind. To run that infernal sex den over his offer of protection. She'd taken Jai Li out of that obscene cage and given her over to him to save instead. When he turned the princess over to his brother Marcus, he'd have paid out that obligation.

The train jerked itself into a slow start and gradually left what looked like three families out there along the track for the fat woman's brother to stuff in his wagon and transport to Oklahoma City. Tears stung Junyur's eyes, but when he dropped Jai Li off with his brother, he'd be free to return.

Junyur felt dismay watching those families congratulate each other out there just off from the tracks, but he felt horror when the barrel of Miss Berrigan's pistol jabbed him in the ribs.

"What the hell do you think you're doing? Get that damned thing off me!" he hollered.

"Get up and gather what you think you need, young man," Miss Berrigan told him, her voice icy with disdain. "You, too, Princess. We're getting off this train and going back to Guthrie for my goddaughter. Right now! Before the train's moving too fast."

"The train is already moving too fast, madam," Jai Li observed. For a minute Junyur thought he had an ally against the older woman. None of them were going back to Guthrie.

But then Jai Li continued. "But it's still in the realm of possibility. We can jump. I'll wait for you."

Both Junyur and Miss Berrigan faced the princess, Junyur absolutely shocked at her statement, Miss Berrigan sporting a big grin. The princess made a dignified exit from her seat, leaving all her possessions behind, and walked unhurriedly down the aisle to the exit as if she hadn't a care in the world.

Still bristling at the indignity of the pistol jabbed into his ribs, Junyur didn't take Jai Li's comment about jumping off the train seriously until she suddenly vanished to the cries and yells of all the other passengers, who then began pointing.

Jai Li must have landed on her feet beside the moving train, then lost her balance and fallen back into the dirt. He saw her sprawled gracelessly on the ground with her skirt in disarray, but she moved as if uninjured.

"Oh, hell," Miss Berrigan commented. "Come with us or don't," she told him. "Somehow I think our little princess might be more use to me than you would. Wish us luck," she said, removing the pistol from Junyur's side and following the girl out the front of the car.

"Oh my God," one of the passengers cried a moment later. "She has to have broken an arm!"

It was an insane act, but Miss Berrigan had jumped off the moving train to join the princess. Junyur got a glimpse of her through the window as he walked briskly to the same exit.

Junyur didn't bother to question the diagnosis. Broken arm or not, a woman had probably been injured. He couldn't return home and tell his brother he'd lost both May Ling and Jai Li, and Miss Berrigan. Not that Marcus knew anything about it at this stage anyhow.

Nor would he let a sixteen-year-old Chinese girl and a middle-aged white woman jump off a damned train to rescue the woman he loved.

That was his job.

The race was little more than three days off. If he could get everyone to Oklahoma City, he could hire some muscle to take the two women down south to Marcus in Texas. Then he could run the race, claim his land, then return to rescue May Ling.

Who probably didn't need his help anyhow.

6
Running after the princess

Junyur Wilde had a difficult time throwing himself off the train.

If he'd been the kind of hero his brother Marcus was, Junyur would have already *jumped* off the train. Here he was, countless minutes later pondering *throwing* himself off. Between the two words lay a world's difference in heroism. Junyur sighed loudly. He certainly wasn't the man May Ling thought he was.

The train had picked up speed while Junyur deliberated, but he could still see the two ladies of his out on the ground, away from the train tracks, and off to the right. They were getting farther and farther away with every second. Were they up and walking already? Without waiting for him! Or was this an optical illusion?

He had to do it. He had to jump. And he had to jump *now*, before the train ate up even more distance between him and his companions.

But he just couldn't do it. At least not without all their stuff.

"Oh hell!" Deciding he had no choice, Junyur galloped back to his former seat and then returned twice as fast to the train exit door with the hastily retrieved leather carpetbag clutched close to his chest.

"Jai Li," he asserted, raising his voice so he could hear himself in the wind tunnel created by the still-open door.

"And Miss Berrigan. Not just companions. Women in peril. Here I come!"

With a silent prayer, Junyur shut his eyes and fell backward off the train, leaving it to fate whether he survived or had just killed himself. For a couple of heartbeats (that felt like all of eternity), Junyur flew through the air.

A creosote bush struggling for its own survival at the bottom of the incline supporting the train tracks saved him. He bounced off it while unconsciously curled into a ball, then went flying head over heels, skidding to a stop in the dirt. His traveling bag cushioned him from the plunge through the arid Oklahoma soil. When Junyur finally came to rest, he'd created quite a dust cloud to announce himself.

Junyur decided to stay put. Miss Berrigan and Jai Li would reach him any minute. He would take the time to regroup. And get his wits about him.

Staring up at the blinding blue sky suited him right fine, for the moment. The ache in his chest subsided just a little as he waited for them. He carefully flexed all his limbs. Nothing broken. After a while, his breathing returned to normal and his back hurt from lying flat. He propped himself up with his elbows and looked for his ladies.

He saw the tail end of the train disappearing to the south as the track veered into a curve. Three people throwing themselves out of a moving train plainly hadn't warranted another unscheduled stop. Junyur allowed himself to feel a little miffed at that. He'd paid good money for those tickets. The least they could have done was slow down and send one of the conductors out to see about them.

His ladies ought to be close to him any minute now. No use getting angry about the train and its passengers. Instead, he needed to figure out a way to get the three of them to Oklahoma City, and in one piece. Junyur twisted around to look for Miss Berrigan. She should have gotten to him by now. He was surprised she wasn't already lecturing him on the etiquette of train jumping, or something else equally stupid.

Finally, Junyur sat up and looked down the north direction of the tracks. Just at the edge of his eyesight was a big blur alongside a smaller blur, and both blurs were blurrily walking away. As if they didn't even know he was there.

"Hey! Hey, you! Stop! Wait a minute! Come back!"

Junyur had yelled loudly enough. Maybe they couldn't hear him because he was sitting down.

Junyur forced himself to his feet, nearly tottering into his luggage and losing his balance. He windmilled his arms to stay upright, all the while yelling as loudly as he could up the train track toward his former companions.

But call as he might, neither Miss Berrigan nor Jai Li turned around to run back to him.

For a split second, Junyur felt rage rise up in his heart, but it vanished just as suddenly into a wry grin. These two ladies of his had gumption, he begrudgingly conceded. But companions of his they no longer were. Maybe they didn't know he'd jumped off the train? Either that or they were both mentally unhinged.

Two women alone and walking along the train tracks weren't going to get far without attracting the wrong kind of attention. They'd need him to protect them. No doubt about it. Marcus would just have to wait a little bit longer for his Chinese wife. This was going to take a while.

Junyur dusted off his banged-up cowboy hat and put it on his head, shouldered the leather carpetbag, and with his tongue checked that all his teeth were still attached.

As he trudged after the two women, Junyur wondered just what Jai Li was up to. He could understand Miss Berrigan. Blood called to blood, there was no denying that.

But Jai Li was another matter.

The lusterless girl he'd fled Guthrie, Oklahoma, with and had started to feel protective of hadn't had it in her to pluck up the courage to willingly return to the lion's den that Guthrie represented, either with or without him.

He was sure of that.

But the Jai Li with her flawless English who looked down her nose at him, the one who'd abruptly appeared and just as suddenly disappeared while sharing his train space, she just might be the personality driving the action over there.

Or maybe Miss Berrigan was just dragging her along.

And was Jai Li some demented young woman with two disparate personalities warring for her soul? Or just an excellent actress?

All this thinking was giving Junyur a headache.

Junyur rearranged his bag over his other shoulder and began to run after the two, first at a trot, and faster when his muscles warmed up. Alas, the blurs representing Miss Berrigan and Jai Li sped up, too. He didn't seem to have any chance of catching up to them.

"Wait up!" he called fruitlessly.

He picked up speed, careless of what prairie dog holes might do to his ankles, and equally careless of rattlesnakes, tarantulas, scorpions, raptors, vultures, and broken bottles. Miss Berrigan and Jai Li clearly weren't going to wait for him. Instead, it looked like they'd started walking faster, even running, which made no sense to him at all. They needed a man by their side.

"Jai Li!" he called out after realizing that, in the condition he was in, he'd not catch them any time soon. Surely, the princess felt some residual gratitude toward him. After all, he'd offered her his brother as a husband. That ought to count for something.

He glanced up from watching where his feet were stepping just in time to see one of the blurs studying him. At least one of the blurs had stopped. Junyur thought she'd seen him.

"Miss Berrigan! Jai Li! Wait for me!" he cried one more time, stubbornly determined not to beg.

Finally, both blurs remained stationary. Fifteen minutes

of unmitigated hell later and he was at their sides, his breath coming in ragged gasps as his eyesight gradually cleared.

"Stop your begging, young man," Miss Berrigan said when it became clear he didn't have the breath to talk.

He hadn't been begging.

"We didn't know you were there," she said. "We'd have stayed for you if we'd known."

Even while panting for breath, Junyur recognized a lie when he heard it. They hadn't wanted him with them. The last fifteen minutes—the last thirty minutes, after he'd finally realized the women had no intention of letting him gain any distance on them—he'd run full-out and only stumbled into their midst when they'd stopped.

But if they didn't want him with them, they could have just kept on walking. He would never have caught up to them. Someone had changed their mind.

"Why ... why didn't you ... didn't you ... wait?"

If that sounded like begging to Miss Berrigan, then so be it. Why hadn't they waited? And why had they changed their minds?

It was stupid to leave him behind.

As he watched the older woman put together her next lie, Junyur had a sudden flashback to May Ling spinning her own elaborate fabrications. Despite the difference in their races, in their ages, and in their clothing styles, Junyur could see the connection between the two for the first time.

He laughed. He was never going to rid himself of May Ling's influence, was he?

"Never mind," he told Miss Berrigan. He was with them now, and he'd make damned sure they didn't ditch him again. The plan had changed. No longer was Oklahoma City his goal. Now they had a whore to rescue, and he doubted they'd be able to do much about it without him.

Junyur measured his steps to the older woman's pace, all the while thinking of May Ling. He had to force himself to watch the ground for those prairie dog holes that his older brother Marcus had once lied about. Telling him they were snake holes. For *giant* snakes.

Fantasizing about May Ling was a lot more interesting. At some point, he was going to have to tell Miss Berrigan that May Ling was a prostitute. And he didn't relish the task.

He figured Miss Berrigan had never even seen a whore.

Jai Li, however, had come way too close to the profession. He winced, remembering the cage. He glanced at Jai Li as they tromped closer to where she waited impatiently. She'd had plenty of time to rest, not tiring herself walking back to him like Miss Berrigan had done. Jai Li had gained some color back into her cheeks. The minute they caught up to her, Jai Li took off again.

Neither woman showed any signs of flagging. It was only Junyur flailing around. He could barely keep up with them, and nearly twisted his ankle stepping in one of those holes he was supposed to be looking out for.

Jai Li kept moving away even as Junyur fought to stay upright. At least Miss Berrigan kept looking worriedly at him, as if he wasn't up to the task of walking to Guthrie. Junyur ignored her as he recovered. In a few minutes, he had pushed himself to a steadier pace and was shadowing the girl.

Jumping off the train had to be one of the stupidest stunts he'd ever pulled. But after the women had escaped him—

"Whoa!" he said. Then he grabbed for Miss Berrigan's arm, knowing instinctively not to touch Jai Li. "Stop right where you are," he told them.

To his surprise, they stopped.

Miss Berrigan swatted his hand off her while Jai Li watched incuriously from her mysterious Oriental eyes. Dust settled on their shoes. Miss Berrigan coughed. "Well," she said. "What do you want?"

"Where are we taking *her*?" Junyur asked, gesturing at Jai Li while looking all around them for any sign of civilization.

"I understand why *you* need to get to Guthrie, but we can't drag the girl back there."

"What do you expect me to do with her?" she asked. "I need you back in Guthrie. Did you think Jai Li could just continue to your brother's home on her own? Or that we could just leave her in Oklahoma City?"

Yeah, actually, that *was* what he'd been thinking. Leave her with someone trustworthy in Oklahoma City.

"Do you actually know anyone in Oklahoma City, young man?"

Nope, he didn't. Wasn't going to admit to it, though.

All he really knew was that it was dangerous to take the girl back with them.

Jai Li would be no help whatsoever rescuing May Ling. Not this skinny, erratic, calla lily of a girl. No matter which personality she put on for the moment, she'd only get in the way.

Miss Berrigan, however, had the personality of a battleship. He could see her bowling over the bad guys with her presence alone.

And Junyur Wilde? He hadn't set out on his own to pick up May Ling in Guthrie just because everyone else was busy. He could take care of himself, and of anyone in his care.

Everybody knew that.

7
Squash Blossom is a what?

BIG JIM AND RICHARD SIDLED back through May Ling's office door a full fifteen minutes after Squash Blossom's arrival. May Ling narrowed her eyes at the two. In a whorehouse, a fifteen-minute time span had special meaning. If either of her bodyguards had taken advantage of their positions here to satisfy themselves with any of her girls, willing or not, she'd let Squash Blossom cut off their offending appendages.

And she'd have Richard mutilated first. He'd been warned.

With barely a nod at Squash Blossom, May Ling indicated her order, knowing she understood what was needed. Squash Blossom had done this before. Seemed to enjoy the rough contact. And especially the shock. Squash Blossom really loved seeing the shock as it got to the man's eyes.

Without a word, the graceful and mysterious Squash Blossom, attired in a dizzying array of colorful clothes, walked over to Richard and pushed herself into him as if she wanted to disappear. She ground herself into him mercilessly, keeping him still with an iron-strong arm around his hips.

Richard's jaw dropped in shock. As Squash Blossom rubbed herself more tightly into his crotch, Richard's lust changed to outrage. His face flamed red. Only the frosty stare directed at him from May Ling prevented him from wringing Squash Blossom's neck. He carefully kept his hands to himself, and allowed Squash Blossom to finish her teasing and disengage without getting into a fight.

The young beauty returned to her place on the office couch to look at her nails. Richard sputtered, choked, and then finally swallowed his shame.

When calmed enough, Richard righteously declared his resentment. "That ... that mutant!"

May Ling fixed him with a glare.

Richard took a deep breath and started again. "The girls. The girls upstairs. Are they all like *him*?" he asked, pointing at the delicate beauty on the couch.

"You know they not," May Ling hissed under her breath as she stared him down. Richard had problems, but he'd proved loyal. Plus, he was sharp. At that, May Ling chuckled. Not so sharp as to have figured out that Squash Blossom was a young man masquerading as a woman, but not many had.

"No," she replied. "He only one."

"She," Squash Blossom corrected her boss. "In this place, I am *she*." And then with an artful scowl at Richard, Squash Blossom informed him that she was also a master assassin, skilled equally with bow, knife, gun, and poison. "And courtesan," she added.

Big Jim poked Richard hard on the side of his arm. "Apologize to the lady and let's get those girls out of the cage before it's too late. That's what we're here for."

May Ling remained seated, but nodded her gratitude to Big Jim. He never failed to appease. She'd found him a natural diplomat. "You have plan?" she asked, hoping for the best.

But he shook his head. Richard took the initiative, calm at last. "We can haul the cage away in the dead of night," he said. "Get the girls out of town before trying to break the bars."

"Guards," May Ling reminded him.

Squash Blossom stood and made her way toward the bodyguards. "It's not a bad idea, Miss May Ling. I can distract the guards."

"Or scare them to death," Richard blurted angrily.

"Oh, grow up," Squash Blossom retorted. "Half the whores on the West Coast are men in women's dresses. Most of the time the customers are so hurried they never even notice." Then she gave Richard a smug smile and continued her sentence. "The rest of them like it."

"Stop bickering," May Ling commanded. "That wanted poster. How long?"

Richard and Big Jim exchanged looks. Big Jim asked for clarification. "How long have the posters been up in the sheriff's office?"

"Yes, how long?" Her expression was stony. With an effort, May Ling tamped down her irritation. She knew she didn't speak proper English. She'd had years and years of Jai Li's taunts about it, but this wasn't Jai Li. Richard and Big Jim were employees. They had better learn how to interpret her pidgin talk right fast or she'd find them jobs elsewhere.

"Doesn't matter," Squash Blossom interrupted. "Valentin is here already. The empress's swordsmen are another problem, for later."

May Ling shrugged. This was why she'd brought Squash Blossom downstairs in the first place. Along with all his other sinister accomplishments, he was also a master strategist. "So. Get rid Valentin?"

Squash Blossom's smile held no merriment. "He's no longer intent on murdering Jai Li, right? Has other plans for her. Like his for you? Then send him after that train and the cowboy. Save yourself."

May Ling inwardly cringed while keeping her face passive. It was her job to protect Jai Li, not let her get recaptured. Also, despite her tender feelings toward Junyur Wilde, he was no Squash Blossom. Valentin would overcome him easily. A recaptured Jai Li and a dead or mangled Junyur Wilde were not viable options.

So why did Squash Blossom suggest such? May Ling raised an inquiring eyebrow.

Before she could get an answer, Sherriff Patton and his

son, Deputy Patton, were at the door. May Ling pursed her lips. Had they recognized Jai Li from the posters at last and come to secure the prize?

May Ling's personal maid could not restrain the pair. Holding her arms across the threshold, she'd attempted to deny them entrance, tears of defeat ruining her elaborate makeup.

Crying wouldn't deter those two.

But to May Ling's surprise, they stopped just shy of the maid. She'd not suspected any chivalry from the Pattons. With a nod to the brave young darling barring entry, May Ling indicated her approval, then invited the men inside.

"Feisty little thing," the deputy commented, but he refused to let her take his hat. His father growled. He let her have his hat, but kept his firearms.

"All is good," May Ling announced. "Welcome." Then she added, "gentlemen," and "no go. All stay."

Richard maneuvered the two lawmen into sitting by Squash Blossom on the couch. Then he hovered at one end while Big Jim towered over Squash Blossom on the other end. The maid either didn't hear or didn't understand May Ling's orders and scurried out of the room. Both the sheriff and his deputy followed her with their eyes.

"We're here," the sheriff announced testily.

"Late."

It hadn't been May Ling objecting to their manner, but Squash Blossom. The beauty looked sideways at the lawmen from under half-lowered eyelids. They squirmed. Squash Blossom grinned.

"We want to free the girls from the cage," Big Jim announced. Squash Blossom expressed displeasure at his interruption by arching an eyebrow. The lawmen attempted to stand. Squash Blossom caught their attention with a quick, flirtatious flick upward of her costume. Both plopped back into their seats.

When Sheriff Patton got his breathing under control, he

objected, "Getting one cage of girls out of this town won't accomplish anything, Miss May Ling. Valentin will just order more cages and more girls."

May Ling had already figured that out. Valentin and his political machine controlled all the evil in Guthrie. She'd been planning an attack on the cage system right from the beginning, soon after arriving there. The pieces were almost in place. Only the swordsmen from the empress and Valentin himself were missing. May Ling was going to use the caged girls' escape to lure the villain back to town.

These petty lawmen were the first stage of her assault.

8
Valentin makes his move

A STARTLING HISS ESCAPED May Ling's lips, and with that, she jumped out of her chair and was out the door before either of the lawmen had time to fill her in about Valentin's newest scheme. May Ling stopped just past the threshold to eavesdrop on the conversation. Her secret peep-hole allowed her to see much of the room as well.

Deputy Patton didn't get as far as the door. May Ling's bodyguard popped up and pulled him roughly back into the center of the room by his belt before forcefully propelling him into the chair both he and May Ling had just vacated.

The vacuum she created was immediately occupied by the shorter of the two bodyguards, Richard. Just how she'd planned it.

"Nice try, varmint," Richard said. He then crossed his arms over his chest and gave the deputy and his father a glare that dared either of the lawmen to try any further moves. Outside spying, May Ling smiled as if she harbored a precious secret.

"That woman's worth ten thousand dollars to someone," Deputy Patton said.

"Miss May Ling is worth quite a bit more to those of us living here," Richard countered. "No tricks of yours will get you anything," he continued. "And Jai Li is the one worth ten thousand dollars. They won't pay a thing if she's dead."

May Ling's smile broadened, thrilled that her employees

valued her so highly. And perversely elated at the amount of bounty for her ward.

May Ling didn't know if any of that was true, but it sounded right. The empress dowager never forgot any of her supposed enemies. May Ling straightened her skirts and composed her features. It was time to return into the fray. She re-entered her office the way she'd exited, with a hiss of disapproval and a rush toward her desk.

A spark of interest flamed in the deputy's eyes as May Ling headed for her chair, which he currently occupied. She was betting he'd vacate her spot before she had to force him out, but she was wrong. Seemed he wanted to bargain with her. Or have her in his lap.

"Help me call those people. I'll split the money—"

Sheriff Patton cut his deputy off. "Mind your manners, son. Give the lady her seat back."

Unexpectedly, Squash Blossom exploded with laughter, which made it difficult for May Ling to keep her tranquil composure. She made little shooing gestures with her dainty hands to hurry Patton Junior along. And wondered what was animating Squash Blossom all of a sudden.

So, the pair of lawmen were interested in sharing the bounty money with her? That was not unexpected, but it was disappointing. She thought they had more imagination than that.

Too bad she didn't have the time to explore their motives. Nonetheless, May Ling had dashed out of the room for a reason. Now she had her answers.

If the Pattons were susceptible to profit sharing, maybe they were open to bribes.

And Squash Blossom was full to bursting with a dangerous secret. Just itching to let everyone know who she really was. Not a good thing, but May Ling wasn't sure she could control her for much longer.

Sheriff Patton was right about Valentin being in their way. Although Alain Valentin had allowed May Ling full sway over her business, and had not interfered with any of the girls under her roof, she was under no illusions about who was really in charge. Valentin had *allowed* these things. Nothing had happened here that didn't have his stamp of approval. Even letting her cowboy suitor, Junyur Wilde, come and go unmolested must have fit in with his nefarious scheme somehow.

So why were the sheriff and his deputy suddenly in May Ling's office concocting an escape plan with her that would divest the villain of one of his more profitable investments—the girl cage?

Something was going on that May Ling didn't know about.

She flicked her hand fan out and flipped it closed five times in succession before giving it up. A noise from outside had finally gotten so loud it came through the walls.

"What in the hell is that?" Sheriff Patton cried.

"Stampede from the sound of it," Big Jim replied. "No, don't open the damned ..."

Deputy Patton had thrown open the office door and stalked all the way into the entryway before anyone could stop him. May Ling stood up to watch. When he stuck his head outside, dirt from the street filled the doorway, giving him a coughing fit that left him blind. He soon stumbled over the threshold and out onto the slipshod planked platform that led from Miss Adelaide's to the street.

The men all rushed to help him. Even May Ling followed. Big Jim had been right. It was a cattle stampede, and now they were in the middle of it. Richard and Big Jim scrambled out of the way of the longhorn steers that had jostled one another up onto the platform. May Ling was sheltered behind them and was pushed almost back to her own front door. A piebald steer knocked Deputy Patton off his feet, then kicked him in the chest.

Screaming in pain and sounding just like a little girl getting her fingers caught in a door for the first time, Deputy Patton lashed out at the frightened steer. The steer retaliated.

Its horns grazed the deputy's shirt, ripping it right off him. And then it jumped clumsily back into the street and raced after the rest of the herd bolting crazily down Guthrie's main thoroughfare.

May Ling breathed a sigh of relief. The thundering sounds of hooves were fading away when May Ling heard a familiar voice soaring above it.

The noise of the agitated cattle had confused her senses. For a moment, May Ling thought her cowboy had come back to get her. That Junyur Wilde was behind a scatterbrained plot to confuse everybody with a stampede through downtown.

Her hopes rose tumultuously in her throat at the certainty that Junyur had come back for her, but then dashed her just as suddenly into depression and fear when she came to terms with reality.

Valentin.

It was Valentin.

Everyone around her recognized that voice. May Ling was surprised she hadn't. The deputy seemed scared. While he clutched at his bruised and trammeled chest, Big Jim cautioned him. "Better pour some spirits over that, and I mean right now. Wrap some cloth around it. Tight." Everyone else stood stupefied, even the previously manic Squash Blossom.

May Ling wanted verification that it was truly Valentin out there. To see with her own eyes. She stood on tiptoes in her own entryway, swaying perilously back and forth. Big Jim pushed her gently back into her establishment. "It's him all right. No need to meet him head-on, Miss May Ling."

"They're gone," Richard told her, talking over his shoulder in her direction. "The stampede's gone." Richard wafted his hand in front of his face to disperse the settling dust. "And here he comes," he added. "Earlier than I expected." Richard shot a glance at Big Jim.

"Who?" Deputy Patton asked.

"Get some alcohol on that bruise like I told you," Big Jim snapped.

Richard took a brief look back at the rest of them and then laughed. "I'd do what he says if I were you. And quickly before May Ling's cowboy's brother sees it."

May Ling had started tearing strips out of one of the pillow-cases for the deputy. "What you mean, *brother*?" she asked sharply.

Richard and Big Jim exchanged a sheepish look. Richard held out a placating hand. "Now, don't get yourself all bent out of shape, Missy," he said. "Valentin told us he'd raised this proposition with you, but there's been a change. When you contacted the bounty providers, he had to work fast to stop them."

May Ling blinked rapidly in confusion. She hadn't contacted anybody about Jai Li yet.

Whoever this cowboy's brother was that the bodyguards were talking about couldn't possibly be of any help. And if it was who she thought it was, then things had just gotten a whole lot messier.

God help them all if it really was Junyur's oldest brother. The one she was supposed to have married.

9
Who the hell are you?

"Yog," Junyur ordered, pointing at Jai Li. "Sit down. Over on that little stump, or anywhere. Just sit. Miss Berrigan and I have some conversing to do."

Things hadn't gone as he'd expected. Not by a long shot. One scan of his surroundings confirmed the desolation of the terrain. The Sooners, who had stopped the train to take on their relations, were long gone, not even a dust trail left in their wake to guide him and his two ladies to anywhere.

The train was long gone as well, but soot left behind by its steam furnace still floated through the dry air like blackened snowflakes. Junyur batted them away from his expensive cowboy hat to no avail. When all this was over, price be damned, he was getting himself a new hat.

Junyur didn't even watch to see if Jai Li followed his instructions but immediately fixed Miss Berrigan with his eyes. He coughed, then began.

"It's time we get this straight," he told her. "We're not going any farther until we understand each other."

He searched again for a bit of shade to stand in, for something a little more comfortable to sit on than plain dirt, and didn't find it. He faced the older woman, crossed his arms in front of him to try to exert more control over the situation, and stared her down. In the corner of his eye, Junyur noted stunted bushes, tumble-weeds, and the now vacant train tracks. He coughed some more.

Miss Berrigan finally spoke. "I'm afraid for May Ling. If

you had even one shred of decency left in your degenerate male brain, you'd never have left my goddaughter that way. Even now, it might be too late. We've got to get back to her as fast as we can. Jai Li can help. She's more important than you know. I'm not letting go of that young lady until May Ling's safe."

Junyur sputtered, surprised she actually stopped lecturing him. Boy, had she ever got it wrong! May Ling was nobody's victim. At least not now. She was a dragon. He wouldn't be surprised if she controlled the whole town by the time they got back, even though it had only been a day since they parted.

But he did understand Miss Berrigan's interest in keeping Jai Li by her side. If Jai Li really was a princess, the older woman might be planning on swapping her for May Ling. To whoever was threatening her. The question was, should he let her?

In a way, he was sorry Jai Li wasn't the quiet, scared skinny girl that had been dragged away from the sex cage. He had a sneaking feeling that the princess would turn out to be more than anyone could handle. That she had her own agenda. Jai Li had seemed happy with his plan to take her to his brother's ranch and marry her off. But that had been before Miss Berrigan appeared. And before Jai Li had shown her true colors.

Miss Berrigan's plan would only work if Jai Li and May Ling had a true commitment to one another. May Ling had certainly sacrificed herself to save Jai Li. Until now, though, Jai Li had shown no signs of wanting to reciprocate. Jumping off a moving train and walking through this wasteland seemed more like running away to him, and he wondered at Miss Berrigan interpreting it otherwise.

He looked dubiously back at Miss Berrigan who was regarding him with suspicion. Best to ask her outright just how Jai Li and May Ling were connected. His judgment said Jai Li was a liability. She should simply wait in Oklahoma

City, with a chaperone or something, for his brother Marcus to come up and collect her.

Junyur opened his mouth to accost Miss Berrigan with his misgivings, then immediately resumed coughing. A sheen of dust rose from behind him to lodge in his throat.

Miss Berrigan reared away in shock and spoke for him. "What in the world! Would you look at that!" And she pointed beyond his shoulder.

He turned. A wagon drawn by a draft horse approached slowly from downwind, barely making any noise. Junyur had heard that some buffalo hunters would sheathe the wheels with hides to muffle their rumbling, but he'd not seen it personally until now. No buffalo out here, however. Just what or who were they creeping up on? One last bout of coughing almost drowned out the stranger's greeting.

"Good afternoon, my friends," the big man at the reins hailed them from a distance. "Is that her?" He continued riding right up to them, pulling the horse to a halt in front of Junyur and looking hard down the tracks where Jai Li sat on a stump just down the incline. "The princess? That's got to be her," he said. "It sure isn't either one of you."

The stranger hopped down, not waiting for answers. The well-trained horse stood solid where he left it. Thinking that the big man meant to engage Jai Li out of their hearing, Junyur grabbed the man's arm as he pushed his way past. It was like swatting at a particularly nimble fly. The big man simply flicked his shoulder and brushed right by without a glance at him.

It only took a moment before everyone understood his intent. Before Miss Berrigan had time to berate Junyur for his failure to protect them, Junyur had leapt after the stranger to stop him before he reached the girl. But he wasn't quick enough.

The big man didn't plead or argue with the princess, he simply bopped her in the face with his fist. She fell limply into the dirt, saved only at the last minute from hitting her head on a rock when the man grabbed her arm and jerked her up. Immediately, he slung her over his shoulder and began his return trip to the wagon. Jai Li swung from side to side like a slaughtered deer.

Junyur went wild. His face flamed; his eyes glared. He ground his hands into fists. Certain triggers just immediately sent him over the edge into a sort of berserker frenzy, and seeing a man hit a woman was one of them. At home they had a saying just about him: Wilde by name, wild by nature. He knew it was apt.

"No! Don't!" Miss Berrigan protested. "You'll hurt the girl."

Miss Berrigan's voice echoed as if Junyur were in a barrel and someone called to him from outside. No matter. Nothing Miss Berrigan could say was going to stop him. Junyur bolted right into the man carrying Jai Li and knocked both of them to the ground. Jai Li fell from the man's embrace to tumble down the incline. Miss Berrigan scrambled after her.

The big stranger and Junyur struggled in a tangle of limbs, Junyur on the bottom. He grappled with the man as they plummeted down the incline head over heels, headed toward Jai Li. Out of the corner of his eye, Junyur caught movement. Again, he ended up underneath the big stranger as they came to a rest. No amount of struggling did any good.

With the stranger's grinning face just inches above his, Junyur had the sudden recollection of May Ling's first kiss. The comparison brought bile flooding up his throat, but all his thrashing around did nothing to help him get away. The stranger just grinned more broadly.

The click of a cocked pistol brought both men to their senses. Junyur freed his head to swivel around searching for the source of the sound. He expected it was Miss Berrigan. After all, it was she who had the gun.

Jai Li's coldly determined face behind the expertly leveled pistol truly confounded him and gave him hope that not all was lost. This wasn't the scared skinny girl, this was her alter ego.

"Desist your altercation," Jai Li commanded.

Junyur correctly guessed this was the proper English for *Stop!* He let the other guy face the brunt of her displeasure. He had a feeling that the real Jai Li didn't tolerate disobedience. Keeping totally still, Junyur waited for the inevitable. The big guy with the wagon who was trying to abscond with her ignored Jai Li as if she was an ordinary woman.

Mistake.

When the big guy pulled away from Junyur instead of staying in place, Jai Li took a huge stride forward and kicked him directly on the side of the head with those delicate ballerina slippers still on her feet.

Junyur expected her to fall away in great pain, and with a sprained ankle. He wasn't prepared for the big guy to collapse unconscious back on top of him with what was most likely a concussion. Junyur sure as hell didn't want Jai Li to kick him in the head, so he remained quiet, confused about what to do.

The two women spoke loudly, conferring with one another and standing almost above Junyur. They made no effort to pull the big man off him.

"Leave him there," Miss Berrigan said. "I'll bring the horse and wagon over."

"I think not," Jai Li told her. "He'll be my brother-in-law by and by. Did you know? If I mind my p's and q's I'll be married to a wealthy land owner before long. I heard you talking. Why should I go back with you? This marriage should keep me safe from the empress dowager."

Shocked to his core, Junyur couldn't keep from interrupting their conversation. He'd already forgotten his objections to dragging Jai Li along for the rescue.

"May Ling saved your life." Junyur struggled to push the big man off him and failed. "Don't you want to save her?"

Junyur had a good view of the girl's face as she digested the condemnation he'd tossed up at her, and he wished he hadn't. Jai Li was cold as ice and twice as treacherous.

He'd seen snakes that looked more appealing. That looked more human.

"That is May Ling's job," Jai Li told the two of them, her eyes narrowed to mere slits, her voice clipped and precise. "She was paid to protect me. She failed. You should be grateful I won't take revenge for her negligence."

Junyur scrambled from beneath the stranger, almost growling in rage. This was May Ling she was disparaging. The woman he loved. The woman who'd given up her chance with him in order to save Jai Li.

"Who the hell *are* you?" he demanded, clumsily pushing himself to his feet, kicking away the inert body of the would-be kidnapper. Looking into the alien eyes of Princess Jai Li, Junyur watched her mouth work itself into a weird semblance of a smile.

"Nobody you'd want to cross," she answered. "Now, get out of my way."

10
Appropriating the stranger's horses

Junyur got out of her way.
Jai Li and Miss Berrigan quickly moved out of his hearing range, the older woman gesticulating wildly. The pair seemed to have started another argument. The last thing Junyur heard was something about taking the horse. He only hoped it didn't involve Jai Li's callous plan to abandon him amongst the tumbleweeds. Horse stealing was a bad choice as well, but he could live with that. Maybe.

Junyur shook his head, a little bemused with his irrational admiration of the chit, and a lot worried about his immediate prospects. Jai Li with the bit between her teeth was proving to be unstoppable.

The fourth person of their party took his time returning to consciousness. Junyur decided to help him on his way with a boot to his ribs. The big man's eyes flashed. Then he seesawed on his back until he could flop onto his side. He must have been semi-alert for the past five minutes or more because he knew what they'd been talking about.

"Those are my horses," he yelled toward the two women, still muddled in his speech. "That's my horse, I mean, not yours. My horses. My horse. My wagon. And the bounty on your head, Princess, that's mine too."

Junyur knew what Jai Li was going to do before she did it, and he lunged toward her with all his might. The bullet she'd aimed at the big man's head was redirected now toward Junyur. Thank God, it went wide, hitting only dirt.

The girl fell during his tackle, and the gun dropped from her hands into the rocks. Miss Berrigan hurriedly got to it before anyone else.

Junyur drew Jai Li up from the ground and kept her tightly wrapped in his arms, hoping with all his heart that she didn't bite the hell out of him. And that he hadn't seriously hurt her. She seemed quiet for the moment, almost like the abused girl from the whorehouse, so he gave her back into the older woman's care. "Will you behave?"

Jai Li didn't answer. Just looked sullenly at her feet. He wanted to give her a shake, but didn't. "Let's all get more comfortable," he told Miss Berrigan. "Go sit in the wagon," he told her. "And keep the gun. Don't let the princess get it again. That will be your only job until we get things settled."

Jai Li clambered onto the wagon after Miss Berrigan.

Junyur took his attention off the women to look down at the big stranger. "And you, who the hell are you?"

The man glared, then sneered at Junyur. His eyes greedily studied the cowboy, then veered onto the women in his wagon. His voice came out as a growl. "Mike Shale's my name. My sister Missy was on the train with you. She saw the posters."

Junyur took his attention off Mike Shale to see if Miss Berrigan needed his help controlling the girl. A slight nod of her head toward him settled that question. They were all right, for the moment.

"What posters?" he asked.

Shale acted astounded. As if Junyur had denied Christmas.

"The posters the Chinese government has plastered all through the west. They're in every station and hotel. There's a ten-thousand-dollar bounty on that one's head. They want her back real bad." Shale stopped to take a breath, jabbing a finger in Jai Li's direction for emphasis.

"When I picked up Missy, she pointed her out. Should have grabbed her right there and then. But I had to double-check back at the camp just to be sure."

Miss Berrigan called out from the wagon, "What camp? Find out what camp he's talking about."

Junyur couldn't help rolling his eyes in exasperation. That woman thought she was running the whole show. He hadn't had a minute's peace since she'd invaded their train compartment.

"Who's at this camp?" he asked Shale. "And how far away is it?"

Shale took his gaze off the two women and stared up at Junyur. Before deciding to answer, he spit blood into the dirt and wiped his mouth. "We be five," he said. "Missy and her husband and their oldest boy, and me and my son. About thirty minutes out. I drove out with mine to get Missy and her family from the train so we could bunk up in Purcell for the race."

The race.

The land race Junyur had placed all his hopes on.

He'd almost forgotten it in the middle of this May Ling, Jai Li, and Miss Berrigan mess.

If they hurried back to Guthrie, and Junyur could show the two of them what May Ling had become, and better yet, that she didn't want rescuing, then he'd have just enough time to get back to one of the staging areas for the race. Jai Li and his brother Marcus would just have to wait. May Ling had those two bodyguards. Surely, they could protect the women for a short time.

But if he took the opposite option, ignoring Miss Berrigan's plea to save May Ling (who probably didn't need saving anyway), and he ran with Jai Li to his brother's ranch, then he'd still have enough time to get back to the race. There were still several days left. It was all this being ordered around that was ruining his life. First from Marcus. Then from May Ling. And now from Miss Berrigan.

"Get in the wagon," Junyur brusquely told Shale, hoping the tone of his voice hid the uncertainty in his heart. If May Ling needed rescuing, that was one thing, and he'd sacrifice almost anything to help her. But he was pretty sure that wasn't the case.

"Go on, get over there and get up."

One thing was damned certain, though. The cat was out of the proverbial bag. Jai Li couldn't show her face in Oklahoma City, nor in this man's camp, and probably not on any train either. Ten thousand dollars was killing money. And fierce as she was when she played the princess role, she wasn't a match for *any* man out to take her.

"Now what?" Miss Berrigan's acerbic question broke Junyur's concentration.

She occupied the shotgun position on the wagon. Beside her on the bench seat sat Jai Li, who fiddled with the horse's reins as if she didn't know what to do with them. Seemed the princess had reverted back into the tearful, fearful girl she'd been when he'd taken her away from Guthrie. He really hoped that was the case. Because the other Jai Li scared the hell out of him.

"Let Mr. Shale ride in the back," he told Miss Berrigan. "He has to come with us."

Shale shot him a totally expected look of malice, resignation, and irritation before shrugging and clambering into the wagon bed. The wagon pitched to the left with his weight. Junyur found himself the only one left on the ground and decided to check on the traces, on the state of the horse's harness, on its hooves, and then on the scant bit of cargo that still sat in the wagon bed with its rightful owner.

Junyur had a sudden thought. *Was* Shale the rightful owner? He could have stolen the entire rig.

It didn't matter. Junyur shrugged. He was the owner now, at least until he got the women to safety. Then he'd think about getting Shale his equipment back.

"Miss Berrigan, you've got to get in the back with Mr. Shale," he announced. No way was he putting Jai Li so close to the man who wanted her bounty. And even if Miss

Berrigan could drive the rig, which he doubted, he wouldn't be much of a man if he let her do it.

Miss Berrigan looked as if she would refuse. Junyur opened his mouth, prepared to argue with her, but to his surprise, Miss Berrigan left the front bench with great dignity, and she even raised her arms indicating that Shale should lift her up into the wagon bed beside him. Shale surprised both Junyur, and probably himself, by helping Miss Berrigan without protest, and without any unnecessary jostling.

"Where did you find this marvelous horse of yours?" Miss Berrigan asked Shale when she'd finished arranging her skirts about her on the hard bed of the wagon.

Junyur was also curious. The type of farm horse in the traces was rarely used in this part of Oklahoma. He'd never seen one before.

"My sister's husband's family breeds them," Shale told them proudly. "This gelding was a wedding present."

Junyur was thinking that if it was a wedding present, then it was a pretty old horse by now, when he felt the man glaring straight at him. Suddenly Shale pointed. "You'd better not hurt my horse, boy. If you do, you'll be the sorriest cowboy this side of Texas, I swear!"

At first affronted that any man could think he'd knowingly harm a horse, Junyur stopped and thought before he spoke. He'd left his favorite horses back in Guthrie, hadn't he? On Jai Li's obviously suspect orders so they could take the train. God only knew what had happened to them. And he hadn't even given them a single thought since.

Even if his original plan to whisk May Ling back to the Texas ranch with him had worked out, hadn't he been planning to use the same horses to do that, and then only a short time later use them in the race? Where the horses were almost certainly going to get injured, either through overexertion or some sort of accident?

Seemed Mr. Shale had made an uncomfortably accurate assessment of Junyur's character, at least as far as horseflesh went. And he didn't appreciate it. Junyur eyed the newest member of their party with distaste. No one liked getting caught out for being less than they should be.

"I'll deal with your horse as needed," Junyur told him coldly.

11
The arrival of Marcus Wilde, the older brother

MARCUS WILDE IN CAHOOTS WITH **Alain Valentin?** May Ling reeled at the implications. Had Junyur tricked her into putting Jai Li in harm's way? She tapped her fan furiously against the upholstered chair blocking her path before tossing the frivolous thing into the cushions.

May Ling pushed past her bodyguards. At the door leading down to the street, she paused to study the features of Valentin's guest. The dust from the stampede still swirled. The shadows emerging from them quickly coalesced into the form of a man. Her heart skipped erratically. If she hadn't intimately known her lover's size and shape and way of walking, she'd have mistaken Marcus Wilde for Junyur Wilde. But the age difference told.

Marcus Wilde had lived life. Junyur Wilde had just begun. Her lover seemed almost a blank slate compared to this man. Pain had etched itself permanently into lines around the older brother's eyes and the sides of his mouth. His hair was short. You could barely see any strands peeking from underneath his expensive Stetson. He also had the tanned skin of a man who'd lived much of his life out of doors.

By his side, as if for contrast, slinked May Ling's landlord Alain Valentin, the nefarious, devious, yet deadly charming nemesis of her charge, Jai Li. His short cap of straight black hair had gone to gray above his ears. His artfully concerned-looking brown eyes were the type found on many Midwestern American men, but Valentin was part Chinese, part French.

A gray goatee decorated his chin, and a sparse yet scruffy mustache framed his upper lip.

He looked like a nice man, but he wasn't. May Ling had heard that Valentin's demeanor always remained studiously grave, even as he carried out the basest of the empress's orders. Jai Li had once called him a changeling. May Ling knew he'd started out as a spy. Heaven only knew what his job was now.

Goosebumps rose on May Ling's forearms. The back of her head tingled. Not for the first time did she wonder if Alain Valentin was more than mortal man.

No matter. She'd always suspected they'd battle it out sooner or later. Seemed it was to be sooner. May Ling hoped Junyur's brother was more innocent bystander than accomplice. It dismayed her mightily to see a Wilde in the company of a Valentin. May Ling took a deep breath to steady her nerves, at the last moment mourning her hastily-discarded paper fan. In her capable hands it had often served as a weapon. Now, she felt naked without it.

May Ling moved carefully from the rickety wooden sidewalk in front of her establishment and into the street to confront the pair. She didn't want to slip and fall in the muck, humiliating herself in front of her enemies, so she minced her steps. She slowed even more realizing that her silk kimono robe would be ruined. Making a face, she shrugged. It couldn't be helped.

May Ling looked around for any stray steers before hopping lightly down. She had no wish to be trampled by any of the cattle still rampaging through the town, but other than that, she had no fear of them.

A sea of mud met her eyes. The earlier stampede of longhorns had made a mess of the main street. She'd been lucky to have kept her soft shoes on her feet.

May Ling made it safely to the middle of the street where she stopped in front of the two men, keeping her hands still, leaving all thoughts of cattle behind. This was her first meeting with Valentin since she'd spirited Jai Li away from him.

Behind her was Miss Adelaide's Club for Discerning Men. At the end of the street across from it was the local teahouse. The sheriff's office was on the other end of the street, with five or more shells of half-built store-fronts taking up the space between them. Guthrie was a town growing larger by the day.

"Who you have there?" she asked Valentin, as if she hadn't already figured it out. She really wanted to know the why of it, but etiquette demanded she ask her questions in the proper order. She nodded as cordially as the situation allowed toward the stranger.

Valentin didn't answer her, but instead studied the men at her back. Her bodyguards had followed her out of Miss Adelaide's. So had Squash Blossom, who glowered venomously out of flashing eyes. Valentin crossed his arms in front of his chest and gave back as good as he got. His gray morning coat flapped lightly in the breeze that had just come up.

Marcus Wilde answered her. "I am the oldest of the Wilde family, May Ling." His voice floated to her ears, low and sonorous, like a heavy musical string instrument. She leaned closer to him, as if she couldn't hear.

"Mister Valentin tells me you've made some sort of arrangement with my little brother Junyur. I'm here to tell you Junyur's got no authority to agree to anything on our behalf, so you might as well let him go."

May Ling came out of her self-induced trance with a start. The brother clearly thought she'd shanghaied Junyur. Or otherwise kept him captive. May Ling thinned her smile to a snarl and directed it at Valentin.

Still positioned strategically behind May Ling's back, Squash Blossom snorted in amusement. May Ling would have joined her in laughing had Marcus Wilde not appeared so humorless.

So, they thought she had Junyur Wilde ensconced somewhere in her establishment. Good. That would give him and Jai Li a lot more time to escape Valentin's reach.

"Brother left yesterday." May Ling ventured a sly glance at Valentin who seemed lost in his own thoughts and was still glowering at Squash Blossom. "Took Jai Li with him."

That got Valentin's attention, though it was Richard his gaze turned to. May Ling took this short reprieve to chance another glance at Marcus Wilde. How had he known to come here?

She thought back to a few minutes ago. Richard and Big Jim had said Marcus Wilde was out in the street. They'd let slip something about a plan Valentin had proposed. And about her contacting the person offering the bounty for Jai Li's capture.

She hadn't—

When you contacted the bounty providers he had to work fast.

May Ling gasped in dismay. When she'd telegraphed the empress dowager to stop her from putting a bounty on Jai Li for her safe return, she had expected the spate of *Wanted Dead or Alive* posters that had cropped up all over the west to disappear. The empress dowager didn't really want Jai Li dead, only banished from China—with good reason.

Or did she?

Either way, Richard had the right of it. May Ling had failed to stop the bounty hunters. She fluttered her hands as if she still had her precious fan. She studied Valentin, her emotions in turmoil, not liking the knowing smirk that had appeared on his face.

Valentin didn't have any use for the bounty money. He was richer than God. What he did have was an undying enmity for Jai Li. Probably for rejecting his amorous advances. There might have been other reasons for his vendetta, but unrequited love was May Ling's guess. Jai Li had told her not, but May Ling didn't believe her. Romantic love was

The Cimarron Bride

on her mind constantly since meeting Junyur Wilde in the flesh. Unrequited love, hopeless love, any and all sorts of love. Surely, Valentin was human enough to fall.

The ground trembling beneath her feet jolted May Ling out of her reverie. She began to slip sideways. Panicked, she blanched, fearing an earthquake, and turned to run. And nearly got herself killed.

Marcus Wilde expertly jerked May Ling out of the path of a longhorn thundering back through the town. It would have trampled her if she'd moved so much as an inch. May Ling screamed out a warning to her team. Squash Blossom had been left alone and exposed to the danger that would have killed the both of them if Marcus hadn't intervened, and he hadn't grabbed Squash Blossom, only her.

May Ling couldn't look, but closing her eyes didn't prevent her from imagining the collision between woman and steer that had to have happened. When she opened her eyes, Squash Blossom was safe on the porch, calming a trembling longhorn with her soothing voice.

Marcus picked up May Ling, carrying her all the way back to her whorehouse, dodging cattle right and left with his arms wrapped around her for protection. A few minutes later, he had dragged her up to the rickety sidewalk and almost to Miss Adelaide's front door.

Dozens of out-of-control longhorns raced back and forth in the street in front of them. One frantic steer got itself caught up on the walkway beside them and crashed through it down to the ground. May Ling winced, sure it must have broken a leg, but it quickly recovered. One part of May Ling's mind began figuring the cost of repairing the walk. She couldn't help laughing at herself. She had much more important things to ponder. Fixing a sidewalk was an unnecessary luxury.

"What's so funny?"

Marcus breathed heavily into May Ling's ear, then repeated his question. "What's so funny?"

Saved from having to explain herself by the outlandish sight that met her eyes, May Ling pointed silently. The two or three longhorns closest to them were now kicking the sides of her whorehouse.

And it was funny, to May Ling. Until she figured it out.

This had all been a distraction.

A set up.

A planned drama, meant to keep her off balance. With probably Valentin the mastermind behind it.

But from what was she being distracted?

May Ling pursed her lips, forgetting for a moment that she still stood within the safety of Marcus Wilde's arms.

Was it Marcus himself she was supposed to overlook?

12
Valentin knows all about it

MAY LING GLANCED CAUTIOUSLY UP into Marcus Wilde's face. He caught her at it, grinned, and loosened his grip on her waist. He and Junyur smelled nothing alike. Marcus had the odor of tobacco about him. Junyur smelled of spice.

The town stood silent for once, the rampaging cattle having tired themselves out. As she breathed in the scent of the older Wilde brother, May Ling wondered if the stampede had wrecked her sidewalk beyond repair. She steadied herself using Marcus's shoulder and began limping her way through the broken planks to Miss Adelaide's main door.

"You're hurt," exclaimed Valentin, abruptly materializing in May Ling's path. He was right, she *had* been injured. Hadn't realized it until now. She stared in dismay at her feet, quickly forgetting her puzzlement at the villain's sudden appearance as her ankle began stinging. One of the steers must have nicked her with its sharp hooves.

Before she could stop him, Valentin leapt off the porch, possibly to get help. May Ling figured he meant to look heroic, jumping to find her aid, but he slipped the minute his feet hit the mud and fell on his backside. There was nothing for it but to laugh, so she did. First in merry little tinkles she'd often been told sent shivers down men's spines. Then in an out-and-out belly laugh. People falling down were always funny. Valentin falling down was exceptionally satisfying.

Laughing at Valentin made her ankle hurt even worse.

Without thinking, May Ling put her hand out to Marcus, and he took it. She slowly raised the bottom edge of her kimono to calf level, then stuck out the offending foot to see what was the matter. Above her muddy soft-sole shoes, her ankle looked just fine. She shot a sharp peek at Valentin from under artfully lowered eyelashes. Had she limped before the villain had suggested she was injured, or only afterward? Sometimes with Alain Valentin, reality and fantasy blurred.

Gingerly, May Ling began walking without assistance, determined to get back home without any man's help. Every step hurt, but every step hurt less than the one before. As she passed through her front door, she turned back to stare at Valentin, who'd finally regained his own footing. May Ling glared. Hissed, even. He'd better stay away from her from now on.

A smile emerged on May Ling's face at the reaction she saw. In both men. Valentin reared back as if he feared she'd throw herself through the air and tackle him back to the ground. Marcus whistled appreciatively under his breath and pushed his hat off. Like his younger brother, Marcus was also blond.

"You don't want to see this," Richard told May Ling when she turned around and found him barring the way into her whorehouse. Big Jim nodded in agreement. "Why don't you take Squash Blossom and the both of you get some tea down at the Chinaman's place," Richard continued. "At least give us some time to get some of the glass swept up."

"No," was all May Ling said, but then she had to wait for the two-letter word to percolate through Richard's thick head. He'd understand in a moment. Meanwhile, she tapped her little fan furiously against one of the support posts on the porch, knowing Valentin was enjoying the scene. She was just about at the point of setting Squash Blossom on Richard before the bodyguard reluctantly gave way. May Ling and Squash Blossom entered Miss Adelaide's, brushing past both Richard and Big Jim with a haughty expression that abruptly disappeared once they'd passed the threshold.

"No cows did this," May Ling exclaimed. Pictures were off the walls, chairs overturned with their insides cut to pieces, and excrement smeared the floor leading to the kitchen. May Ling wasn't an expert on cattle, but she knew human shit when she smelled it.

"Valentin!" Squash Blossom replied. "He came from here, May Ling. Jumped out at you from the porch."

Somehow May Ling couldn't see Valentin smearing shit all over her walls. After all, he owned what she managed. Despite her acute sense of proprietorship, this wasn't her business. It was his. Something else was at play here. She pursed her lips in puzzlement until she saw Squash Blossom watching her. No reason to drag Squash Blossom into the fight between Jai Li and Valentin.

Wanting to collapse and recover in one of her precious chairs, May Ling instead straightened her shoulders and pasted a grim smile on her face. She'd heard the rustle of cloth at the stairway. The rest of her ladies were coming down the landing.

She turned to Squash Blossom. "Stop them," she said, shrugging toward the women carefully descending toward them. "Keep them hidden upstairs. We leave now."

She objected to the disguised young man giving her the once-over, rather than obeying her orders. They had discussed running. Had agreed to it as a last resort. She shouldn't be so surprised. Squash Blossom usually anticipated May Ling's needs and filled them before she issued any orders. Not this time, though. Indeed, Squash Blossom still stood, staring at her with an unreadable expression.

Thinking she'd misread her intentions, May Ling grabbed Squash Blossom's arm and tapped her hard on the head with her fan. "All of us leave. Pack. Sneak away. Organize those upstairs. Find everyone. Everyone."

But that was not to be.

What May Ling feared the worst—that Squash Blossom would finally break down from the strain of his deception and proclaim his secret to the world in some horrific crime—started on the bottom steps of her staircase that afternoon with a willful narrowing of Squash Blossom's eyes and a smug smile on her lips.

"My father will no longer hold sway over you!" she declared, loudly, and with her true, masculine voice. "I will stop him here."

Before May Ling could prevent her, she'd leapt past her, pushing down the two bodyguards who stepped forward to detain her. Without a single look behind at them, she ran out the door, silk skirts flying.

May Ling, Richard, and Big Jim stood frozen for a second, then followed Squash Blossom back outside. They were just in time to see her grab one of the over-excited horses let loose from the stable and hoist herself up on its back. In another moment, she would have been out of sight.

If anyone hadn't already guessed her secret, they'd have gotten a shocking eyeful once she'd jumped onto the horse's back. Her skirts ripped right down the front, exposing the all-too-revealing underclothes that had come from Sears Roebuck. As she fled, May Ling dejectedly watched flecks of mud rise up from her horse's hooves. After a moment, Squash Blossom was gone.

Seemed he didn't need her protection anymore, May Ling mused, biting at her lip. A yard or two away lay Squash Blossom's favorite kimono, soaking in one of the mud pools that had collected from the stampede.

He must be mostly naked by now. At least his upper half. If his hair had come undone, someone might mistake him for one of the American Indians May Ling had read about but never seen out here. Painted face and all.

The question was—and here May Ling turned to face Valentin who'd come up behind her, still scraping mud off his pants—had Valentin recognized his own youngest son amidst all that now-discarded and tattered silk and satin in the road over there?

May Ling couldn't decide. Neither did she venture to guess at Squash Blossom's plan. It would be a waste of her time, and there wasn't much of it left to her anymore.

Valentin finally pulled himself together. May Ling tottered with the sudden and intimate weight of his arm across her shoulder. Seemed he thought he could use her as a crutch.

Or maybe he just wanted to whisper into her ear.

May Ling braced herself against being maneuvered out of her spot, but it turned out to be conversation that was on his mind and not further bullying.

"I've known for a long time, May Ling," Valentin said, pointing with his goateed chin in the direction his youngest son had taken. His shrug seemed to indicate he didn't care one way or the other. With his next anguished words, he confirmed it. "He's been dead to me ever since he was a small boy and murdered all my cats."

May Ling recoiled in shock. She liked cats as well as the next person, but family was family. And none of this explained Valentin's pursuit of and determination to kill Princess Jai Li. Or his determination to debase May Ling herself. For a second, she was tempted to ask.

Marcus Wilde coughed behind them. She and Valentin turned as one to the stranger in their midst, Valentin pulling himself up to his full height. May Ling curbed her urge to rearrange her skirts, and stood silent and still under her lover's brother's scrutiny. With another cough, or maybe it was a harrumph, Marcus walked away from them and away from her sporting house as well, leaving her the choice to follow or to keep Valentin company.

"My son must have run off to find your cowboy," Valentin announced, making sure May Ling was listening by pinching her on her upper arm.

"I've got a proposition for you," he whispered. "I know

you want the cage business discontinued. I'll guarantee it. If you can get the Wilde brothers for me."

May Ling furrowed her brows. Why would he want the Wilde brothers, and what exactly was she expected to do about them?

Valentin recognized her confusion. "It's their land I want, May Ling. Even more than I want that damn girl brought low. I'll trade you the girl, the girls in your house of disrepute, and discontinue the cage in exchange for the Wilde ranch."

Before May Ling had time to disguise her feelings, she knew that Valentin had recognized the tiny smile of surprise she'd let show on her face.

At last, here was a way out for all of them.

If she could understand Valentin's motives. If she could trust in his word.

Weighed out logically, what was more valuable to her? What mattered most? The lives of the many different people in her care, or the two Wilde brothers that she didn't really know.

No matter that she was in love with one of them.

13
Jai Li's flight

"Where would you go to intercept this train if you were gathering riders for the race? Further north, or south?" Junyur asked the erstwhile kidnapper Shale, the wannabe bounty hunter, from his position by the horse's head. He had yet to decide who would manage the reins.

Shale hunched over and refused to speak.

Miss Berrigan huffed and answered for him. "I don't think Mr. Shale is going to help us, Mr. Wilde," she said. "Do you plan on putting us back on the train? You realize that was how Ja Li was recognized. Do they still have stagecoaches in this area? Maybe that would be safer."

Junyur wasn't native to this area, so he didn't know. Probably only Mr. Shale knew the answer to her question, and it looked like he wasn't going to volunteer any information. In annoyance, Junyur lessened his grip on the horse's halter. Miss Berrigan clambered out of the wagon to confront him face to face. Shale followed a minute later after telling them he wanted to move about a bit. That left only Jai Li in the conveyance. Junyur held the halter, but loosely.

"I think we just need a couple more sound horses," Junyur finally decided, gazing out at the prairie. "I assume you three can ride?" He tried giving each of his companions a confident smile, but failed.

Jai Li ignored him, but Miss Berrigan gave him a concerned look and gently told him, "No."

Junyur entertained the idea of leading two inexperienced women and an unwilling man on horseback for the length of time it took to get to Guthrie, or even Oklahoma City, and shuddered. He'd have to go alone.

These three would have to hide somewhere safe until he got back. Unfortunately they weren't going to be able to let Mr. Shale go. Junyur wondered if Miss Berrigan could handle him on her own and decided she couldn't.

Shale would either have to come with Junyur, or they'd have to imprison him somehow while Junyur was gone. Shale would be a liability staying behind, but he'd be a more formidable liability accompanying Junyur. Shale would have to stay with the women.

Junyur decided not to tell the others of his plan. They could object all they wanted to once he'd found them a refuge with enough food and water and gotten two swift horses to carry him onward, one to ride, the other as backup. "I'll figure something out," he told them. "Everyone, get ready to leave. And, Shale," he added, "you'd best behave or you'll wish a lot more than good treatment for your horse."

Shale growled, but settled down. His shoulders drooped back into a belligerent slump as he began to hoist himself up into the wagon. Jai Li turned her body sideways on the bench seat so Junyur couldn't see her face, and hissed, "No."

Shale jumped obediently off the wagon-bed and stood stolidly behind it, staring at Junyur.

"Stop it right there, young man!" Miss Berrigan demanded. Although the older woman's words bypassed Junyur's brain as if they were refried beans racing through his digestive system, they also froze him to the spot. He thought she was talking to Shale, but Junyur's body clearly understood otherwise even if his head did not.

Junyur faced the pistol in Miss Berrigan's hands once more. Next chance he got he'd take the damned thing away from her and throw it into a cactus patch.

Junyur looked to Jai Li for help, and got only indifference.

Nor did Shale come to his aid. With a suspiciously sly smirk on his lips, the stranger in their midst held out his hands to indicate it had nothing to do with him.

Junyur instinctively knew to keep his eyes on Jai Li, who convincingly trembled in a hunched-up position on the bench seat as if she were afraid of Miss Berrigan's gun, the reins to the horse dangerously close to her hands. Shale, Miss Berrigan, and Junyur were still standing on the left-hand side of the wagon. Bunched up and dancing around each other for position. Junyur took his eyes off Jai Li for one second, and then had the most horrible premonition.

Nothing except inexperience was keeping that frightening girl from taking control of the wagon and leaving the other three of them in her dust. And before Junyur had the time to let go of the horse's halter and get his feet out of the path of the wheels, he almost lost his fingers.

Jai Li had abruptly stood up in the wagon. "Yes," Jai Li shouted, "stop right there as the lady suggested. And goodbye." Then with a banshee-like scream directed at the three of them, the princess took control of the traces and slapped the huge horse into a dead run.

Junyur leapt out of the way just in time, falling on his face in the road. Miss Berrigan lost control of the pistol. Shale stepped away from all of them.

Within a minute, all Junyur could see of Jai Li was the dust of her passage. Still flat on his back, he kicked holes into the dirt with the heels of his boots to avoid the screaming fit rising up from his diaphragm.

Shale stepped out of range, commenting coolly, "That's ten thousand dollars you just let get away from you."

"Help me up," Junyur said. "I don't deal in bounties, so it wouldn't matter if it was a million dollars."

"Were," Miss Berrigan said, correcting his grammar. She came closer to inspect his injuries, and looked a bit ashamed. "You'll be all right. Whatever possessed you to let the girl go?"

"Yeah," Shale said. "Didn't your Pa teach you not to ever trust a woman?"

"I don't need any advice from the peanut gallery," Junyur groused. He did, however, wonder if his obligation to May Ling concerning the girl had ended with her flight. He wasn't going to be able to go after Jai Li, and go with Miss Berrigan back to Guthrie to rescue May Ling, and also get Shale set up somewhere civilized. All at the same time. Or even consecutively.

There was the race to consider, too.

Shale read his mind. He gave Junyur a broad grin full of malicious humor. "I'd forget about the land race if I were you. Go back to your family. Or go rescue this May Ling you keep talking about. That little girl who just stole my wagon and horse won't be coming back."

Junyur feared he was right. They couldn't just stand here along the tracks. They'd wasted enough time already. Junyur eyed the big man. Shale came from somewhere close to this area, he should know where the nearest house stood. And it didn't make sense for him to refuse aid at this point.

"Where would you walk from here?" Junyur asked Shale, gesturing with his arm to include the whole eastern expanse. "We can't do much without horses. Where can we find horses?"

"And water?" Miss Berrigan added.

"Why not ask for the moon while you're at it?" Shale responded.

At Junyur's glare, Shale toned down his sarcasm. "If it's horses fit to steal, then the nearest place would be what they call the Seguin spread south of here. Fair warning, though. Those Texicans who settled up here hang horse thieves.

"I'd try for the Hauftmann ranch. They usually have horses boarding with them. Plus, there's a barn for shelter. The missus might even be soft-hearted enough to feed us, too. At least once."

Miss Berrigan waited for Junyur to say something,

and when he didn't, she butted in. "How far away are the Hauptmanns? And will our encroachment harm them? Harm them too much?" she amended at Shale's grin.

"They're the rich folk in this area. I'd imagine they can replace whatever it be that we take," he replied.

Both looked to Junyur. Shale had given him the information he'd asked for. Seemed there was a relatively easy remedy to their current plight. So why did he feel so despondent over it? It couldn't be the loss of Jai Li.

The real girl, once she'd dropped her act, had recovered from her ordeal as a dangerous, arrogant, and unlikable misfit. She didn't even have beauty to soften the other attributes.

So, was it that he planned on returning to May Ling instead of his long dreamed of land race that had Junyur down in the dumps?

That rescuing the whore meant sacrificing the ambition?

Whatever it was, Junyur realized this was not the time to mope about it. He looked both his companions in the eyes and nodded.

"Mr. Shale. I thank you," Junyur said. "When we've settled accounts at the Hauftmann's ranch, I will be sure you have what it takes to get you back to your own family."

Shale crossed his arms in front of his chest and glowered. "You'll no longer throw me into a basement and leave me for the rats? That's mighty big of you."

"Yes," Miss Berrigan said. "What changed your mind?"

What Junyur wondered was how both of them knew what he'd been planning.

It was with that thought that he watched the sun set. They'd been bickering for longer than he'd calculated. A little more time contemplating the turquoise, gray, and pink clouds following the disappearing sun into the void wouldn't hurt.

But pink clouds? Really?

Junyur's cowboy soul shuddered, but the poetic sensibility he'd hidden from everyone except May Ling (in his letters to her) soared at the sight.

14
We learn too much about Miss Berrigan

JUNYUR COULDN'T BELIEVE EITHER OF them had actually thought he'd imprison a stranger and just leave him to die. What sort of a man did they think he was? They didn't deserve an answer. His indignant body posture ought to be enough to show them how offended he was. Junyur shook his head at the pair.

"Let's get walking." He pretended he didn't see the look that passed between them, the one that said *I told you so*. He was an expert on that look, having brothers surrounding him all the time. "Do we follow the train track?"

Barking, "No!" as his answer, Shale dismissively pushed Junyur aside. "You'll only get squashed flat that way. Sometimes the trains come up too fast. If you're not paying attention ..." He clapped his hands together to illustrate his point.

"Anyhow," he continued, pointing at the horizon. "That's the wrong direction. We need to go this way."

Miss Berrigan fell in step with the burly stranger, leaving Junyur to bring up the rear. The rising full moon helped them avoid hazards, still Junyur took note of the times Shale helped Miss Berrigan cross some suspect spot, and stepped with care when he came close to it as well. He had to. They could have voiced their warnings to him too, but they hadn't. And they didn't the whole long trek through the darkling Oklahoma plains.

It was beneath Junyur's dignity to call out for them to

slow down, and he especially wouldn't ask for a break. So bit by bit, Junyur fell farther and farther behind. It was only because of the flickering light shining out of a ranch house kitchen window that he found his way to safety and caught up with his cohorts.

Only later did Junyur wonder if Miss Berrigan *meant* to leave him behind. Or if she'd changed her allegiance to Shale, thinking the bigger man would be more help to her than Junyur in the business of getting May Ling out of the whorehouse and into her motherly care. Of course, Miss Berrigan still didn't know about the whorehouse.

Part of him sort of wished that was true. But the bigger part of him remembered May Ling and the taste of her kisses. He wasn't going to let Shale have even the slightest glimpse of May Ling. Shale would not go any further with them.

Miss Berrigan and Shale had concealed themselves in the barn where Junyur found them easily enough. They told him they were waiting for him. He almost believed them.

Junyur considered complaining, decided against it. If he couldn't keep up with them on foot, he knew with certainty that they couldn't keep up with him on horseback. And the next part of his plan depended on those promised horses. He'd give Miss Berrigan and Shale this little taste of winning one over on him. It meant nothing in the long run.

The moon was higher in the sky now. Slits in the barn walls and holes in the roof allowed enough light that he could see his companions.

"That the Hauftmann place?" Junyur used his head to indicate direction while keeping an eye on the two. "Shouldn't their livestock be in this barn?" he asked.

Except for their own heavy breathing, no noises emanated from the structure. It had hay arranged in stalls and spread over the floor in abundance, but no animals. Shale began to laugh.

Holding out his hands to forestall Junyur's complaint,

he said, "You don't know the Hauftmanns. They sometimes keep their animals in the house. Yes, the house. I've seen it."

Wondering why anyone would do something so bizarre, Junyur saw his answer in Shale's face. He was telling the truth, but how did Shale know so much about this family? Maybe because he was a cattle thief or a horse thief and had a history of hanging about this place to get the lay of the land? And that was why these people kept their horses in the house. To keep them out of reach.

Shale saved Junyur the trouble of asking. "Yep. I steal horses from them. Sometimes. People have too much to themselves as it is. I spread it around to other folks."

"Are you comparing yourself to Robin Hood?" Miss Berrigan sprang up from her spot on the hay mound and punched the big man in the chest. "You're nothing but a thief. Who do you think you're fooling? You've never given any of your ill-gotten goods to the unfortunate! No one ever does. Don't you lie to me even one more time, son!"

For some reason, her outburst tickled Junyur's funny bone. What started out as an amused snort quickly escalated into giggles. When he accidentally met Shale's startled eyes, it caused both men to break out laughing. Junyur wondered if Miss Berrigan had some sort of soft spot for the Robin Hood character. He didn't know why Shale laughed so heartily.

"I'll tell you," Shale said between bouts of guffaws, somehow reading Junyur's mind for the second time. "People used to call me Little John because of my girth. Made me curious enough to read the story. I ain't lying. Them horses from here that I took are working out real well at the Mission at the top of the river in San Antonio."

"That's a hell of a range," Junyur commented. He caught movement out of the corner of his eye. He managed to deflect Miss Berrigan's next swipe at their resident thief, but caught the brunt of it himself. "That hurt," he complained, rubbing his shoulder. "That's not ladylike behavior, either," he added. "I expected more from someone like you."

Miss Berrigan raised herself up to her full five-foot-five-inch height and ripped her hat off. Both men gasped. They'd not seen her without that hat on her head the whole time they'd known her. Instead of the carefully coifed long hair they'd expected from a woman of her age, Miss Berrigan's short-cut cap of hair brought to mind pictures of Joan of Arc, to Junyur, at least. He had no way of knowing what Shale thought, other than he looked shocked.

"What happened to you?" Shale demanded, brutally to the point.

Miss Berrigan raised her head, suddenly fierce with pride. "I was one of the Parkerites," she explained. Then seeing that neither man knew what she was talking about, she continued, "I vowed to keep my hair short like the Indian captive Cynthia Ann Parker until she was returned to her family. Her Indian family," she emphasized.

"She's dead," Junyur said. He knew the story quite well.

"I know that!" Miss Berrigan snapped. "I grew to like it this way."

"Then why do you keep hiding behind all that headgear?"

"Don't be stupid, young man. People pester me with questions otherwise. Little children try to look up my skirt."

Both men tried to stifle the burst of laughter bubbling from their mouths, and failed. Miss Berrigan promptly boxed each of them on their ears.

"Mercy!" Junyur cried, shielding his head with his arms. "Mercy, madam!" But as she backed off, he gave her a sly grin and added, "But why do the children try to see under your skirts?"

"Because asshole men like you put them up to it," she yelled. "Just leave me alone. Leave me be for a moment."

Junyur didn't figure either he or Shale was bothering the old maid all that much. It had only been a small bit of teasing. *Broke the ice, didn't it? Made Shale act like he was one of the group rather than outside it.*

After stalking away and brooding in the corner for a

quarter of an hour, Miss Berrigan stalked back, interrupting Junyur's contemplation.

"I feel that I made a mistake," she announced, nose in the air and eyes directed anywhere but at either of the two men in her company. "You two can go your own ways. I'll engage transportation from one of the Hauftmanns, and go after May Ling by myself. It never really concerned either of you to begin with, at least not now that the princess ran away."

Rather than feeling relieved, Junyur's first response was anger, which he quickly quelled. This was an old woman he was dealing with. She was probably going through the change. With a quick grimace, Junyur tore his thoughts away from that unseemly tangent.

Strangely enough, though, Junyur never considered following Miss Berrigan's orders to cease and desist. To go away and leave her alone. It didn't even cross his mind, even though it would have set him free to run the race.

For once the great land race wasn't first in his thoughts. It was maybe third or fourth.

He interrupted Miss Berrigan's tirade. "All that just because we made fun of your hair!"

"This doesn't concern you anymore," she said, looking determined to stand her ground.

"It sure as hell concerns me since it sure as hell concerns my brother Marcus who is going to marry her!"

Miss Berrigan stepped back a pace. After a moment, she pointed straight at him and cried, "Jai Li is gone, young man. Good and gone, and your little scheme right along with it. So why don't you just go back to where you came from? And leave May Ling to me. I no longer require your services."

Junyur took a deep breath, trying to clear his mind. He guessed Miss Berrigan really did plan to ask the Hauftmanns for help, what with Shale confessing to horse thievery and himself to an overwhelming desire to leave everything behind and join the great land race.

And he wished he could.

Leave the two of them.

Wished he could trust May Ling to take care of herself—after all, she'd done pretty well for the past year—if you didn't count turning to prostitution. Wished he could trust Shale not to try claiming the bounty on the missing Jai Li. And trust the Hauftmanns to be decent people. And Miss Berrigan not to get herself killed.

Unfortunately, trust didn't come easily to any of the Wilde brothers. Sometimes not even within the clan itself.

Maybe it was a good thing that Jai Li had run off like that. Junyur winced at the thought of Marcus's reaction to his planning a marriage between the two of them. If he knew his oldest brother, and he did, Marcus would take the easiest way out of the mess. With guns blazing.

15
Put her in the cage!

STANDING IN THE MUDDY STREET with only her bodyguards and that villain Valentin for company, May Ling realized too late that she'd misinterpreted Valentin's reaction to finding his son Squash Blossom under her protection. She struggled to keep that knowledge off her face. Wished mightily that Marcus Wilde would saunter back over. She could use someone with his broad shoulders and lithe frame. Though they were strangers to each other, May Ling felt a strong connection to Marcus. Because of Junyur.

Valentin! She needed to keep her mind on Valentin, who now watched her like a cat contemplating the mouse in the corner. He licked his lips in anticipation as May Ling fought to keep her contempt concealed. Big Jim and Richard were there to help her. Even Valentin wouldn't dare hurt her out here in the street.

But when Valentin's men converged on the planks alongside the barely-built businesses across from them, she visibly shuddered. Ten men at least. Shuffling against one another, their boots beat an annoying rattle on the wooden platform that served as a sidewalk. The grin on Valentin's face was all it took to deflate what had been her rising confidence.

May Ling had always assumed Valentin indifferent to his son. Both in Valentin's tone and in his words, there had never been anything to show he even knew where his son was, nor cared. But now a subtle shift of shadow over

Valentin's face revealed an unexpected depth of pure self-hatred. It disappeared as soon as it materialized, leaving May Ling unsure it had ever existed. Valentin had always oozed power, and arrogance, and what she saw as false concern.

May Ling had nothing to do with his son's life choices, but she had stepped forward to shelter him. As Squash Blossom. A boy of Eurasian descent hiding out in a whorehouse disguised as a Chinese girl.

Disconcerted, May Ling rubbed some of the mud off her sleeves, only succeeding in spreading it further. Onto her fingers, her face, and even into her mouth. Dirt tasted like dirt. She spit it out.

One of her shoes was mired in the muck near her nemesis. No chance in hell that he'd help her with its recovery. She could see the wheels turning in Valentin's mind. Plans within plans within plans.

Valentin didn't want the Wilde brothers' estate! He wanted to crush Marcus and Junyur under his heels like he'd done with this poor street where she'd finally found a home.

Valentin wasn't going to free the girls from the sex cages, either. May Ling barely disguised her sneer of contempt. She still had to play nice in order to get what she wanted.

Valentin still stood before her, waiting for her nod of agreement. Richard and Big Jim flanked him, looking proud of their pact. Did they understand what she'd just realized? Would they still protect her? Fight alongside her? No way was Valentin's aim to take over the Wilde brothers' ranch. Something much bigger was afoot.

Evidently, some of May Ling's consternation escaped her carefully placid countenance, for her two bodyguards stepped slowly away from Valentin. Over the past half year, they'd learned to read her body language. They were not mistaking her intentions now. The sucking sound their old boots made as they temporarily escaped the mud set her teeth on edge. Richard and Big Jim, and maybe Mr. Wilde, were all the help she was going to get.

Squash Blossom had run. May Ling bet she meant to go for Junyur, but it was too late for that. She hoped she'd keep on running. Forget all about May Ling and her plight.

Jai Li should have been in Marcus Wilde's protection by now, but clearly she wasn't. May Ling could only hope Jai Li wasn't returning to Miss Adelaide's. Valentin wouldn't let her get away from him one more time.

Junyur should be back at the Wilde property by now. Or preparing for the great land race coming up. She wished him luck. She wished him happiness. She wished him prosperity in his future life.

May Ling stood practically alone against her adversary. For a moment she wished she had her fan in her hand. She wanted nothing more than to strike Valentin across the face with it. What could she think to do with this smirking criminal? He didn't give her any more time to plan.

"Enough," Valentin suddenly commanded.

No longer mildly dangerous, Valentin rose and stretched his arms to the sky as if imploring lightning to strike her dead.

May Ling's thoughts scattered. She jumped. Big Jim reached across and kept her from sliding all the way to the ground, but she lost the other of her shoes.

Valentin gestured to the group of men May Ling had sensed congregating behind her. All of a sudden, the whole group of them stepped closer to their leader, crowding May Ling between Valentin and themselves. May Ling felt their menace. Smelled their foul body odor.

"Put her in the cage," Valentin ordered, his voice deceptively quiet. "Let the rest of the men know she's now available."

May Ling squeaked. One man had put his hand on her waist. With both hands, she pried him off her—his hands calloused and raspy, hers smooth and soft. The man dropped back, totally startled. As if he'd never touched a lady before.

She saw herself from high above, as if she no longer

inhabited her body. Sudden fear, then an inappropriate calm suffused her mind. She'd survived rape before, she would survive this, too.

Probably.

Big Jim brushed her aside to lunge at Valentin, knife drawn and positioned for a killing blow, screaming high-pitched curses. Richard shouted after him, pushing May Ling down to the mud as he grabbed for his partner. He missed. Big Jim raced at Valentin like a locomotive falling off the tracks.

Someone was going to die.

From behind May Ling, one of Valentin's men shot a hole through Big Jim's back that barely missed Valentin himself. Blood sprayed from the wound and drifted down into the mud. For a couple of seconds, Big Jim didn't know he was dead. He completed three more steps toward his target, then tottered. The knife fell from his hand, his knees buckled, then he landed on his back in the muck.

Her heart caught in her throat. No one had ever died in May Ling's employ until now. Big Jim had just become the first. She'd have swayed and fallen if Richard hadn't had his arms around her. By rights, May Ling belonged on her knees in the muck rending her clothes in mourning. She barely contained the first of her sobs. But if she wanted to kill Valentin, she'd have to remain calm. The man who'd actually murdered Big Jim was only a pawn.

Richard released his hold on May Ling and prepared to spring at Valentin. As May Ling readied to stop him, Valentin took control.

"Stop right there," Valentin ordered. "Or I'll have them kill this other man of yours, too."

May Ling caught fiercely at her remaining bodyguard's sleeve and pulled him back. He glowered down at her, but May Ling remained focused on Valentin, her face pale with the effort. She'd have preferred to kill him with that decorative fan of hers, but the stiletto secreted in her sleeve would work just as well. She just needed to get close to him once more. It still felt like she was in a dream.

"Now," Valentin continued, pointing to Richard. "You take her to the cage and shove her in."

May Ling mutely gave her permission. She let Richard draw her up from the mud. Began to limp alongside. Any moment she was going to fall onto Valentin and slit his throat. If Richard could only get her close enough.

Richard stumbled to a halt at something Valentin said that May Ling didn't catch. She heard the growl rising from her bodyguard's throat, and she jabbed him in the stomach in warning. It got Valentin's attention back on her. His smile would have cut diamonds.

May Ling stared into Valentin's eyes, willing him to come closer, ever closer. He needed to be a little closer still, and it looked like it wasn't going to happen. May Ling would have to cross the distance herself.

Richard choked. They were almost at the cage. Starving, abused, and dying Chinese girls clamored for mercy as May Ling came in reach of them. She wondered for the first time how she hadn't heard them from her office these last few months. Suddenly May Ling lost her balance, falling into the arms of one of the men who meant her ill. Valentin lost interest and walked away.

The killing moment passed and was gone with Valentin's confident exit. But May Ling had changed her mind anyhow.

If she murdered Valentin in the street, his men would retaliate. Big Jim had already fallen. She didn't want to lose Richard, too. He'd been the one who'd rescued Jai Li from the sex cage. If she didn't have him, they wouldn't be able to save any of the rest of the girls.

Valentin might just have set in motion their means of escape.

May Ling would not be a cowering victim. And she wasn't above using sex to achieve a goal. She wouldn't have survived as long as she had otherwise. Putting her into the cage might have been the stupidest mistake Valentin had ever made.

But these girls, these women, they were going to have to fight.

Maybe even to the death.

Everything would depend on the mettle of the girls left in the cage.

Only now did May Ling acknowledge how devastating the loss of Big Jim was to her. As the sobs came, she did nothing to control them.

16
Waking up to a nightmare

JUNYUR ROLLED HIS EYES IN exasperation, shutting his mouth against the threats he'd been prepared to spit out at Miss Berrigan, at Mr. Shale, and at the big wide world itself. At everyone. Nothing was going as planned. Absolutely nothing. Even the smell of newly-mown hay in the barn had begun to cloy. And Junyur usually enjoyed the sweet, pungent tang of hay bales. It brought back good memories.

Instead of making preparations for the most important race on the continent, he was babysitting a couple of strangers. Instead of May Ling at his side (the most beautiful woman he'd ever seen), he'd gotten Jai Li (a skinny, conniving chameleon of a trickster).

And now, he didn't even have Jai Li!

Junyur repressed a sneeze, his eyes watering. His two companions wavered, doubled, and then faded back to their normal selves as he spasmed, ending with a violent waving of his arms. Junyur covered his mouth too late. His *achoo!* was so loud it probably had reached the farmhouse up the sloping incline from where they hid.

If his traveling companions didn't stop screaming and yelling at one another out here in the barn, it would be them drawing the attention of the people who lived in the big house. And not him. Junyur sniffed. Didn't matter what exposed their presence here, his hay fever or Miss Berrigan's bossy voice shouting down Mr. Shale. Everyone needed to be quiet.

Junyur glared at the two. He wasn't going to lose his chance at those horses Shale said were at the house. But the big guy and Miss Berrigan evidently weren't going to stop bickering. Junyur's sneezing had simply overwhelmed their argument. Junyur bet neither of them was listening to the other anyhow.

"I need some space away from you two," Junyur announced when there was a lull. "Fresh air. I'm going to take a walk."

Junyur turned his back on Miss Berrigan, pretty sure she wouldn't interfere. She was too busy berating Shale for pursuing Jai Li. She broke off her tirade just long enough to fluff up what was left of her hair, then resumed her verbal attack. Mr. Shale stepped away from the barn door, but didn't let Junyur pass, solidly barring Junyur's exit while simultaneously letting Miss Berrigan's invectives roll off his back. Or maybe not.

"I'll go with you," Shale said. "I know this place, can keep you out of trouble. You're not going out there on your own."

Junyur choked. Sure. It had nothing to do with the middle-aged woman screaming in Shale's ear and hitting at him with fists full of hay. Nothing at all.

Junyur shrugged, agreeing to the company. When the other man backed warily away from Miss Berrigan to slip out the barn door, Junyur followed, his mind racing. Most of what Miss Berrigan had been yelling about was the bounty on the princess, which was troubling. Even though Jai Li was no longer under Junyur's protection, he wondered who wanted her so badly that they'd spend ten thousand dollars on it. As he'd said before, that was killing money.

It was also enough money to buy himself a ranch anywhere in the world. All he had to do was deliver Jai Li to those who coveted her.

Once outside with Shale, Junyur glanced back at the barn, shame-faced. He was glad Miss Berrigan hadn't seen his eyes right then. He'd watched greed poison several family friendships back when Marcus first built their ranch. He didn't want Jai Li swamped by bounty hunters, that was for sure. Miss Berrigan would never have forgiven him, and to his surprise, that mattered to him. May Ling, however ...

Damn it. All he had to do was consider betraying May Ling's trust and his mind filled with pictures of the vixen. In the loose, colorful robes she seemed to prefer, specifically the yellow silk with the red and blue flowers. The smell of her, even. Some feminine perfume, made of flowers, and just a sniff of bath soap. Her calm, soothing, low-pitched voice, so lyrically seductive. Even when she mispronounced every tenth English word she attempted. All this came rushing back at him.

Hadn't Miss Berrigan just told Junyur to go away? Said that she no longer wanted anyone's help rescuing May Ling, especially not Junyur's. She didn't want him.

Jai Li obviously didn't want Junyur around. The princess had run away from him, intent on her own adventure, and Junyur didn't think he'd see Jai Li ever again. Was counting his blessings that way. That skinny, small-breasted hooligan could stay lost as far as Junyur was concerned, though he pitied whoever ended up with her.

Even May Ling had sent him on his way. Wanted him to take Jai Li to safety more than she wanted Junyur for herself. She'd literally pushed him out the exit, with a dainty pass of that damned fan toward the door of Miss Adelaide's, no less. May Ling didn't want him at her side. Not then, and probably not now, either.

So, what did he owe any of them?

Why not take one of the horses and go on his way? Things would work out. They always did.

"Where are those horses you told us about?" Junyur asked Shale. "You say they keep them in the house? Where in the house?" Junyur, having made up his mind to abandon his companions, was now in a hurry to do so.

Shale seemed to be wondering whether to tell him or not, his head moving back and forth in what might have been a dismissal, so Junyur left his side and began jogging up to the house on his own. He heard a hissed protest behind him but didn't stop.

The house was a simple, sturdily built one-story cottage. Someone had added to it willy-nilly along both sides so that it stretched on and on and on. Luck had taken Junyur straight to the front door. Soon he saw the horses through the gap in the window curtains just like Shale had said. Both horses were close enough to the front door to be handy, if only the door wasn't locked.

Nothing for it but to try. Junyur jumped to the porch, then turned the bolt.

The door opened.

Two horses were right there in front of him.

Junyur even had to push them out of the way in order to enter the house. Whinnying mild annoyance, they lumbered to the side. To Junyur's amazement, he saw that the Hauftmanns had turned their dining room into a makeshift manger. More than the two horses were stabled there. A couple of goats, at least one chicken, a piglet. The heavily-carved wooden furniture had been pushed to the far end of the room to get it out of the way.

Junyur shrugged. He didn't have time to ponder the eccentricities of people he'd never meet. It was obvious they expected thieves. Plus, the house was cooler than the barn. They needed a guard, however, if they could sleep so soundly as this. Luckily for him, they didn't have one.

Quickly he returned to the two horses that were snuffling their irritation at his intrusion, and led them out onto the porch where he hobbled them. Back in the house, he found their saddles, their bridles, and their horse blankets.

It was a good thing he didn't have to go back to the barn for anything. Seeing Miss Berrigan would engender feelings of guilt. Junyur didn't want to acknowledge feelings of guilt. No telling what that woman would do with that gun of hers.

If Miss Berrigan realized Junyur was striking out to rescue May Ling, she'd insist on accompanying him. Junyur no longer wanted or needed either of his two companions. Best that they thought he'd abandoned them. Maybe he and May Ling would swing back this way as they headed south again. Catch them up. He'd play the hero. Introduce May Ling back to her godmother.

"What do you want to do?" Shale asked, coming up into the house and making way too much noise.

Junyur abruptly abandoned his pleasant fantasy of returning this way. Junyur just wanted to leave, and leave Shale and Miss Berrigan behind. Neither of them would be amenable to that, however. Even in so short a time, Junyur knew them that well. Best he didn't go back to the barn, then.

As he contemplated riding one horse while leading the other, Junyur shook his head. It could be done. "I want the horses saddled and then off the porch and into the yard over there," Junyur answered at last. "Without waking anyone. You helping with that?"

Shale nodded. And went right to work on it. Within a few minutes, he had the horses eating out of his hand (sugar, Junyur bet), and had moved them halfway off the porch. One horse was a roan mare, the other a spotted gelding. Both a little on the chubby side. Shale guided them very slowly and very carefully.

Junyur felt a twinge of guilt letting the big man calmly coax the horses out of the haven where they'd been cool and safe. And after what Shale had earlier said about Junyur's treatment of his own horses, he hated to earn that reputation for real when he stole and then ran the horses full speed. But Junyur was going to do what he was going to do.

"Gently," Junyur chided. Shale shot him a look that was suspiciously observant. Junyur would have to work quickly. "Get them down the steps gently," he repeated. "Don't want no broken legs." Junyur jumped down first and positioned himself safely out of kicking range. He'd learned that lesson early, and often.

Once both horses were on the grass, Junyur accepted their reins from Shale. Then Junyur trotted beside them into the front yard, making sure the saddles held. He also got a clear view all around him. The house on one side and the barn on the other. Junyur was surprised Miss Berrigan had kept to the stable, and that Shale still remained on the Hauftmann's porch.

It wouldn't do to linger. He'd jinx his luck if he did.

"See you," Junyur told Shale, jumping onto the back of the roan mare and setting the horse twirling in a couple of circles to get the hang of its temperament.

The painted gelding whinnied. It knew what was going to happen, unlike the hapless Shale staring stupidly at Junyur from the porch. Junyur gave one last huge whoop and galloped rapidly off with the other horse trailing behind like a kite's tail.

"Good-bye and good riddance," he yelled over his shoulder. Dust from when he'd just circled the yard rose up and clogged Junyur's throat. He hacked it down with a strangled grimace.

Junyur didn't look back again. And he didn't return. Junyur firmly pushed all thoughts of Mr. Shale, Miss Berrigan, and Jai Li back into the nether portions of his mind where he kept everything he didn't want to think about right then. It was a pretty big pit.

Things might have gone differently for him and his family if he had returned. But he didn't, and it didn't.

Within a day's travel, Junyur got himself hopelessly lost, was hungrier than he'd ever been in his whole life, was dirtier than a pig in a sty, and was as despondent as a bride left at the altar. His fantasies of May Ling now had a distinct tilt toward her being angry with him, of her disapproving all his plans, and of no sex whatsoever. *She loves me. She loves me not.*

Junyur chose to rest for a while.

After making a fire to stay warm in the late spring evenings (and to discourage coyotes and cougars), Junyur hobbled his mounts and fell asleep. Against all his common sense, he dreamed longingly of May Ling. He dreamed lustily of May Ling. And woke late the next morning with his arms and legs tightly cocooned around a skinny half-naked woman who had to be Jai Li.

Junyur's budding erection abruptly shriveled.

He felt his consciousness leave his body. Was soon looking at himself and the girl on the ground from some distance above.

She had the form of Jai Li, she had the smell of Jai Li, and even had the hair of Jai Li. With a rush as his consciousness returned, Junyur fully awakened, more alert than he'd ever been in his life.

Very, very carefully, Junyur disengaged himself from the human rattlesnake in his embrace.

"If you don't get your hands off me this instant, that thing between your legs will be the least of your worries."

Junyur froze in terror. The voice had come from the night visitor.

He'd heard tales of what Jai Li could do, although he hadn't witnessed it himself. Didn't want to see it now, either. Didn't get the chance to say so.

Junyur's mouth dropped open in shock as the blanket fell from his sleeping companion's shoulders and bunched in a pile too close to the dead campfire.

This wasn't Jai Li.

17
Preparing for battle

It was May Ling's second day in the cage. The moans, coughs, and plaintive soft cries of her companions created a constant wail of noise. It was difficult to block it out so she could think. She knew Marcus Wilde was expertly hidden somewhere nearby. Possibly behind the partially overturned water trough in front of the deserted stables. Or he could be behind her, watching from a shadowed doorway belonging to her very own whorehouse.

Whorehouse!

May Ling cringed at the image he must have of her. That her lover's brother imagined she was a whore. Or whorehouse operator. She winced at what he was probably thinking that very minute. The last meal she'd eaten a whole day before threatened to disgorge. She burped. Nothing ladylike about it at all. More like a costermonger after sampling his own goods. A rotten egg aroma filled her nose. She fruitlessly patted at her rumpled kimono, trying to get it back down below her knees instead of rucked up around her hips.

Running a whorehouse had never been her plan. Seemed it was her destiny, though. Her shiver this time had more to do with the heat than the Wilde brother's imagined covert stare. Maybe not so imagined, though. She felt someone's steely gaze on the back of her neck, and hoped it was Marcus Wilde.

She wondered if he planned a rescue. Didn't want that.

At least not so soon. Neither she nor the girls crammed in with her were quite ready.

May Ling especially was not ready. She should be leading by example. Instead, she cowered, like the rest of them. Twenty-four hours of this hell and no one had intervened. It was past time the girls organized themselves. That would give Marcus Wilde something to stare at. And Valentin's minions, too.

May Ling used the image of Junyur's brother riding to the rescue as a goad to get her on her feet. It worked by fits and starts. It hurt to stand more than it hurt to sit. The cage had no solid flooring, just more bars. Was probably eight feet by twenty feet. May Ling had measured it out many, many times the previous day, weaving herself around and between the other captives.

In her fantasy, she and her fellow prisoners saved themselves before Marcus arrived. But after only one day of confinement, the reality of the cage had masterfully unhinged her. She'd only thought she knew what these young women were experiencing. Nothing had prepared her for this. Not even being raped in the New York slums when she and Jai Li had first stepped onto American soil.

The bars that imprisoned her and twenty other women shone slick with condensation. Too many bodies confined in too small a space created its own kind of heat. The bars were slick with handling. Rain had splattered down on them in chubby droplets during the night.

May Ling gripped the bars in her hands and shook them until her fingers stiffened. The rattling iron bars silenced the inmates. For a second or two, all was quiet. May Ling could hear herself breathing, surprised at how calm she seemed.

Beyond the cage, May Ling could see Richard standing in the Chinaman's tea shop doorway fiddling with his gun belt. Why hadn't he done anything?

And, never one to discount women as fighters, May Ling wondered what the residents of Miss Adelaide's were doing.

Would they run like she'd told them to? Or were they busy risking their own lives to free her? No way would her girls carry on with business as usual. Neither would Valentin have murdered them. They were his property, after all. Part of his livelihood. It wouldn't make good business sense. May Ling hoped they'd run.

A sudden screech of panic brought May Ling to her senses. What happened outside the cage was out of her control. She needed to concentrate on what happened inside the cage. One of the girls had given in to her panic. She'd gone over and calmed her.

"You get us out?" a voice asked behind May Ling's ear. The young woman who had been crying pulled gently on May Ling's hair, then also stroked her ear. "Some of us are strong," the girl said. "Not all. Sorry, miss. But not all."

May Ling deliberately did not turn. Her eyes overflowed with tears. She gulped several times trying to get the words out of her suddenly raw throat.

"How many?" she asked, keeping her lips as still as possible, keeping her voice as low as she could and still be heard above the misery. Valentin had men hidden along the street. She'd caught them watching them. "How many strong?" she asked.

"Seven," the girl answered.

It wasn't enough. And even if the girl at her back thought those seven women were strong, that didn't make it so. All May Ling had seen from them was dejection, despair, and the frailty of women already cursed with fragile bodies trying to survive brutal exposure.

May Ling cursed herself for waiting too long. With Richard over there, and Marcus Wilde somewhere near, that gave them ten fighters. May Ling no longer counted on the girls from her house. With only the two men having access to weapons, her plan wouldn't work. She and the girls in the cage with her were doomed.

With a sob, May Ling gave way to the despondency that

had gradually crept up on her. The heat, the intermittent drizzle, and what happened to any of the girls who got too close to the bars of the cage where male passersby had been grabbing them ...

May Ling abruptly realized her own precarious position, then quickly backpedaled her way to the center of the cage, taking her mysterious new ally along with her. As she caught her breath, May Ling began counting their advantages. Some of the women were naked, but not all.

With a shudder, May Ling decided not to follow that logical thread. It took a strong will to live for a woman to disregard both being caged like an animal and the psychological distress of nakedness. They had also been systematically starved. They had no weapons, at least none she'd seen. Most of the captives were peasant girls, as well, which meant no formal training in self-defense.

But this wasn't counting their strengths. This was cataloging their weaknesses. May Ling turned her back on her fellow inmates and hobbled to the one blanket that had been thrown in the center of their cage, where she collapsed.

Despite the fire of outrage running through her veins, May Ling surprised herself by falling asleep. A nightmare about the British army in China woke her up. Or had it been the tepid drip of water hitting her head that brought her back?

May Ling gave a short, heartfelt prayer of thanks for that rain-drop. Without it, the nightmare would have been forgotten as soon as she awoke. She wouldn't have remembered the square.

May Ling had watched British battalions muster to arms outside the walled city of Peking, and in processional displays through the Forbidden City all through her childhood. Most marvelous to her was the soldiers' ability to quickly form themselves into a square formation to defend themselves.

She sent another prayer of thanks up to her gods for the British and their squares.

May Ling now had a strategy that would get them all out of the cage. All it needed was one horny villain with a gun at his side crawling into their midst, his mind blanked out by lust. May Ling figured there were more than enough such men in the shadows.

All she needed was one.

18
Squash Blossom finds help

JUNYUR LET OUT A HIGH-PITCHED scream of relief at finding a half-naked boy in his arms, rather than the mercurial monster Jai Li. It woke the horses, woke the snake sheltering just outside of his sleeping bag, and woke the sun into rising. Or so he told Squash Blossom once they'd disentangled their various limbs.

Junyur grimaced as he pushed himself away. The boy's skin had felt tantalizingly feminine, soft and pliant in his hands, and he hoped with all his heart it was because of a dream. Junyur had camped late evening in a sparsely forested copse that could have been Indian territory, as far as he knew. And fallen into a deep sleep, alone. No one should have been able to find him.

The boy had had nothing to do with the sun rising, of course, though by the astonished look on his face, Junyur thought he'd convinced him otherwise. With the sun straight in Squash Blossom's brilliant black eyes, he looked less girly-girl than usual. Junyur didn't understand how anyone had ever mistaken him for female. Though to give the boy credit, the gauzy robes he usually wore hid all manner of clues.

Once Junyur had finally chucked the snake safely away from them, he began thinking about breakfast. Junyur followed the snake's progress in his peripheral vision. When it vanished, he turned his attention back to Squash Blossom who had continued to glower. And had moved closer. He felt the boy's breath in his face. Smelled him, too. Jasmine, though how he'd managed that after a half-naked, barebacked ride through Oklahoma grassland was quite a trick.

Junyur retreated as far as he reasonably could, and kept his eyes focused on the boy. Breakfast was going to have to wait, even though the thought of the crisp bacon he wished he had was making his taste buds ache. Junyur gnashed his teeth with frustration. Too bad he'd have to make do with some sort of oatmeal concoction fashioned into a bar.

"You knew already, didn't you?" the half-naked young man commented, a scowl on his handsome Eurasian face, and his hands clenched into fists, his voice sullen.

Junyur didn't want to admit it, but Squash Blossom was wrong. Until this morning, Junyur hadn't a clue. The younger man was damned good-looking, whichever sex he chose to represent. His skin, flawless, his posture straight, his black hair shiny, abundant, and fanned out by the breeze into a halo that was getting into Junyur's face. Squash Blossom's obvious Chinese heritage made him all the more appealing. Junyur decided to lie.

"Boy," Junyur said, brushing Squash Blossom's hair out of his mouth and looking around for his unnecessary cooking gear, "I've been with enough women to know you weren't one, but since it seemed to be a secret, I decided not to let on. But why are you half-naked like this?"

Squash Blossom shrugged. Then grudgingly gave Junyur room to move out of his space. "I didn't have time to change into pants. Lost my skirt on the street when they jumped May Ling."

Junyur stopped dead in his tracks. His heart plummeted down near his boot tops. "Someone attacked May Ling, and you ran!" he squawked.

The boy reacted slowly, with what Junyur saw as callous unconcern, by only giving him a nod. It was as if running away from a woman in distress carried no stigma in his mind. Not a smidgen of shame nor of cowardice did Squash

Blossom show. Nor did any hint of femininity remain to grace his form.

It was with great effort Junyur didn't raise his hand and strike him down. His fingers itched to smash the dispassion from the boy's eyes.

Squash Blossom hadn't answered Junyur's question. Not with any information, he hadn't.

"Who attacked her?" Junyur asked.

With suddenly slumping shoulders, Squash Blossom answered. "My father finally lost patience. Valentin," he explained in case Junyur didn't already know that Valentin was his father. "He attacked your lover. Put her in the cage. He's gotten new instructions from the empress dowager, and neither Jai Li nor May Ling are important to anyone anymore. I expect he'll let her out in a bit."

Junyur blanched. It wasn't what he'd expected to hear.

Squash Blossom looked up through his lashes at him, not finished with the bad news. Squash Blossom set his jaw as if he didn't want to continue, but felt he must. Junyur was gratified to finally see sadness in the boy's eyes.

"If we don't get back there before dawn tomorrow, everyone will be scattered. May Ling may go with them. It wouldn't surprise me."

Go where with who?

Junyur only cared about saving May Ling, and was about to say so, but stopped. Maybe he'd been fooling himself, because all of a sudden Junyur choked up about the girls in the whorehouse, the girls in the cage, the sheriff, his deputy, May Ling's two bodyguards, and all the horses and attendants in the stable who had been so kind to him.

He let a soft whine of distress escape his lips. This was going to be a lot harder than he'd anticipated.

So Squash Blossom's father was the villain Alain Valentin. Junyur didn't understand Valentin suddenly giving up his profitable sex-based businesses, and, what had Squash Blossom said, *scattering*?

Maybe he meant *running*.

May Ling had said that the empress dowager of China had threatened to send swordsmen after them. The idea of Chinese swordsmen parading down Guthrie's streets searching for that aggravating princess gave Junyur a fit of the giggles. He sounded like one of May Ling's girls, which embarrassed him more than giving into laughter.

Squash Blossom stared daggers at him, which turned Junyur's giggles into hiccups. Eventually. It took a few minutes and more disapproving glares from the boy for Junyur to control himself. A few minutes more and the two young men faced off against each other, sober-faced.

Junyur still hadn't gotten any breakfast. Seemed he'd be going hungry this morning.

"You need some pants, kid," Junyur observed. What Squash Blossom had covering his butt and thighs looked like woman's bloomers.

"No, I don't. These are fine. I need you. With you leading us ..." Squash Blossom's voice faded as Junyur turned his back on the boy and walked to the stolen Hauftmann horses.

Out of the corner of his eye, Junyur studied Squash Blossom, who had clearly misunderstood the situation. Squash Blossom approvingly watched Junyur throw a saddle across the back of the roan. And listened with a smile on his face as the horse whickered.

Junyur regretted that he didn't have any sugar in his pockets to reward the poor horse. By the end of the day, it was going to have deserved it. He took the time to rub the horse's velvet-like mouth instead.

As Junyur hurriedly tightened the girth, he tossed a question back at Squash Blossom. "Just who will I be leading into battle? May Ling's got those two bodyguards, to be sure, but little more if I remember rightly."

"She's got Miss Adelaide's girls," came the proudly-stated reply.

For a second, Junyur pictured the dainty, colorfully-clad ladies of Miss Adelaide's fighting hand-to-hand with

Valentin's brutal toughs, but couldn't make it work. The women were sex toys. Entertainments. None of them could defend themselves, much less attack a group of men.

Junyur finally decided to eat his oatmeal concoction. As he shook his head sadly at Squash Blossom's misguided but grand vision, Junyur soon had both his horses in readiness. Squash Blossom had his horse feverously prancing in place, desperate to be gone. Junyur wisely didn't tease them any longer. He washed down the now-gummy counterfeit biscuit with tepid water, shuddered at its cardboard taste, and made himself ready.

"Yee-haw!" he cried, spurring his horse into a controlled gallop and leading the other. To his surprise, Squash Blossom and his horse kept pace, which wasn't what he wanted. And not what he'd planned. Junyur noticed uneasily how the three mounts threw up a cloud of dust in their wake, but as Junyur didn't figure anyone would be following them, he ignored the wide trail they left.

All through the first hours of their trek, Junyur worried about May Ling. It was Squash Blossom who forced them to rest and water the horses.

Junyur would have pushed on for longer, and meant to argue about it. Then what Shale had said about him and his treatment of horses came back to haunt him. He eyed the roan who hadn't gotten its sugar cube this morning. With reddened cheeks and a deep pang of shame, Junyur vowed to keep the pace slower from then on. A couple of hours more weren't going to make much of a difference.

Surely by now, Valentin had May Ling shut up in her comfortable Miss Adelaide's office space. Where Junyur would find her reading one of her books, comfortably wrapped in one of those sumptuous silk robes she favored. And the other girls would be locked in the rooms upstairs. Gossiping. Eating cookies and drinking tea.

Maybe this would be a simple breaking and entering caper, no fighting required. Just get the girls out and run.

No, a little more rest wouldn't hurt a thing.

19
To the rescue

SQUASH BLOSSOM AND JUNYUR DIDN'T talk much during the hard ride north. Single file suited the both of them. Junyur let the boy take the lead. That way Junyur wouldn't have to keep looking over his shoulder for him. For the first time, he *did* have to eat another man's dust. It tasted like dirt. Junyur kept hacking it up and spitting it out. The clop, clop, clop of the horses' hooves would have made him drowsy were their task not life-or-death. The only reason they weren't racing at breakneck speed this very moment was to keep from killing their horses.

When Junyur and Squash Blossom did talk, the words seemed to float out of the boy's mouth and evaporate in the air before they got to Junyur's ears. He figured he wasn't missing much. Maybe Squash Blossom's ideas for a new dress design. Or out-and-out gossip from the whorehouse. Didn't try to make Squash Blossom repeat himself. Junyur just kept on plodding down the trail, leading his other horse. And trying to stay awake.

Idly, while checking the ground for prairie dog holes and watching the horizon for trouble, Junyur wondered what a whore did when she wasn't with a client. He'd never given it much thought before, but just as he tried focusing his mind on that pleasant conundrum, more mumbled sentences bounced through the space from Squash Blossom to Junyur. The only thing Junyur understood was the name *Marcus*.

A shiver of shock ran down his spine. Junyur took his

hat off and wiped his brow. How did a boy disguised as a girl and living in a whorehouse even know who Marcus was? Junyur kicked his horse forward and grabbed at the other horse's reins.

"What did you just say?" Junyur yelled, jockeying to keep himself in the saddle and not bump into the other horse. "You said my brother is where?" Junyur heard his voice crack with the strain. That hadn't happened to him in years.

"Probably with my father, if I know Valentin."

Junyur waited for him to say something else. When he didn't, Junyur's face flashed red. He reached over Squash Blossom's mount and grabbed a handful of the boy's hair. It was as if silk threaded through his fingers, and smelled of fragrant flowers. All anger faded as Junyur wrinkled his nose. He barely controlled an oncoming sneeze.

"Ouch! Let go of me," Squash Blossom demanded.

Junyur studied the younger man while loosening his grip. Aggrieved, and also anxious, Junyur finally relented. He didn't have the time to waste. He backed his horse a few steps farther away before stopping.

"Then talk," he said.

Squash Blossom took his sweet time plaiting his hair back into a single braid after wrenching himself out of Junyur's grasp. And chattering. The boy talked so fast and clipped it was impossible to follow. Junyur studied the horse instead, expecting frazzled nerves from the boy's mare. But Squash Blossom must have had the most docile of horses. It contemplated Junyur right back. Placidly. Like a cow.

All the while Squash Blossom had been talking, Junyur hadn't heard any of it. He had to force himself to get his mind off the horse and pay attention to the boy. The boy chattered on. Like a magpie. The flower scent wafting from Squash Blossom distracted Junyur too much. He'd just about decided none of Squash Blossom's gibberish had been important, anyhow, when he finally caught a sentence that grabbed his attention with a vengeance.

"Once he realized which sort of Wilde you were, he cabled your brother," the boy said.

That got Junyur's notice. He even raised an eyebrow. *What sort of Wilde he was?* He studied Squash Blossom for any indication he was playing a practical joke. A Wilde was a Wilde was a Wilde. The three brothers had different personalities and likes, to be sure, but—

He had a sudden inkling. Maybe the kid meant their money. Or his oldest brother's power. Or maybe it was the ranch he meant.

Squash Blossom hesitated, and then stopped outright as Junyur's eyes glazed over, deep in thought. When Junyur finally figured out *what sort of Wilde* to his satisfaction, his attention snapped back to the boy. *Valentin was after the ranch.*

"With some tall tale of you being railroaded into a dangerous situation by May Ling," Squash Blossom suddenly continued, running the words together as he speeded up his talk.

Junyur glared. Was the boy afraid of him now? Junyur set his jaw, raised an eyebrow even higher, and prepared to sigh, almost missing the last sentence.

"He came to take you back home."

Junyur's horse shied as he pulled back on the reins. Squash Blossom seemed to be raring up to continue his one-sided conversation. Junyur needed him to go back to the pertinent stuff.

"Stop," Junyur demanded. "Just stop for a minute."

Squash Blossom sulkily shut his mouth and reined his horse to a halt. Junyur rounded him a couple of times in a fury before pulling his mount and his pack horse to their side and stopping. "Marcus thinks May Ling is the villain?" he said. "Instead of Valentin?"

"*Mon pére* is devilishly tricky, Mr. Wilde. Whatever he wants your brother to think, he will."

Junyur sat on the horse, poleaxed, his mind running

all sorts of scenarios. He didn't want Marcus in May Ling's company. Especially when she was alone and vulnerable. For God's sake, Marcus would fall in love with her. How could he not! And May Ling belonged to Junyur. Jai Li would have to do for his older brother. Marcus couldn't have May Ling.

But the longer it took Junyur to get back to Guthrie, the more time Marcus would have had with May Ling. With *his* woman. Damn it, where was Jai Li when he needed her!

"What's wrong now?" Squash Blossom asked.

"Everything."

Enough of this. He didn't need Squash Blossom. Junyur gave the boy an angry look, and then he lashed his two horses into a gallop and set his face toward Guthrie. No more lollygagging.

Clods of dirt and mud and grass flew all around Junyur as he raced to the rescue. No longer did the dry odor of dirt cloud his smell. What came up from his horse's passage hit him in the face and tasted of cow patties. Junyur wanted to gag, but controlled himself by thinking of May Ling.

Fifteen minutes later, Squash Blossom caught up to him. And jerked Junyur to a halt by grabbing the reins and not letting go, no matter how hard Junyur lashed at him. The sound of his quirt whacking Squash Blossom's flesh brought back memories Junyur didn't want. The Wilde boys' father had never been one to spare the rod.

When all three horses finally stood still, heads outstretched and hanging, breathing hard, Junyur stopped hitting at Squash Blossom and favored him with another ferocious glare. The boy heaved a sigh so loud it finally took the rest of the anger out of Junyur's heart. But, what the hell—

"Guthrie is that way," the boy told him, pointing at a forty-five-degree angle from where Junyur had been headed.

Golden grass stood three feet high, extending as far as Junyur could see, waving and bucking with the wind that had suddenly whipped through. It was as if a sea of grass had suddenly materialized at Squash Blossom's beck and call. Junyur had been following a well-trod road that led elsewhere.

"Oh."

Then they were off. Junyur was thankful Squash Blossom hadn't waited past that one-note exclamation of contrition. The boy set off immediately on the correct course. Junyur rapidly followed. He hadn't been this embarrassed since he was caught in bed with Maria Gonzales.

As they galloped forth, Junyur worried mightily about prairie dog holes that might be underfoot, but also about what May Ling was going through. He had all the time in the world to imagine all manner of torments.

Gone were all his fantasies of girlish gossip, and tea and cookies, of May Ling quietly reading novels, her dulcet voice slowly sounding out the words she did not know. The ground sped by, sometimes without Junyur even noticing. His thoughts were far ahead of them, in Guthrie.

After half the day had spent itself, the next segment of their rush to save May Ling went by in a blur of creeks they leapt, fields they flew through, and gardens they trampled. The scant remnants of civilization they passed through were proving more difficult to navigate than the previous wilderness.

Junyur's saddle blanket was damp from the creeks, but also from his mount's sweat. Junyur's hat was off his head and dangling across his back from just the strap. It was a miracle he hadn't lost it entirely. He wiped perspiration off his brow with trembling and equally wet fingers before putting his hat back on.

And he was finding it hard remembering those creeks, those fields, those gardens they'd ruined. It was in a daze that Junyur forged ever forward, thinking only of May Ling.

In the final hours of their mad rush, they endured passenger trains they madly raced to crossings. Curious riders they ignored who didn't ignore them back. And finally what Junyur thought might be the beginnings of a tornado in the far distance.

It wasn't.

The storm coming from the north reached Guthrie before they did. Outside the city limits, it dumped an inch of rain over what the people in town magnanimously called the streets. On Junyur's previous visit, he'd called them quagmires. This time the streets were more like mud pits.

Their horses slipped and slid, but kept their feet under them, barely. Squash Blossom managed to keep his seat as his horse almost went down, helping the animal to balance and then to force its way to safety on a small tuft of grass.

Junyur's horse fared both worse and better, skidding in the center of what was usually a mud-plastered avenue, but ultimately stabilizing itself by digging all four feet into the mess. Junyur went cartwheeling over the horse's head.

To say that Junyur fell off the horse was putting it charitably. Those who witnessed Junyur's spread-eagled somersault over the roan's neck, and his subsequent attempt to stay on his feet once he landed, never tired of telling the tale.

Junyur and Squash Blossom were back in Guthrie, Oklahoma.

Just in the nick of time.

What met their eyes left them stupefied.

20
The new plan

May Ling's hastily built but brilliant plan to save herself and protect the women caged with her out in the middle of the muddy, treacherous streets of Guthrie came to naught.

She almost cried. The abasement and dejection of the past two days demanded a bloody and desperate fight to the death, not a stranger with bolt cutters demolishing their prison with the coming of dawn. The empress dowager of China's long-promised swordsmen had arrived. May Ling hadn't needed their help.

The streets had silently filled with them while May Ling and the caged women slept. She had suspected nothing. The snap of broken steel and the clatter of the damaged lock falling from the bars woke everyone. The black – patterned red uniforms the Chinese troops wore shocked May Ling into action. She recognized their significance instantly, maneuvering herself through the cage door and out into freedom with caution. She pulled her disarrayed clothing into a modicum of order as she went. Tucked her loosened hair behind her ears. Put a strained smile on her lips.

Several half-naked girls followed, clinging to May Ling as if to a lifeline. May Ling's last-minute reparations to her looks made no difference. Both she and her new dependents tripped right into the arms of waiting soldiers.

May Ling trembled with anger and fear. The empress dowager had caught up to her at last. Just when she might have been safe. Or at least safe from the long arm of the royal court. Her plan would have worked. May Ling knew it like she knew the sun would always rise from the east.

Of course, the soldiers had been sent to waylay Jai Li, not May Ling. Not the other young Chinese women now in her care. As if that made any difference. May Ling wondered if once the men realized the princess wasn't there, would they just leave?

One of the soldiers singled her out. Handed May Ling a pair of shoes to replace the ones she'd lost. She felt ashamed of herself. His placid stare forced her to take stock of the situation as it was, not as it had been. The sky was no longer gray, but ice-blue with the promise of even warmer temperatures. The iron cage was surrounded by young Chinese soldiers in uniform. She estimated not a one of them was over the age of twenty.

One by one, every shivering girl was escorted out of the cage, some with clothes hastily thrust at them by one or more of the soldiers. The half-naked girl clutching May Ling ended up with two kimonos too many, but kept the extras tightly wound around her waist after hastily donning the most brilliantly-colored one. Jade green. May Ling apologized courteously for the younger woman's greed, and got a blank stare from the commandant in return. He waved his hand at something past her line of sight.

A disgusting noise caught her attention. One she'd heard before, but not in this country. It had always reminded her of the thunk of a butcher's knife separating a melon in two. The line of distraught women swayed in place, but none of them moved voluntarily from where they'd been directed to stand. Most continued dressing themselves. Some began bartering back and forth for what colors or styles they wanted instead.

May Ling's new companion began to laugh. The young woman pointed to the shadowed area behind the now partially demolished cage, her snickering abruptly becoming shrill and hysterical. May Ling saw a fallen townsman twitching out the last of his life's blood, the flow oozing into a wagon rut. When one of the soldiers reached down and then pulled the head from where it had rolled and held it out at arm's length, May Ling recognized one of their tormentors as the deceased.

"Women to the teahouse," the soldier in command barked. "Take the men to the whore's place and get them in order."

May Ling bristled at being called a whore one more time and refused to budge. The push the soldier gave to her shoulder wasn't exactly gentle, but it wasn't a testosterone-fueled shove either. She followed the guide without further protest, but made sure her newest satellite remained fastened to her and did not drop behind to be lost in the madness that would surely ensue. May Ling expected a bloodbath any second, but shortly realized she'd underestimated the empress dowager's cunning. She evidently knew her men.

A crowd of twenty or so townsmen already stood corralled under the eaves that backed up to Miss Adelaide's alley access. They stood silent and fearful, watching the women march past them. None looked like they'd been rousted from the beds. May Ling figured they'd been caught in whatever evening activities they'd been enjoying. A couple of them had on formal dining clothes the likes of which she'd been used to in England, making the rest look shabby by comparison.

For the first time, May Ling saw no lust in their eyes. There was fear, and oddly enough, there was hope. Some seemed to be appraising her. But it didn't seem to be for sex. Many of them seemed lost in thought. The boldest of the bunch studied her for a moment, which made her stop and stare. When he raised his hand to brush his dark hair out of his eyes, she saw that he was shackled.

"Take me," he yelled. "Choose me."

"Leave the lady alone," May Ling's guide gruffly told the group of prisoners, for prisoners they seemed to be. "You'll get your turn to plead your case once the ladies have had time to rest."

What in the world!

The young man who had yelled out looked like he wanted to verbally accost May Ling a second time, but he didn't, fading back into the shadows where he leaned back on the wall for support. *Choose him for what*, she wondered, but soon forgot all about him. After walking around the block and onto the sidewalk across from and down the street from her own establishment, the former prisoners arrived at the stoop of the teahouse.

Once more, May Ling tripped. It seemed to be her curse. Catching her by the elbow, the guide helped her up the makeshift steps to the wooden landing.

Once inside, the unnecessary warmth of the fireplace and the scent of tea and freshly baked bread soothed May Ling into a stupor. The smoky, earthy smell of what had to be *Lapsang souchong* spread from the kitchen, tantalizing her tongue. She could almost taste its residue. No matter how much she always complained, this proprietor always left residue in the cups.

May Ling gazed around the room without really seeing it. Suddenly she was sitting in a chair staring at a highly-polished tabletop. Listening to the shrill demands of the girl who'd attached herself to her side. Seemed like the girl was still refusing to leave her. Quickly, another chair was moved to them and put right alongside May Ling's.

After taking the time to calm herself, May Ling glanced around the room a second time. All the women from the cage were warily drinking tea and nibbling at cookies. May Ling left her chair to move closer to the fireplace's warmth. Despite the heat, she felt chilled. A tug at the back of her kimono told May Ling that her newest dependent was right with her. May Ling extended her hands toward the fire. The girl did the same. May Ling knew better, but she longed to walk directly into the fire and warm all the blood in her

The Cimarron Bride

body. Even right at the fireside, she couldn't get warm. It didn't make sense, unless she was in shock.

As May Ling slowly recovered, she decided to finally to ask the girl her name. At the same time, the Chinese soldiers entered the establishment, one of them making a beeline straight for her.

The girl by her side suddenly stepped between May Ling and the officer. Towering over her, the girl announced, "My name is Xi Chang. Come no closer to me and my lady!" she yelled at the soldiers.

May Ling tried waving her away. It would have worked if she'd had her fan with her, but the girl was proving tenacious. Xi Chang was only making the situation worse with her aggression. The girl stood solid as a stone, facing down the soldiers, arms crossed, shoulders back. It was impossible to move someone standing that way. May Ling recognized the stance. This was no mere peasant girl. She knew kung fu.

May Ling stood on her tiptoes to see over Xi Chang's shoulders and apologized for her behavior. No one seemed to have heard her, however. With a wry grin May Ling changed what she'd next intended to say. If the soldiers didn't know who Jai Li was, then they needed to know now, before things got out of hand.

"Jai Li not with us, captain," she said, finally catching his eyes. When that didn't get the response she'd expected, she continued. "I fail both empress dowager and Princess in this, but no one else responsible."

To her surprise, neither the half-starved waif protecting her nor the soldier paid her any attention. They seemed to be engaging in a death match to see who would back down first, but the soldier did softly disabuse May Ling on one point by saying, "Only half-failed, May Ling. We're making changes in the wily princess's plan."

The princess's plan? Jai Li didn't have any plan as far as May Ling knew. Only running.

The soldier pulled his gaze off Xi Chang, turned around, and stomped out, leaving May Ling alone with all the girls. What was she to make of their unexpected good fortune? Rescued. Clothed and fed. Sheltered in the teahouse.

What plan?

May Ling moved to the window to watch the officer's movements. He was headed to her establishment, Miss Adelaide's. Where he'd told everyone to take the townsmen. And they'd left all the women unguarded.

May Ling was astonished. She and the women with her could now simply walk out of there, which wasn't too different from her hastily-built and brilliant plan in the first place.

But what plan was *he* referring to? Her curiosity aroused to the breaking point, May Ling was as close to abdicating her responsibilities as she'd ever been. Which she'd never do. She continued to spy on the soldiers outside, but her mind raced with other thoughts, other memories.

Until they'd been waylaid in New York City, Jai Li's plan had been for them to lose themselves in this country, and marry herself into a rich man's family if she had to. Junyur Wilde had been May Ling's plan. Had there indeed been another plan? One she had no knowledge of? One concocted between the empress dowager and the princess that was so important the government had sent soldiers after her?

May Ling wouldn't put it past either of them. She'd just have to wait and see.

A commotion erupted right outside the teahouse door, interrupting her thoughts. May Ling narrowed her eyes in frustration, then squinted as a stranger came inside. The rush of wind following the heavily-muscled man almost put out the hearth fire. For just a moment, May Ling's heart leapt with joy. Then drowned with dismay. She'd mistaken the broad shoulders and Stetson hat of Marcus Wilde for Junyur and couldn't disguise the disappointment in her voice as she greeted him.

Speak of the devil. "Why you here?" she demanded,

aghast at the angry words coming out of her mouth. Why so angry? Here was someone who could help get them to safety.

Marcus Wilde had every right to be anywhere he wanted. It was May Ling and her people who had to justify every step and every word.

She did not back down, however, but stood brazenly erect with pointed finger now poked solidly into his chest.

The man chuckled, damn him. And took her hands off him so he could get a cigar out of his pocket.

"I'm part of the new plan," he casually told her, continuing to fiddle with the cigar. "The plan that's going to save your pretty butt and maybe even all the rest of your, well, your employees. So sit down and listen to me."

Before May Ling had moved away from him, the door burst open a second time, thrusting a very tousle-haired Jai Li into their midst.

"Oh no! Oh no!" May Ling almost lost her composure. Everything she'd done had been to get Jai Li to safety. And now they were right back where they started.

Her bodyguard Richard vaulted through the door next. Then Alain Valentin.

Stunned, May Ling waited. Would Junyur Wilde appear next? Or Squash Blossom come back? Maybe all the Chinese soldiers out in the street would come barreling through the door, crowding what was an already overcrowded space.

None of that happened.

Too late May Ling saw that the trap had been sprung.

May Ling, her new dependent Xi Chang, and the poor, abused girls from the cage were evidently to be pawns in whatever diabolical plan Valentin had bullied, bribed, or blackmailed Jai Li into.

How Marcus Wilde figured into any of this was anyone's guess.

21
The empress dowager of China

Jai Li acknowledged May Ling's presence by a slight quirk to her mouth as she passed into the teahouse. Once inside, the princess plopped ungracefully into one of the lounging chairs closest to the fire. Valentin, however, stopped when he reached May Ling and gave her the half-bow she'd often seen him offer minor dignitaries. The scent of rose petals drifted from his hair. By custom, she returned his gesture, and with the same amount of courtesy. He grinned.

"I see that we think alike in this," he whispered, theatrically loud so everyone could hear if they were paying attention. "Back where we started. Everyone back where we started." She smelled his foul breath and winced. Onions! The rose petals didn't stand a chance. For a second, she could taste onions at the back of her throat, but it was her imagination running amok. The only taste in her mouth was the lingering sourness of black tea.

May Ling couldn't help herself. "Except him," she declared, pointing at Marcus Wilde who winked at her as he strode past. "Everyone back where started but him!"

May Ling wanted her fan so badly! Her lover *Junyur* Wilde had been smart enough to learn from her solid whacking strikes, though it took him long enough. By the clenching and unclenching of her right hand, May Ling showed her fury at not having the opportunity to school the older brother as well.

With a deliberate exercise of willpower, May Ling slowly, even sensually, rubbed the feeling back into her hands. It sent pleasant tingles up her arms and calmed her. But now she was too hot.

Wherever Jai Li had come from, she'd clearly taken the time to clean up. May Ling envied her the flamboyant coloring of the long silk cloak Jai Li had just flung off onto the floor. The jade green and red-patterned kimono she'd worn underneath it brightened the modest establishment they all found themselves in. May Ling longed to touch it, to crinkle the material between her fingers. It looked like silk.

May Ling shivered. Her chills had returned. From cold to hot, from hot to cold. The Oklahoma Territory climate wreaked havoc on May Ling's metabolism. Even this close to heat, she suddenly couldn't get warm. The fire crackled with the sound of paper being crushed, and then one of the small logs fell, sending out sparks.

Jai Li raised her voice, her tone a direct imitation of their long-ago English professor's at Oxford University, minus the accent. May Ling properly blamed Alain Valentin for their ouster from the university. She'd enjoyed the college. Wished they were still there.

"Sit down, all of you," Jai Li ordered. "On the floor if you can't find a seat. Circumstances have changed."

May Ling watched Jai Li exchange a triumphant grin with Junyur's brother. They seemed to know one another very well. But how?

May Ling twisted around to study the women in the room, wincing as she strained her back, but still taking stock. Although all the females seemed to be Chinese, that didn't mean they all spoke the same dialect. Most of them probably didn't know enough English to understand what was coming. May Ling decided to help them.

With her arms held out alongside her, and then lowered slowly, she made patting gestures, hoping they'd follow her example and do as Jai Li had demanded. To all sit down.

May Ling gracefully sank to the floor, arranging her kimono to cover her knees as she dropped. She gave up her chair to Xi Chang.

The women from the cage followed May Ling's example, some rustling and rucking up their new dresses in an effort to keep them off the floor, most of them plopping down with a moan. The sound of their sudden activity mimicked the commotion of crickets, though they were trying so very hard to be quiet. Not another one of them took a chair, though there were many chairs to be had. May Ling saw a scowl developing on Jai Li's face, so she raised her voice in hopes of defusing the childish tantrum that threatened.

"Pidgin talk, worthy Princess. You use too big words. Pidgin, Jai Li," she advised.

Marcus Wilde took that opportunity to laugh. Boisterously. May Ling made a face. Junyur Wilde would never have embarrassed her so. She felt shame for Jai Li. Her assessment changed, however, just moments later when the princess and Junyur's brother made their relationship clear.

"She's got you there," Marcus told Jai Li, his warm, chiding words wiping the snide expression off the princess's lips quicker than any complaints from May Ling had ever achieved.

May Ling watched in amazement as Jai Li turned a fond look his way. They couldn't have spent much time together already. Jai Li had been with Junyur while Marcus was here. So how did they know one another so well?

"Maybe you're right, Marcus," Jai Li said. "May Ling, please come up by me and help me talk."

And as May Ling hesitated, Jai Li modulated her voice and held out her hand to her. "This is immensely important," she added. Almost a plea. "It's important to me, to you, and to the empress dowager. And to the men she has sent here."

Looking May Ling directly in the eye, Jai Li added one more thing.

"One more thing," she said. "Everyone needs to understand

what the risks are and make their choices," she told May Ling, and everyone else. "Right here. Right now."

That had been two more things, but May Ling let it slide. Disguising a tiny sigh of annoyance, May Ling rose, stood still for a moment to get her balance, then glided gracefully a few feet closer to the princess by the fire. Now she was too hot again, but preferred it to the shivers.

May Ling was tempted to pat Jai Li's shoulder in sisterhood, but refrained. Jai Li had just issued May Ling an ultimatum.

May Ling had never liked ultimatums.

Getting one from her former ward was especially unappreciated, and she let it show on her face.

Marcus Wilde got out of her way.

May Ling decided *not* to spit on the floor. She gave a ladylike burp instead, a very tiny one, but regretted it when the bitter black tea smell of it reached her nostrils.

Richard moved from the doorway and followed in May Ling's footsteps to where Jai Li presided. He stamped heavily over the hardwood flooring with all the grace of a water buffalo. There he loomed. It was a little like having a mountain brooding over a sapling, but Jai Li seemed unperturbed. She curled her legs under her on the chair and basked in the heat of the fireplace like a cat.

Valentin tailed Richard but oriented himself *behind* Jai Li instead of May Ling. Out of touching distance, but not so far he couldn't order everyone about. That didn't seem to bother Jai Li either.

"Time's wasting," Valentin commented. "Let's get on with it," he ordered, his voice trailing off as if it finally dawned on him that he was no longer in control here.

For some reason, Jai Li let him get away with it. She nodded approvingly as she turned toward May Ling and spoke directly to her. Jai Li's unexpected tidings captured May Ling's attention immediately. What she said was so bizarre May Ling almost lost her breath.

With all the serious decorum of a court courtier, Jai Li began. "The empress dowager has come up with a plan to take from this country what it has taken from China."

And to May Ling's horror, Jai Li's voice didn't once falter, nor her serious mien show any awareness of the ludicrous announcement she'd just made.

May Ling's eyebrows rose involuntarily. A gasp escaped her lips, but Jai Li seemed not to have noticed. Bemused, May Ling rolled her eyes, waiting for more information. What the hell was Jai Li talking about?

When nothing else was forthcoming, and Jai Li stared at May Ling as if she'd imparted the most amazing news, May Ling blurted out what was foremost on her mind.

"Tea? You mean the tea? But there no tea plantations here!"

Marcus Wilde snorted. The noise of it impacted the whole room. May Ling watched him valiantly trying to control his merriment. Even Valentin's shoulders shook. As laughter exploded from both men, May Ling's eyes flashed. She was sorry she'd opened her mouth, but there was no reason for all this derision. Everyone wanted China's tea.

All the foreign nations currently infesting the Heavenly Kingdom had come there for the tea. And taken the land while they were at it. Except for the United States. The American government had yet to make its intentions clear.

"Oh," May Ling exclaimed, her hand suddenly at her face, fingers tapping both cheeks to get the blood flowing. She felt the fool, but the old trick worked. Her mind suddenly clicked.

"The land race!" With horror May Ling heard her voice crack like an adolescent boy's.

"The empress sends soldiers for land!"

22
Three choices

Jai Li crowed. Clapped her hands and tittered merrily. "Yes, the land race your young lover was so anxious to join. You gave the empress dowager much food for thought, you two, with those letters of yours. When we disappeared from New York, the empress bravely vowed to continue the plan without us."

But it had been the empress dowager herself who put a bounty on Jai Li's head for daring to engage herself to the young emperor.

And the empress dowager's own spy Valentin who'd tried to assassinate them in Oxford. And who'd had them captured and put into a whorehouse in New York! Didn't that imply he'd been following the empress's orders?

May Ling was confused, but Jai Li was still talking. Maybe it would make sense in a moment.

"When we resurfaced safe and sound in Guthrie, the empress dowager knew the gods were smiling on her plan. If foreigners continue to appropriate ..."

Here Jai Li stumbled to a stop, possibly remembering May Ling's advice to use small words. She looked to Marcus for reassurance and then continued.

"I mean, if foreigners keep stealing our land, China will retaliate ..." Another pause. "China will strike back by taking American land."

May Ling held up her hands against this surprising turn of events. Her sleeves crept to the juncture of her elbows until she belatedly thought to lower them. Fixing the sleeves back into their proper shape gave her a little bit of time to get her mind in order. The fabric scraped the tiny ridges on her fingertips, like a cat's rasping tongue. She turned her back on the others to protect her thoughts.

May Ling bet the original plan had been to have Jai Li and May Ling killed to keep them away from any and all of the empress dowager's marriageable relatives. Perhaps once they were out of the country, the empress had simply lost interest.

But why had Valentin taken over as their persecutor? *Because he'd failed to kill them?* That was actually a motive that May Ling could understand. Revenge against adversaries of the inferior sex for the unforgivable sin of defeating him.

Was the empress dowager simply spring-boarding off Valentin's persecution of them in order to invade one of the countries that had invaded China? Had her flight with Jai Li into the Oklahoma Territory given the empress dowager of China this very brazen and daring idea?

She thought it very likely could be true. A tiny smile escaped May Ling's mastery. She hid her complimentary chuckle under the guise of a cough.

Amusing, wasn't it, a land grab sanctioned by the very country they wished to steal. Wouldn't work, of course, but this was going to be interesting. How in the world were these villains planning to succeed at it?

"Tell me," May Ling said, swiveling around to face Jai Li, and Valentin behind her. "Say it all again. I pass information to girls."

The congratulatory smirk on Jai Li's face gave May Ling pause, but there was nothing she could do about anything until she knew what was what. Pressing her hands together in front of her stomach, May Ling relaxed her pose and prepared to translate. Jai Li grinned in approval. Tapped her booted feet on the floor.

"You have three choices," Jai Li began. "All of you, unless too many make the wrong choice."

May Ling shrugged. She turned to their audience. "Do as I say," she told the former prisoners of the cage. Then she returned her attention to Jai Li, pretending ennui.

"That's not what I said," Jai Li snapped.

"Too complicated," May Ling replied. "Continue please."

Jai Li scowled, but went on with her instructions. Again, she raised her voice. And stood up so everyone could hear.

"First choice: You can leave this city. No one will follow."

"Next," May Ling replied, not bothering to translate.

"Second choice: You can marry a white man and farm the land we win in the race," Jai Li told them.

It was difficult for May Ling to control her expression with that bombshell. What white men did they expect to agree to that crazy scheme? She almost didn't hear Jai Li continue. Another stir of rustling enveloped the room. Evidently, some of these women *did* understand English.

"And your last choice is to marry one of the empress dowager's soldiers and live as servants to one of the white men now in the whorehouse waiting on your decision." Jai Li rushed her last pronouncement as if she was afraid the room would erupt with protests.

May Ling's mouth dropped open at the preposterousness of what Jai Li proposed. How did any of that constitute the takeover of the American continent by China? This was the Territory of Oklahoma anyhow, and not the United States proper. Oklahoma hadn't invaded China. Didn't Jai Li know that? Marcus Wilde certainly did.

"Was that too complicated for you?" Jai Li demanded, haughtily staring down at May Ling, her voice icy with disdain. May Ling shook her head in negation and struggled to gather her wits.

"I have ... have ... questions." May Ling struggled to get the words out. "Questions. What ...," she stuttered. But then the words dried up. Totally mortified, May Ling stopped trying. She hadn't stuttered ever. Now words died unborn in her unworthy mouth.

"Go on," Jai Li encouraged her.

Abruptly May Ling thought of the impediment that bothered her most. One that Jai Li should have known herself. She took a deep breath and forced herself to address it, the very idea sticking in her craw like an undigested crumb of fried shrimp.

"But some white men, Miss Adelaide's right now, some hurt girls," she said, embarrassed to the core. She really wished she had that fan. Jai Li deserved a smack across the face for even considering such a union.

Before she could continue her question, Marcus Wilde interrupted.

"Not anymore," he stated. Marcus stood with his arms crossed over his chest, studying Jai Li while also watching May Ling. He didn't elaborate on his comment.

It was May Ling's bodyguard Richard who explained. "Every man these girls identified as one of their assailants has been executed."

But the cage had been Valentin's idea! It was Valentin who had thrown May Ling into the cage himself. Not to mention what he'd done to Jai Li a week before. Yet there he was, standing tall behind her in this very room, part master of this new plot.

So, the soldiers had executed some of the citizens of this town. Over what they'd done to the girls! If so, there were a lot more reparations that needed to be made. Maybe ending with the death of Valentin himself. May Ling could not repress a smile.

Just how many men *had* they killed? May Ling decided she didn't want to know. At least some redress had been made. She raised her voice and addressed the other women in the room. Now was the time to translate for them. She spoke from her spot on the floor, equal to the rest.

"Marry white man. Be farmer wife. Want this?"

The Cimarron Bride

"No, no," Jai Li interrupted. "Not this way. Tell them all the options first."

Always, Jai Li's way was not May Ling's way. May Ling wanted to start with the most advantageous option and work her way down. Her huge sigh of frustration rang loudly in her ears. With wary eyes, she looked around. Marcus Wilde shook his head.

"Sorry, Princess. I start again."

May Ling raised her voice. She directed herself to the one woman most recently abused. Xi Chang. "Marry young China man. Be ranch servant. Farm servant to white family."

"Or just get the hell out of here!" Jai Li shouted at the girls, evidently losing patience with May Ling's reticence. "Never come back!"

Boisterous chattering broke out everywhere. May Ling took advantage to get some answers. She scooted closer to Jai Li and said, "Not understand. Servitude not invasion."

Marcus Wilde pushed his way through the excited women. "Listen to me," he said. "With the backing of the Chinese Tongs, an agreement has been drawn up. Whether women marry the Americans or they marry one of the Chinese soldiers sent here, they sign unbreakable legal documents guaranteeing ownership of land to the Chinese government three generations hence. On penalty of death."

May Ling choked. She'd seen some of those Tong contracts enacted. No one had ever been able to weasel their way out of them. "But who men have land?" she finally remembered to ask.

"That's where the land race comes in," Jai Li informed her. "We pair the soldiers with the white men to claim the land. They run the race, either by the rules or not. Failure not allowed." And with that, she fluttered her hands in apparent mockery of May Ling's notorious fan expertise, and smiled seductively at Marcus Wilde, who had been dividing his attention between May Ling and Jai Li up until then. Jai Li had his whole regard now.

Sounded like a recipe for disaster to May Ling.

But it was also just devious enough to work. Assuming that not all of these women wanted to just walk out of here with her when she went. That would derail the empress dowager's devious plot right enough.

May Ling, of course, was going to leave this place and never come back. Every girl from Miss Adelaide's was welcome to come with her. She hoped they weren't headed for a showdown over it, because if enough of the girls wanted to leave with her, that wouldn't leave any brides for the farmers and soldiers. And if they were going to battle over the women, May Ling hoped that Marcus Wilde would remember her regard for his little brother and side with her.

She was going to need all the help she could get.

Valentin caught her eye as she pulled her attention back to the lovey-dovey pair of outlaws, Jai Li and Marcus Wilde. With a theatrical toss of his head, Valentin indicated he wanted a private word. May Ling wondered if she could get away with murdering the villain right in front of everyone.

With a smile and an agreeable nod of her own, May Ling rose to meet him, all the while surreptitiously scanning the room for an object suitable as a weapon.

Americans had a peculiar saying May Ling happily approved of. *Strike while the iron is hot.* If she and Valentin and a weapon with which to kill him all ended up in the same spot at the same time, she was going to put an end to him and the misery he caused.

Even if he was Squash Blossom's father.

23
A death in the family

THE SUITABLE WEAPON MAY LING selected to kill Valentin turned out to be a rusty old sword that had fallen off the wall and been lost and forgotten underneath a lounging couch in the teahouse. Or so she guessed. She'd taken tea here from time to time, but she didn't remember any swords decorating the premises.

It more accurately resembled a Persian Shamshir. It would be a miracle if she maimed or killed anyone with it, as curved as it was. With her index finger, May Ling tested its edge. It took a while for any blood to emerge from the incision. More blunt than she'd like, but still able to slice human skin. And it stung. May Ling held it hidden against her skirts as she left the building to stand in the street. She didn't want any innocents involved.

From the corner of her eye, May Ling noticed that Valentin had also gravitated down into the street and had somehow produced a heavy walking stick that looked suspiciously like a sorcerer's staff. He held it away from him as if it were, and an enormously heavy one at that. It was like he was afraid of it, but still he managed to aim it toward May Ling as if he expected fire to gush out of it. May Ling flinched involuntarily, the sword slipping in her grasp.

They were only supposed to talk to one another. How had Valentin guessed her murderous intentions so quickly? And armed himself so well?

Then she got the surprise of a lifetime.

When Junyur Wilde dashed into Guthrie, Squash Blossom hard on his tail, he nearly mowed the pair of them down. Valentin quickly stepped one way, May Ling the other.

Junyur tumbled head over heels off his stumbling horse, all the while trying desperately to figure out what was going on. Junyur recognized May Ling, even when he was upside down, but not the daunting gentleman shaking a staff in her face. The jolt of landing butt-first in the muck sent an electric shock up Junyur's spine to the top of his head.

He landed smack at the combatants' feet. Addled, Junyur wondered if he was dreaming. His whole torso slumped. May Ling held an antique Persian cavalry sword amateurishly over her head in a way that left her completely exposed to harm.

Junyur instinctively threw up his hands to ward off her blow should it go awry. The man facing off with her must be the infamous Valentin Junyur had heard so much about.

Valentin, who had turned his shocked face to Junyur when he'd cartwheeled ominously close to the pair, tossed the staff rapidly from hand to hand. Junyur thought he was playing *hot potato* with it. Seemed Valentin wanted (and expected) something miraculous. He should have simply knocked May Ling's head off.

Muck flew everywhere as Junyur slipped and slid through the malodorous mud, trying to get out of their way. As Junyur passed the pair, Valentin dropped his walking staff and stared at him. And while directing an unladylike curse his way, May Ling lost control of the stupid sword.

Junyur watched in awe as it spun crazily up and over the spectators who scurried back from it like roaches from the threat of a boot heel.

Junyur slid another yard before his trajectory came to a final halt. He wondered if he still had all his teeth. With his tongue he carefully took inventory. Bad breath he had, but at least all his teeth were intact. For the moment.

Oh, but that wasn't the least of it. Junyur felt he was in the center stage of a three-ring circus.

He'd only just managed to get himself in a sitting position in the middle of the street when Squash Blossom vaulted, still half-naked, off his horse.

The younger man grabbed the heavy wooden staff away from Valentin, who had fished about around his feet and finally gotten it back into his hands. They struggled briefly before Squash Blossom wrestled the staff completely away.

Squash Blossom pushed his father Valentin to the ground. Then stood guard.

Junyur watched in awe, fascinated not only by the amount of mud covering the two men, but also by how quiet the town had gotten. There was no fog, but it felt foggy to Junyur. All eyes seemed riveted on the center of the street. Did no one have anything better to do?

Bereft of his weapon, and violently reunited with his prodigal son, Valentin did what May Ling at first suspected was a ruse. With head bowed almost into the mud, he lost all control. Valentin was crying.

God damn it! It couldn't have been because of Squash Blossom. The two had become mortal enemies.

But May Ling feared it was so. Both Junyur and May Ling stared stupefied at the villain. Great big sobs. Coughing, gurgling, choking sobs, all coming from the man May Ling knew as her nemesis.

He was the author of everything evil that had ever happened to her. And this time she felt sorry for him. It wasn't every man who made an enemy of his very own son.

Across this unlikely tableau, May Ling and Junyur caught each other's gaze. A small gasp escaped May Ling's lips. Junyur acknowledged her with a cheeky grin and an attempted wave that made her lower her guard.

When May Ling turned all her attention to Junyur, he was still helplessly sprawled in the street with a dazed look on his face. He was staring at her in shock, and nothing in her life so far had looked half as beautiful as his mud-stained face did right then. He had the beginnings of a beard, golden, just like his hair.

Junyur's wayward horse decided to rejoin them at that point. After snuffling hesitantly at its master in the street, it then stepped delicately over Junyur's sprawled body and walked all the way to May Ling, where it nibbled greedily at the hem of her kimono.

She heard a dull thud from behind her and turned. It was the sword she'd brought out into the street for her duel with Valentin, thrown at her from one of the disgruntled spectators grown bored with the sudden lack of action.

She glared at the crowd, and suddenly they erupted into excited chatter. For the first time, May Ling realized how quiet it had been before. She turned back to Junyur, unaccountably uneasy with the atmosphere of this place. Had all of this really happened? Or was she in a dream? Still in a daze, she retrieved the sword.

Then a familiar voice shattered the din and destroyed her burgeoning fantasy.

Marcus Wilde stepped back into view and began hooting at them. "Well played, little brother," he called out. "Now it's time to get back to business."

May Ling saw a line of men submissively following Marcus like ducklings to water. Recognized some of them from town. Assumed they were the men who'd been corralled and taken to Miss Adelaide's to await her companions' choices, which she'd derailed with her challenge to Valentin.

Who still sat crying in the street.

Squash Blossom seemed unable to control the situation, but paced back and forth in front of his errant father as if their roles were reversed and Valentin was the child.

May Ling gritted her teeth.

Thinking of Valentin as a helpless little boy would defuse her righteous anger even further, and this she would not allow.

Valentin alone had been responsible for all the misery she and Jai Li had endured. He had followed them west and suborned half their new town into vice. He had killed Big Jim. He had thrown her into that hellish cage. And more. Gone was that brief stab of pity she felt for him.

Valentin was not going to escape punishment. Even if the empress dowager herself had given him carte blanche, May Ling intended to circumvent it. And if she wasn't able to kill this bastard, she had a sneaking feeling that Jai Li would step up and do the job.

Not in this country did villains reap the benefits of their ill-gotten schemes. Not when they'd been caught and tried and sentenced.

Of course, Valentin had neither been caught, nor tried, nor sentenced. May Ling waved her hand airily in front of her face to indicate that inconvenient facts didn't matter in this case. This part of the country was long accustomed to individuals who took it upon themselves to be judge, jury, and executioner. May Ling determined to join their ranks.

She tried to get Valentin squarely in her sights, but Junyur Wilde was in her way. As was Squash Blossom. And the horses. Otherwise she'd have already wielded that rusty sword right into that bastard's gut, even with the whole town watching. Her fingers itched for violence.

"Business, I said," Marcus roared.

May Ling jumped. The horses scattered. The line of men following Marcus stood still and listened.

"Get this boy some clothes," Marcus ordered. "And take that silly sword out of that woman's hands before someone gets hurt."

"No," May Ling protested. Not again would someone steal her glory. She didn't even remember how she'd gotten the sword she gripped in her hands.

As she startled, her grasp on it unfolded. Bewildered, she let Richard divest her of it without protest.

All the violent noise made her head ache. Squash

Blossom made enough of a racket for an army. She thought he screamed that he wanted kimonos instead of jeans. Who wouldn't? Chaos reigned around him.

Squash Blossom had stomped away from Valentin, deep into his hissy-fit about clothing. Valentin sprawled in the mud, seemingly forgotten by everyone else. If May Ling could pull herself together, she still had a chance. But it seemed that Marcus caught the sudden gleam in her eye. Before she knew it, he'd picked her up and deposited her among the men, all of whom took a step back. As if she'd bite.

"Choose me, pretty lady," the stranger closest to May Ling pleaded. He tentatively reached out his hand to touch her shoulder, and May Ling recoiled. The stranger's hand retreated.

"Save it for the meeting, Mr. Price," Marcus said. "Sorry I deposited you in his lap, May Ling." Then, nodding his head in the direction where Junyur still struggled to gain his footing and recover his wits, he said, "Make yourself useful, May Ling. My little brother must have landed on his head or something. See that he's not really hurt. Please."

Her eyes narrowed. Maybe she didn't need that silly sword. Junyur struggled within spitting distance of the villain Valentin, didn't he? And Junyur had a gun in its holster hanging from his hip, didn't he? Fortuitous fortune indeed! She didn't need the sword to dispatch the cretin. Junyur's modern-day weapon would do very well in its place.

"As you wish," she told Marcus, her eyes demurely directed to the ground, her lips rigidly controlled to keep her grin from breaking out. Carefully she sidled from out of the group of men and hopped down from the sidewalk back onto the muddy street.

Where she slipped and fell on her butt. Disaster struck before she could right herself.

As May Ling watched in horror, Richard rushed forward and struck Valentin through the chest with her sword. And then promptly dropped it into the mud before making his slow way back to her.

"This way there is no blood on your hands, my lady," he explained, his tone matter-of-fact, while she shivered at his feet. "My gift to you for the last six months of our lives." Then he stumbled out of her view.

May Ling wanted to scream, cheated once again of her responsibility. Cheated out of her revenge. Watching Valentin fall forward in death, right in front of his son, had not been what she wanted. She cried inconsolably.

It shouldn't have happened like this.

24
By any means necessary

S QUASH BLOSSOM HAD RUSHED TO May Ling's aid the same time Jai Li had dashed out into the street from the opposite side. Valentin's slumped-over corpse telegraphed his murder to anyone sophisticated enough to understand.

His son, Squash Blossom, faltered at first, then smiled grimly while standing above the body. Jai Li kept walking. May Ling tentatively beckoned the boy to her side, but he ignored her. Might be for the best, she thought.

Unconscious of the death in their midst, the ladies who had been rescued from the cage followed Jai Li across the expanse of the muddy main street. Everybody talked at once, except for the few who screamed. To May Ling, it was like being trapped in the marketplace back home in Peking. No one paying any attention to anyone else. Everyone concentrating on the sale. Or on the butchering.

During the ruckus, May Ling clambered out of the mud and stood up, desperate to get away from Valentin's body before Squash Blossom came back to himself and rightly blamed May Ling for his father's death. Since she hadn't killed him, she didn't court the consequences.

The street teemed with living, breathing obstructions between her and safety. Unthinking, May Ling scratched her nose. Left a big streak of mud across her face that smelled rank.

Fortuitous fortune had just slipped through her fingers,

but maybe Richard had been right. May Ling had yet to murder anyone. Her bodyguard had been considerate to have saved her from that horror. At least Valentin was dead.

Marcus Wilde, with his wide shoulders and determined pace, cut through the crowd at long last. Here to save the day. Probably grousing that he'd get it done if no one else would. May Ling could see his lips move, talking to himself.

She wondered what he'd make of the death in their midst, but needn't have worried. After giving a brief, cool glance at the father and son tableau just yards from her, Marcus shook his head and bypassed them all. He strode quickly to the still-dazed Junyur and unceremoniously slung him over his shoulder. For a moment, May Ling thrilled to think he was bringing him to her.

Wasn't quite so pleased when he passed her and then made his way back to Miss Adelaide's.

Frantically, she raised the hem of her kimono out of the mud and trotted after the two. With a last glance back to the murdered villain Valentin, May Ling decided to leave it to Squash Blossom.

Or maybe not.

She stopped.

Then, sure she could leave. This was Squash Blossom's joss, not hers.

Her feet carried her forward.

May Ling shook her head at the thoughts suddenly paralyzing her. Maybe she'd just lost her best chance at taking over Valentin's turf, but she'd be damned if she let herself get distracted once again from claiming the love of her life for her own. Junyur needed her now. Later she'd figure out a way to disband Valentin's criminal mob. Maybe Squash Blossom could be persuaded to take it over.

All thoughts of Valentin's death and of Squash Blossom's future prospects left May Ling's head when she crossed the damaged entry door to Miss Adelaide's. Marcus was laboriously trundling up the staircase with Junyur in his arms when she looked up. The bedrooms were upstairs. And bedrooms were for ... well, for more than sleeping in this place, that was for sure.

Slowly, she followed, her heartbeat galloping, her cheeks turning rosy with embarrassment, and the death she'd just witnessed threatening to bring up bile. May Ling fought it back down with a series of unladylike burps which embarrassed her. Tears flooded her eyes from the shame of leaving Squash Blossom out in the street alone with his grief, but she was going up to Junyur, no matter what.

Marcus couldn't possibly know which bedroom was hers, but any bedroom would do. May Ling couldn't keep up with him, her steps alternating between mincing and cautious, but he was still in sight when she made the landing. And still stomping like a barbarian.

By chance, Marcus decided on Squash Blossom's room. May Ling watched him nudge the door open and disappear inside with his burden. The door squeaked like a hurt animal. Squash Blossom hadn't used this room often. May Ling followed Marcus, her heart battering against her ribs with anxiety, and stopped just inside the room, uncertain of the older brother's intentions.

After dropping Junyur's inert body into the middle of the bed, Marcus opened the window, which also creaked with disuse. After turning all the way around, May Ling suddenly saw the room as he must. This bedroom was nothing more than a rutting station. It had a bed. It had a spittoon. It had a chamber pot and a washing bowl. No decorations or personal items adorned the walls.

Junyur had often called her a whore. It was humiliating that he'd been tossed onto a whore's bed, though Squash Blossom was about as far from being a whore as anyone could be. Did none of the Miss Adelaide ladies adorn their rooms to make them more homey?

Marcus read the dismay in her face. May Ling colored once more, her cheeks flaming with mortification. She hadn't thought to check on these rooms even once after first acquiring the building. Had left it to her bodyguards. As she sighed, the bitter smell of green tea brewed overlong met her nostrils. Someone in the next room had left the door open.

"Keep my brother here, Miss May Ling," Marcus instructed her.

She switched her attention back to him. Watched him with shaded eyes, pretending to be modestly retiring.

"By any means necessary, if you know what I mean." He gave her a look that indicated he knew she was acting. "I'll get the legal stuff done myself. Don't want either you or Junyur mixed up in it."

And with that very tempting suggestion, Marcus Wilde left May Ling and Junyur alone together in a bedroom, although it hadn't been a suggestion so much as an order.

May Ling caught her breath. Grew faint with the implications. He'd *ordered* her to keep her lover occupied. By any means necessary. An order May Ling planned to follow right to the letter.

Even with the chaos reigning in the streets and death maybe at the door, she and Junyur Wilde were going to have their time together. It was written.

She only hoped she and Junyur were on the same page.

And that whoever was in the next room wasn't who she thought it was.

She'd had a godmother who always cooked the tea too long. No way that could be the same lady, though. And if by chance it was, May Ling had other more important things on her mind.

After studying the bare room, and giving a quick glance to Junyur, she walked calmly to the door and locked it. Effectively keeping Junyur captive. And leaving irritating, know-it-all, middle-aged, twice-removed spinster relatives out of it. Unable to interfere.

If anyone wanted to listen in, then they could.

There wasn't much May Ling could do about that, though

the thought left a bitter taste in her mouth. But no one would watch her with Junyur, and no one would stop them. She clapped her hands together as if to say *and that's that!* Smiling slightly at her paranoia, she onerously dragged the four-foot high dresser chest to the door and pushed it flush. Just to be sure.

That would keep anyone out.

May Ling flounced to the corner of the bed farthest from Junyur's head to catch her breath. Sat sideways on the mattress and studied the young man laid out before her. He was either passed out, or asleep. It would serve her right if he slept the whole time she had him here to herself, wouldn't it? A punishment for her many sins.

May Ling shrugged. What would be, would be. In a minute, she'd have the energy to move, but first she needed the rest. And a bath.

But there would be no bath. Profound disgust colored her emotions. With a huff of exasperation and an angry look at her feet, May Ling realized she'd just locked herself away from any chance of bathing. And since Junyur was just as covered with mud (and who knew what else) as she was, Marcus Wilde had done them no kindness in taking them up the stairs to the bedrooms. Unless he *meant* to keep them apart.

That would have made a devious sort of sense.

May Ling shoved her way off the bed to walk around it to Junyur's head. She wanted to be standing when he first saw her. She wanted to be pretty when he first saw her. She sniffed. Was that stench coming from him, or from her? Couldn't actually smell anything but her own odor without bending down, so she leaned over him, perversely tempted to kiss his mouth as if she was the prince in the *Sleeping Beauty* fairy story. She closed her eyes and swayed with exhaustion.

"I love you," she told the unconscious form, his mouth so close to her lips, realizing with a sudden jolt that she'd said that out loud and that she was telling the truth.

She pulled back a little bit. All those times she'd woken repeating *I love you, I love you, I love you* about this man, every time she'd stopped in her accounting duties and thought about Junyur Wilde with lust, with wonder, with an aching need, all that had been real. Not a dream or a fantasy, but real. As was the man under her hands right now.

"Wake up. Wake up." May Ling shook Junyur by the shoulder, gently at first. Then she clapped her hands loudly near his ear. "Up!"

Junyur snorted and choked, then thrashed his limbs. May Ling heard laughter from the adjoining room where the burnt tea stink still lingered. She lowered her voice and pulled Junyur's hands down from his face. Clear blue eyes met her surprised gaze.

"Oh!" May Ling reared back.

"What happened?" he asked. "And where am I?" Junyur struggled to sit up.

Momentarily dismayed he hadn't asked, *Where are we*, May Ling lowered herself to the bed to get closer to him. After a moment's hesitation, Junyur managed a sitting position. A second later he had her right hand in his and was pulling her closer and closer. She resisted, but he didn't let go.

"Squash Blossom room. Miss Adelaide's," she said. "We there."

After looking her straight in the eye, Junyur blushed, all too well remembering the morning he'd woken up with that damned boy naked in his arms. He was pretty sure he and May Ling were alone in this room, but he turned his head to check anyhow.

"Who is that laughing like a loon in the next room?" he asked, still not letting go of May Ling's hand.

"My godmother," she replied, making a very educated guess that Miss Berrigan had finally caught up to them. She bet Marcus Wilde had something to do with it, but Junyur's moan of dismay changed her mind. "You know godmother?"

"Miss Berrigan? She met us on the train out of here.

Recognized Jai Li right away." He sighed loudly, and then took a long look at May Ling. Her lovely face showed mud streaks, her fragile kimono had stiffened with a layer of the stuff, and her feet were a disgrace.

"You been wallowing in the mud?" he commented.

May Ling's eyes instantly flashed, until she caught the implied endearment in his soft and gentle tone of voice. She went weak at the knees.

Junyur quickly pulled her to him, uneasily aware of his own filth-covered clothes.

There was only one solution.

The only question was, who would get naked first?

25
The chapter-long love scene

May Ling and Junyur stared hungrily at each other. May Ling wondered why she continued to watch him as if they were perfect strangers thrown together by accident. And was that a touch of embarrassment on his face? Indecision even? This was the man she'd been pining for all during the trials and tribulations of the past year. Why wasn't she tearing his clothes off? Or tearing her own clothes off?

To cover her hesitation, May Ling pursed her lips, bewildered at all the different emotions racing through her, wondering if he felt the same. She looked down at her body. She'd already muddied the sheets with her filthy kimono. There were a few swaths of bedding not yet befouled. Damn it! Everything was so dirty! Tears began tracking down her face. She tasted salt.

Junyur also felt ill at ease, but his discomfiture came from the certain knowledge that Miss Berrigan was in the next room listening to every noise they made. He was used to dirty clothes. All you had to do was take the damned things off and throw them in the corner for later. He just needed to block Miss Berrigan out of his mind. Already he sensed May Ling's attention slipping away from him. As he reached out, Junyur's much-abused shirt split up the back.

Junyur laughed out loud. In bed with May Ling was where he'd dreamed of being for the whole of last year. And here he was. He placed his arm around May Ling's waist to stop her flight with gentle restraint. He felt her tremble against him.

"Nothing to be ashamed of, May Ling," he whispered into his lover's disheveled hair. He gently kissed her temple, amazed at the smoothness of her skin. Got a flake of mud in his mouth and tried to pretend he hadn't.

Junyur had only seen May Ling a few times before, but never had she had a single hair out of place. He took the time to separate some of her mud-caked strands and arrange them properly behind her ears. She smelled of mud, but then so did he.

"I heard someone say people in Europe pay a mighty high dollar to bathe in mud," he chuckled. "And we got ours for free today."

May Ling couldn't prevent the smile from creeping onto her lips. Nor the soft giggles that followed. Junyur had pulled her fully into his chest by now. And the shirt he'd split up the back came off easily as she dragged at the cuffs.

The button fly to Junyur's jeans threatened to evade May Ling's ability to manipulate with her fingers, however. She got the first two undone, mightily distracted by Junyur's sharp intake of breath each time she touched him, but eventually he had to pull the rest of the buttons open himself. Her giggles distracted him the way his gasps had distracted her. After staring warily into his face, May Ling decided he'd given her permission to proceed. Her hand found the crotch of his pants before he was ready.

"Damn it, girl, your fingers are like ice!" Junyur yelped.

But he didn't let her remove her hand. With *his* hand, he kept her fingers pressed into his groin until they warmed up. "That's better," he said. "Let me help."

"No," she said.

Junyur raised his head and met May Ling's gaze straight on. She'd come up to a kneeling position at his side, and with him half-reclining on the bed, their heads were even. Her depthless black eyes mesmerized him, but he didn't know what she wanted him to do. As she gently pushed her free hand against his naked chest, he followed her lead and lay back down into the temporary warmth of the bedclothes. Her fingers tickled until she spread her hand fully open against him. Inside his pants.

May Ling had surprised herself. Seemed she wanted to be the one in charge for a while. An amused smirk decorated her lips, and she tried to control it but couldn't. At least Junyur hadn't seen it. His eyes were shut. She could stare to her heart's content at the golden hair on his chest that led all the way in a tapering line straight to her heart's desire. She licked her lips, wondering if he'd taste salty, like her tears. All of a sudden, thinking about it wasn't enough.

May Ling pulled her captive hand away from him and used all her skill in pleasing him. Junyur gasped while lifting his butt off the bed for her. With a grin and a sudden wrench, she pulled his jeans all the way off, freeing the rest of him for her appraisal. Without thinking, she took him in hand. Junyur convulsed in ecstasy, spending himself the moment she touched him. Then rolled to his side, taking her down with him, saying, "Sorry, sorry, so sorry."

With a huff of disappointment, May Ling began to divest herself of the remains of her kimono. Seemed that Junyur had the same idea. Before she knew it, she and Junyur had traded positions almost exactly, with him kneeling beside her prone body and staring avidly, lustfully, lovingly down at her, and she gazing up at him with surprise. All she had to do was get herself rid of these disgusting clothes, open her legs for him, and they could proceed.

Or they could have, had she not precipitated his first orgasm with the grasp and pull of her hand.

After another furtive glance up at him, her eyes rolled back with stoic fatalism. They probably only had a short time left to them, and she'd spoiled it all.

Junyur, however, hadn't stopped to feel sorry for himself. He moved her gently aside so he could slide off the bed for a second, and then returned almost as quickly, his pants remaining on the floor where he'd thrown them.

And with his weight momentarily off her, May Ling had been able to yank off the tattered kimono and toss it to the floor. When she then spread her legs and tried to relax, things began to look up. After that, it only took a bit of fumbling, one vigorous thrust, and a satisfied gasp for the two lovers to position themselves properly.

Groans and whimpers, and what started as barely uttered gasps of excitement soon escalated to shouts. Miss Berrigan began banging on the wall after twenty minutes of it, yelling at them to shut up.

May Ling turned shy after their first successful coupling. By now all her clothing was scattered onto the floor. Junyur lay blissfully on his back beside her, naked as the proverbial jaybird.

All thoughts of jaybirds quickly left his befuddled brain as May Ling resumed exploring his nether parts with her talented fingers. He felt inspired to return the favor, but she soon straddled him, rocking and squirming and twisting around so much he thought he'd gone to a special cowboy version of heaven.

When he couldn't take it anymore, he abruptly whipped her around and began working her into a frenzy, his emotions as out of control as his name. May Ling sent him wild with passion. He hoped her response meant he had set her afire as well.

Later, with Junyur sprawled on top of her, totally spent, May Ling wondered if she'd made a mistake. Such wild passion was alien to her. She held her hand over her breast. Her heart hammered in her chest as if it were trying to escape.

"Ssh. Ssh," Junyur whispered into her ear, gingerly sliding off her but not loosening his hold. He stroked her hair, pulling much of the remaining dried mud out of it, then gathered her to him and massaged her back, all the while talking nonsense. Much later, his voice took on the cadence of poetry, and May Ling wondered if it *was* poetry, not recognizing any of the words.

And while she pondered the conundrum of an ill-educated cowboy reciting poetry in bed with a whore, she found herself surprisingly calm, blissfully at peace, dreadfully sore, and curiously happy.

Even with Miss Berrigan banging on the door like a bill collector.

26
We're married!

EVENTS HAD JUST WHIZZED PAST, leaving Junyur with mush for brains, a huge headache, and an overpowering desire to do more than just bed the whore who was meant to have married his brother.

At some point near the end of their carnal fun, he and May Ling had removed the furniture barring their way out and quietly left Squash Blossom's room for May Ling's personal quarters.

In the anteroom to her personal bedroom stood an absolutely huge bathtub. One of her maids had anticipated them. Hot water stood at hand. Junyur reckoned they spent an hour at least playing around before actually getting clean.

But Miss Berrigan must have heard them leave. Mid-toweling-off, Junyur's headache returned with the force of a true migraine when *his brother!* marched through the anteroom door big as life with Miss Berrigan right behind him. The surprising aroma of green tea seemed to belong to Miss Berrigan.

Before Junyur could stop her, May Ling threw off her towel in brazen anger, and, naked as the day she'd been born, rushed the two interlopers. "Out!" she ordered. "Out now!"

Junyur took his hands away from his forehead. He had to see this, headache or no. The sight that met his eyes was worth it, too. May Ling was glorious. A wildcat, a warrior queen, and Aphrodite all rolled up into one petite and voluptuous package belonging only to him.

Marcus Wilde looked taken aback. As he should have. Junyur wasn't sure if it was May Ling's beauty that floored him or her ordering him to leave. Marcus was lucky May Ling didn't have that damned fan with her, but even so, May Ling looked poised to attack.

But as the seconds ticked by, Junyur wondered why she'd frozen in place so suddenly. Then Junyur saw Jai Li peeking from behind their two visitors, and understood.

He, too, swiftly lost his nerve, becoming as spineless as a fishing worm in that human tornado's presence. He'd hoped to never cross paths with that sorry excuse for a princess again. But there she was, as oppressive and tyrannical as ever. She'd cleaned up nicely since he'd seen her last. Was clothed in elegant silk pajamas patterned with colorful bird designs, and most miraculous of all, she kept her eyes down, looking at the floor as if it held all her answers.

Something bad was going to happen.

After a few seconds pretending to be demure, Jai Li mostly gave it up, marching boldly into May Ling's personal space by pushing past Miss Berrigan and elbowing her way around Marcus. Still keeping her eyes shyly contemplating the floor, or her own feet, she suddenly twirled around, curtseyed to Marcus in a half-assed way, and then walked across to the tub in her swaying manner. When she got to May Ling, she held out her hand for May Ling to kiss.

Junyur chortled. He wasn't gonna let May Ling kiss any woman's hand. And Jai Li wasn't happy when someone crossed her. Junyur wanted to see the sparks fly so badly he forgot about his own nakedness and let the towel drop.

Miss Berrigan raised her hand to shield her eyes from the sight of Junyur struggling to cover himself, but Jai Li chuckled with amusement. Then deep masculine laughter filled the room. It was Marcus. The familiar scent of his favorite tobacco drifted from his clothes. He always smelled that way to Junyur.

Marcus Wilde looked everyone in the eye, as if he wanted

to clue them in on the shared joke he found so funny. Then he returned his stare to Junyur, who was sorely tempted to bend down to grab another towel and cover himself twice over. Marcus had that no-nonsense father-to-son type of face on, something that always sent Junyur's hackles rising.

"The more things change, the more things stay the same," Marcus boomed.

Junyur reared back from the blast. He was so loud!

"Right, little brother? I reckon this was the very pose I last saw you in. Minus these beautiful ladies, of course." Marcus swayed forward, pretending to get his first real look at his younger brother.

"What the hell happened to you?" Marcus asked. "It looks like you've been rode hard and put up wet."

Junyur bristled. It wasn't very far from the truth, and he resented this crudity coming from a family member.

"What are you doing here, Marcus?" he asked. It was with great effort he didn't dive for the towel again. He really didn't like the scrutiny, or the lecture he knew would come.

"You didn't make it home with my bride, little brother," Marcus replied, his voice now dry with repressed humor. "Then the sheriff sent me a wire. I've been here a few days already."

Junyur started to explain, but Jai Li immediately shut him down, interrupting as if it was her due.

After puffing up like a peacock, and looking like she could hardly contain her news a moment more, Jai Li blurted, "What your brother is doing here, Mr. Junyur Wilde, is marrying me!"

Her news plunged the room into dead silence. Which *she* didn't seem to notice. "We're married," Jai Li said. "Already married."

Junyur thought she'd bounce from the floor to the ceiling, she was so excited. Jai Li hopped from one foot to the other like a little girl playing one of the chalk skipping games that had come into vogue.

Miss Berrigan blanched. May Ling's astonished face turned to Junyur for clarification. And Marcus Wilde just stood there looking full of himself. Proud. A little shame-faced. Not going to take any guff about it from anyone.

That's how Junyur figured it was true.

And as Junyur opened his mouth to object, Jai Li rushed up to him and shoved her left hand before his face where he saw it shiny and clear. His former sister-in-law's wedding ring adorning Jai Li's immaculately manicured finger as if it belonged there.

Jasmine floated from the princess's pajamas and up Junyur's nose. He sneezed.

Marcus's eyes narrowed as he studied Jai Li with Junyur. Then he flicked his attention to May Ling, who still stood naked at the side of the tub. "I gather that the beautiful lady over there was supposed to be my wife," he observed. "And you took her for yourself, I see," he added, staring sternly down his nose at the younger man.

Junyur cringed. Marcus didn't know Jai Li as well as he did. Was Marcus really married to that hellion? If so, he'd better not express any opinions, good or bad, about May Ling. There was no telling what Jai Li would do.

Junyur half-expected the princess to whip out some sort of sword and castigate his stupid older brother on the spot. Some part of him even wanted to help her. But no explosion of violence occurred. Jai Li continued to hide her true nature under an on-again, off-again demure demeanor. Behind the protection of that wedding ring.

God help us, Junyur thought. Jai Li would expose her ugly side at some point. No doubt about that. Then where would they be? He wasn't about to give up May Ling, that was for sure. Marcus had picked the wrong wife, thank heavens.

May Ling moved from her spot beside the tub to walk proudly into the spotlight. As was her due. This was her establishment. She should throw everyone out, except him, of course.

Still naked, she stood quietly while Jai Li flittered about in the small, crowded room showing off her ring to everyone. May Ling gave it an appraising stare and then a nod as Jai Li minced by. Then May Ling faced Marcus. She bowed. Marcus inclined his head in a sort of mini-bow, all the while watching Jai Li's antics.

Junyur surveyed the exchange, dumbfounded. How could any man keep his attention fixed on Jai Li when May Ling was in front of him? And naked, no less.

"I May Ling," May Ling said, introducing herself, making Marcus look at her. "My charge named Jai Li. She is princess. I servant."

"And prostitute as well," Jai Li added, still looking at the ring.

May Ling hissed. Junyur feared she'd spit on the floor again. But Marcus chose that time to comment.

Junyur's brother briefly took in May Ling and the way she was handling his blunt stare. "Yes," he said. "The whore."

Junyur flinched. *He'd* been calling May Ling a whore all along, but hearing the hateful description come from Marcus's lips struck Junyur like a kick to the groin.

With a gasp, he watched as May Ling pursed her mouth and stepped back one pace. "Yes, whore," she admitted. For the first time, Junyur felt ashamed of himself.

"You're the one I was supposed to marry," Marcus continued. "The one we contracted for and paid transportation for?"

"Yes," she said. But Marcus couldn't seem to take his eyes off Jai Li long enough to really see May Ling. Junyur, however, could. He saw the beginnings of tears in her eyes. He saw the tremors in her hands she tried to hide for the first time. He saw her head beginning to bow.

Enough was enough, especially if his brother had indeed married Jai Li. There was no call for him to emotionally destroy the woman Junyur loved.

"That was then," Junyur declared, pushing his way

around Marcus until he stood by May Ling's side. "This is now," he told his brother as he took May Ling's hand in his. Junyur wished the both of them weren't naked, but it couldn't be helped. "She's going to marry me," Junyur declared, shocking the hell out of himself and evidently his brother, too, whose eyes opened wide and whose grin disappeared. It hadn't been what Junyur had meant to say.

He'd meant to say May Ling was responsible for saving Jai Li, and all the women working in Miss Adelaide's. That she had put the other girls' welfare before her own. That she'd survived horrible assaults. That he'd never seen a stronger or more beautiful woman.

"There won't be any more marrying going on here," Marcus replied, still not able to take his eyes off Jai Li.

Shocked, Junyur stepped back a pace, moving May Ling with him. He tightened his arms around her. It was cold standing naked like this right in front of the window.

Marcus refocused on the pair, watching them closely. Junyur bristled at the scrutiny, but refused to cower.

"Tell them what's going on here," Marcus abruptly ordered Jai Li, his tone curt. "I'm going to find some clothes for these two rascals."

Jai Li didn't even wait for Marcus to leave the anteroom. She was so excited that she started talking a mile a minute.

Finally, Junyur had to stop her, and have her start over. He hadn't understood a word she'd said.

Miss Berrigan made herself a spot against the wall and folded her arms across her chest, seeming fully prepared to listen in. Junyur was glad he had a reliable witness. He didn't trust anything Jai Li might say.

"Mr. Wilde," Jai Li began. "As a child, I made a very big mistake."

May Ling snorted.

Jai Li glared at her and changed her tone of voice.

"My mentor is correct," Jai Li said. "I was a bit more than

a child, and it wasn't really a mistake. It was a gambit. And I got caught."

"Tell," May Ling instructed. "Tell all."

Evidently, May Ling already knew the tale.

"Oh, hell," Jai Li commented. "You're spoiling the story, so I'll make it short." Jai Li compressed her mouth into a serious expression. Junyur thought she was trying not to laugh.

"I talked the boy-child emperor into an engagement," Jai Li confessed. "We were engaged to be married. We are engaged to be married," she amended. "Still." And when no one commented, just stood waiting for her to continue, she lost some of her self-possessed hauteur and began stumbling over her prepared speech.

"Legally and binding," she assured them. "But also a secret. Until someone told his mother, the empress dowager."

Miss Berrigan laughed quietly, as if she knew who'd betrayed the pair and was pleased. Jai Li hissed for silence. May Ling looked at Jai Li impassively, waiting for her to continue. Junyur didn't believe a word of it. It was a fairy tale.

Jai Li resumed her story.

"That's when the empress dowager put out a contract for my death. May Ling and I had to run. We thought we were safe in England, but that was a delusion."

"More," May Ling demanded. Junyur began to fidget. He knew part of that story was true. He'd already heard it from May Ling. But did that mean all of it was?

"The empress dowager sent Valentin after us. He and his men nearly killed us in New York when we arrived in America, but May Ling got me safely away, and eventually here, where we've been hiding in plain sight ever since."

"But what does Mr. Wilde have to do with any of this?" Miss Berrigan asked. Junyur didn't have to ask. He'd already figured it out.

Jai Li looked at Miss Berrigan with contempt. Then continued talking.

"I have married Marcus Wilde. Consummated the act, too. Naturally, I am no longer a threat to the empress dowager or her son. No way can he marry me. Good plan, is it not?" Jai Li held up her hand. "Don't speak," she told Miss Berrigan. "I'm not finished talking."

And when Miss Berrigan shut her mouth, Jai Li cackled with anticipation. May Ling and Junyur exchanged glances over her head.

Then with all the pompous arrogance that was Jai Li's natural personality, she announced, "Empress dowager has a great plan for this territory. And she's put me in charge. You have to do what I say."

27
Rudely interrupted too soon

MAY LING REFUSED TO LET Jai Li continue her spiel. She'd gotten the gist of it from the soldiers who'd deposited her inside the tea shop with the rest of the women they'd rescued from the cage. She wasn't going to let Jai Li take credit for what was obviously the brilliant plan of an especially crafty female—the empress dowager. Jai Li was a babe in arms compared to the old sovereign.

Watching Jai Li strut and posture and look down her nose at the rest of them, and in her bathroom, no less, had tried May Ling's patience to the breaking point. Any more of it and she'd spit on the rug in disgust. Already she felt the acid burn the back of her throat in anticipation, but she restrained herself. Although she was still naked, May Ling marched right up to Jai Li and socked her in the mouth instead.

How dare she claim to be in charge!

And a moment later, *Damn, that hurt.*

The pain came so far after the shock of her assault that May Ling feared her brain was askew. She reeled away from Jai Li with her closed hand held up to her own mouth as if to kiss the pain away. And tasted the perfumed soap residue on her nails. Junyur was watching, she'd better not spit.

This was the first time she'd struck anybody with her naked hand. She was used to clobbering miscreants with her fan. Her fist burned from the shock.

Jai Li howled with rage from the floor where she'd fallen,

her eyes huge with alarm. As luck would have it, Marcus burst back into the anteroom right when May Ling struck Jai Li, but he made no move to break her fall.

Instead, Marcus stared at May Ling who was sucking on her knuckles. Junyur shook his head. Marcus had clearly seen May Ling knock Jai Li down. Junyur wondered why his brother seemed to support May Ling's actions rather than his newly acquired wife's.

"She'll be all right," Marcus casually commented, as if May Ling's assault on Jai Li meant nothing to him. He'd dropped all the clothes he'd carried through the door, and with his right foot kicked a bundle of them across toward Junyur.

"Get dressed, you two. I want everyone dispersed properly and out of here as soon as possible. A storm's coming."

A storm's coming. Hardly any other warning would have worried May Ling as much as this one. The last time she'd been told *a storm's coming,* half the town she'd been visiting had been blown away. She wanted more information, but Marcus had quickly walked out on all of them without a backward glance.

As May Ling made her way to Junyur and the borrowed clothing, he watched her carefully avoid Jai Li, who remained struggling to right herself and was paying May Ling no mind anyhow. Junyur groaned. What the hell did *dispersed* mean in these circumstances?

A storm coming? *That* Junyur could understand. They'd better dress for it, then.

He rifled through the bundle for pants and a shirt. The clothes crackled with his touch, as if they'd been starched to within an inch of their lives, but beggars couldn't be choosers. He donned the clothes, all the while wondering what Marcus meant by his talk of dispersing people, and what Jai Li meant about having a plan she was going to enforce?

He was *this close* to opening his mouth and demanding explanations.

One look at the hastily-clothed woman he loved, and Junyur knew better than to ask anything. The set of her jaw spoke volumes.

As May Ling carefully adjusted the buttons to the meager cotton dress shirt she'd put on, Junyur had second thoughts about putting his two cents in on anything. He was a newcomer to the scene. May Ling had been living with it for half a year at least.

He took a deep breath, relieved she'd just added some garishly colorful pajama pants to her outfit. That shirt had been way too skimpy. He hadn't needed to guide her, though his hands itched to smooth the sharp creases from the darts visible on the back of her shirt-waist. They looked as if they'd cut buffalo steak.

Wasn't it time he trusted her instead? She obviously understood Jai Li's innuendos better than he did.

While Junyur dressed, Marcus bounded back into the anteroom to gather Jai Li from the floor and set her on her feet. He laughed quietly all the while, as if he had a secret to keep. The mellow tone of his voice set Junyur's teeth on edge. Marcus would get what-for any minute now, if Jai Li stayed true to form, which she would.

Junyur expected Jai Li to go for the fan. And then to beat the hell out of Marcus. It was the first thing May Ling did when riled, if the fan was handy. Today was the first time he'd seen her actually punch someone.

What he didn't expect was for Jai Li to throw her arms around his brother's neck and draw him down into a long, excruciatingly graphic open-mouthed kiss he wished he hadn't seen, and especially wished he hadn't heard.

Junyur was about to cover his ears with his hands when May Ling poked him in the back to get him moving. His ears burned with enough heat to warm an oven. Once through to the hallway, he felt compelled to slam the bathroom door behind him. Junyur didn't want to think it, but he bet Marcus and Jai Li would soon be availing themselves of one of the bedrooms on either side of the anteroom that held the bath.

The disgusting noise he heard, however, hadn't come from the room he'd just vacated, but from May Ling.

She'd just spat on the rug.

And not in any ladylike sort of way, but more like a lumberjack. A big glob of nauseous-colored—

Once more, the look on her face warned him not to make any sort of comment. On anything.

Junyur followed May Ling carefully down the stairs, holding on with both hands to the railings. That tumble off his horse was beginning to tell, not to mention all the carnal shenanigans of the past afternoon, and evening, and this morning. He ached all over.

He stumbled through her office door. The place was in shambles. Papers lay scattered helter-skelter, plants in pots lay overturned on the windowsill, and Squash Blossom sprawled on the one remaining lounge couch, dressed in a feminine kimono and once again painted up as a girl.

Junyur wished Squash Blossom would make up his mind. Junyur never knew whether to address the young man as he or she—Well, *hey you* would do as well as anything else, he guessed.

Junyur limped to the window to look out.

There was a line of young Chinese women walking toward the stable as if they were schoolgirls, and a line of townsmen coming the opposite way toward Miss Adelaide's and talking excitedly among themselves. Neither group looked at the other as their paths crossed.

May Ling broke the silence. Ignoring the mess about her, she addressed the boy. "You pick partners, Squash Blossom?"

She sounded weary to Junyur, but then the activities of the past day had been strenuous on her, too. He couldn't keep a smirk off his face as he remembered, but May Ling waved her hand haphazardly toward the front door of her establishment, clearly expecting Squash Blossom to leave.

Junyur wondered what partner she'd expected the boy to pick. What was all that about?

"Nope," the young man said. "I'm going to stay here."

May Ling stopped fluttering her hand. Junyur saw just the hint of a shock in her expression, then saw all the worry leave her eyes. Wished someone would tell him what was going on.

He watched, slightly jealous, as Squash Blossom left the comfort of the couch to cross to May Ling and put his arm around her comely shoulder. May Ling gently ran her hand up to Squash Blossom's elbow, as if she wanted to test the material.

More than Junyur's ears burned then. It was Junyur's shoulder to caress, Junyur's woman to comfort. But if he wasn't careful, he'd make a total fool of himself and swat Squash Blossom away from her like the pesky fly he was.

Junyur's blood pressure climbed just thinking about it, but no way did Junyur want May Ling seeing him explode. He looked elsewhere for a couple of minutes. Concentrated on picking up the scattered papers, even though it aggravated his back to bend down so many times. Got himself composed eventually.

After watching Junyur cleaning her office floor, May Ling raised her voice to include him in the ongoing conversation she'd been having with Squash Blossom. She started several times, only to stop after the first word. Each time she halted, she also lost her voice, and fingered her heavily starched collar as if it was responsible for strangling her words.

This proved agonizing for Junyur. He wanted so badly to finish her sentences for her, but knew better. Finally, she gave up.

"You tell him," she ordered Squash Blossom. "You talk better." She gave him a little push of encouragement.

Junyur warily kept his expression neutral. It wouldn't do to laugh at May Ling. She had made a reasonable choice in her spokesperson. Squash Blossom had the same mastery of the English language as did Jai Li.

For a second, Junyur wondered why May Ling was sadly lacking in that skill. She'd been enrolled at Oxford University, for God's sake. But Squash Blossom was talking already. Junyur composed himself to listen to him.

"I'm going to stay here with Richard and take over my father's organization," Squash Blossom calmly told Junyur for the first time, and repeated for May Ling's sake.

Junyur's jaw dropped. He turned to May Ling. She seemed resigned.

"Miss Berrigan has decided to return home," Squash Blossom continued. "She told me she's seen you into safe hands," he told May Ling. "That was all she ever wanted for you."

"That big man with her ... he's already left to return to his family. That just leaves the girls," he commented, a sly smirk to his lips.

"And here it really gets interesting," he added.

Squash Blossom laughed as if it was the best joke ever.

28

The insanely stupid plan to take over the Oklahoma Territory

MAY LING QUIETLY PONDERED THE eccentricities of her godmother Miss Berrigan. It was just like Miss Berrigan to travel halfway across the world to save May Ling, but then leave without a word, without even taking the time to see her. Mostly, it was sex that was the problem.

May Ling knew that for Miss Berrigan, the sex act didn't exist. The fact that Miss Berrigan had actually spent the night in a whorehouse, listening to May Ling and Junyur making love one room over, must have been acutely uncomfortable. May Ling was impressed Miss Berrigan had stayed as long as she had. Until both Junyur Wilde and his brother had guaranteed May Ling's safety. And Richard had killed Valentin.

Now her former guardian was seeing to her own safety. And comfort. Going back to her house full of cats most likely.

That was the way of things.

Squash Blossom left May Ling's side when he realized she was paying him no attention. He sat back on the couch, fluffing up his skirt while motioning for Junyur to join him. No longer half-naked, clothed only in women's bloomers, Squash Blossom had taken advantage of Marcus's raid on Miss Adelaide's clothes closets and chosen something wildly inappropriate for the young man he was.

Junyur gave him wide berth, taking his rightful place

beside May Ling. By the way Squash Blossom fingered the elaborately flowered material covering his legs, it must have been satin. Junyur threw his arm possessively over May Ling's shoulders, passively waiting for some explanations.

"I'll just talk louder, then," Squash Blossom said, sounding slightly piqued.

"In case you don't keep up with world events," he began, looking straight at Junyur, "China has been invaded by Western countries who then steal our land. Mostly Great Britain. But even the United States has been tempted," he added at Junyur's dismissive wave.

"The empress dowager has a long-term plan for the Oklahoma Territory that will even the score."

Junyur couldn't help the snort of amusement that escaped his lips. May Ling whacked him with her new fan, creating a reddened welt on his arm. Junyur rubbed at it, hoping that would lessen its sting.

May Ling raised her perfect eyebrows. "Quiet," she demanded. "Learn something!"

Junyur pressed his lips together and vowed to behave himself. No matter what idiocies anyone proposed. He hadn't liked hearing that commanding tone from May Ling, however. Never did cotton to being ordered around.

"Empress dowager sent Imperial Troops here to enter the Oklahoma Territory Land Race," Squash Blossom informed him.

Once more Junyur laughed.

"That won't do you any good."

His voice rose to a screech. The idea that Chinese citizens could join in the Oklahoma Territory Land Race was utter stupidity. Another snort of derision erupted from his lips.

May Ling struck Junyur again.

"Damn it!" he cried.

Briefly, the two of them slapped at each other in an attempt to possess the fan.

"You two! Stop it!"

But even Squash Blossom couldn't keep a grin off his face when he added, "You two need to leave your sexual foreplay for bedtime. Where'd you get that fan, girl? I need one."

May Ling and Junyur both glared at him.

Squash Blossom put his stern face back on and continued to educate the young cowboy from Texas. Junyur listened, but it was hard to keep a straight face. He was beginning to think that not only was something rotten in the state of Denmark, but the Oklahoma Territories as well. Like soured milk.

"We know it won't work for us the way it would work for you," Squash Blossom complained, at last sounding rattled. His face showed red. Despite Junyur's resolve to hear him out, Squash Blossom recognized the beginnings of derision in Junyur's eyes.

"We're smart," Squash Blossom said, trying to get through to Junyur. "We know the way to make it work from behind the scenes."

"Do tell," Junyur said, rolling his eyes. This was going to be good.

Squash Blossom noticed Junyur's disparagement, narrowing his own eyes in return. Then like good con men everywhere, he spat out the rest of his speech so fast Junyur couldn't understand him.

Junyur lost track several times, but what he had heard and understood beggared sanity. These people were clearly delusional.

He made Squash Blossom write it down, but it was so bizarre he never forgot it anyhow:

The Chinese women here will marry the empress dowager's soldiers. That is their purpose. Then as a team, the marrieds will pick one of the American men in that line you just saw. The Americans will run the land race with the hidden aid of their new Chinese dependents, if needed. In return for their lifetime work for the American, the deed to the land they win will be entailed for the descendants of the Chinese couple, who will forever remain with the townsmen's family. Forty years hence the land will change hands. Enforced by the Tong.

Junyur laughed long and heartily at their naïve expectations. And for once, he didn't care which of them he affronted. His face reddened with his explosive hilarity, finally leaving him with a coughing fit. If he'd been drinking anything, it would have been snorted out through his nose.

So many things could go wrong that he didn't take the time to count them. Junyur was left with the ridiculous scenario of every large ranch and farm having some sort of Chinese servant attached to it. Dressed like a coolie from a rice paddy, with a long braid, no less.

And even then, forty years from now no one would be able to enforce that kind of contract! Certainly, the Oklahoma Territory would be part of the United States by that time, which would make it doubly impossible.

When Junyur stopped laughing, he saw that neither May Ling nor Squash Blossom shared his humor.

"Not going to work," he quietly asserted, not understanding their almost identical concerned glances at him. It was as if he was the one who didn't understand the facts of life. What was he missing here?

"Tong will enforce," May Ling declared.

Junyur knew what the Tong was. Sort of like the gangs in New York City who were causing all sorts of political problems back east. "But nobody's going to—"

May Ling interrupted him with a flick of her fan. Junyur shut his mouth.

Squash Blossom gave him that look again.

"You don't understand the Tong," he said. "Forty years, a hundred years, it makes no difference to the Tong. What is written is what will happen. The British will learn that by and by, and so will the United States."

Junyur shrugged his shoulders. If they wanted to believe in fairy tales like this, so what. It wasn't his concern.

Let them run in the race. Let them work alongside

Americans the rest of their lives thinking the place would be theirs in time. It was no skin off his nose.

Junyur barely heard the continuing conversation between May Ling and Squash Blossom, but he did hear the end of it.

"As I told you," Squash Blossom continued, "Richard and I will stay. The girls from the cage have mostly chosen to follow the soldiers. Of the Miss Adelaide's residents, only Sara Beth will stay with you. One of the girls from the cage, also. Xi Chang."

"We go now," May Ling said, her tone curt. She wanted to get out of this room before she started crying again. She'd thought the girls from Miss Adelaide's might follow her down to Texas with Junyur. And they weren't going to. The land race held great sway, indeed.

"Right now," she ordered.

At least someone had their heads screwed on straight. Junyur was relieved that May Ling had rejected the prospect of marrying one of the Chinese soldiers. For a minute, he thought she might not.

The heady scent of jasmine perfume flowed off her borrowed top as she raised her arm and pointed the way out the door. Junyur inhaled deeply, wondering why he'd ever thought it was the tang of starch coming off her clothes.

Junyur was prepared to follow May Ling to the ends of the earth. It warmed his heart to see that she was just as prepared to put all her trust in him.

But evidently *right now* didn't mean the same thing to May Ling as it meant to Junyur. After Squash Blossom left, May Ling had quietly returned to her desk, where after fruitlessly searching for something in its drawers, she sat perched on the edge of her chair.

Her feet carelessly scuffed the rug in a mightily irritating way while Junyur stood frozen in the doorway. Fifteen minutes went by. If he heard much more of that *scritch, scritch, scritch* of shoes rasping against rug, he was going to yell.

The Cimarron Bride

To take his mind off May Ling's nervous fidgeting, Junyur planned out his future with May Ling. Then he planned out his future without May Ling. And even pondered the futures of Squash Blossom, Richard, Miss Berrigan and Mr. Shale.

Junyur wished everyone else would hurry up. Just leave everything behind and go. It was only May Ling and two other girls. How hard was that?

Finally, May Ling left him to his own devices, and by the time she was coming back down the stairs, he'd managed a tiny nap. One look at the new May Ling and he was bowled over.

No longer his China doll, May Ling was the very picture of a working cowpoke, but just a little bit too much on the feminine side of the scale to pass. She wore blue jeans, a blue cotton shirt that wasn't tucked in, and had boots on her feet.

She looked like a young girl dressed up for play. One whose parents had capriciously put her in the cowboy outfit instead of the princess dress.

Before Junyur had time to comment, two other Chinese women rushed down from the second floor on May Ling's heels, almost falling down the stairs. They caught themselves just in time to avoid crushing her.

Junyur heard May Ling hiss from clear across the room. He fully expected to see her use the fan on them, but she merely shrugged herself to her full height and gave them their instructions.

"Kitchen. Put food in baskets."

One young woman ran off. When she returned empty-handed, Junyur wasn't surprised. May Ling's establishment had been thoroughly torn apart by Valentin's men. They probably either ate or stole every bit of food they'd had.

May Ling didn't turn a hair, but proceeded to issue orders, in sequence.

"Stable. Pick out horses," she said.

The two women looked at each other for a second, and

then walked rapidly out the front door while May Ling was still talking. It took a while for Junyur to realize she was addressing him. May Ling in pants was mighty distracting.

"You. Mr. Wilde. Guns in pantry. Take them."

For just a second, Junyur swayed under the command in her voice and almost did as she directed without discussion. But he already had his shotgun and a pistol. He had no plans to carry any other weapons.

When he stopped, and when May Ling saw that he hadn't obeyed her, they turned to face each other and stood staring for a long time without talking.

Junyur gave up first. If she wanted him to sling a parcel of rifles over his horse, he'd comply. But the horse would sure hate it, and hate him as well.

"I'm going over there to get a horse for myself," he told her, still lustily eyeing her cowboy costume with dismay. It sure showed off her shapely curves. And she certainly didn't look like a boy.

And with that on his mind, Junyur escaped out the door and into the street where he stopped to take a deep breath.

May Ling in pants aroused him more than he'd ever admit. No sirree, she didn't look like a boy. But there was something in the idea of her shapely legs residing in the material that had probably housed masculine equipment only the day before that sent his blood racing.

Christ! He sure hoped she couldn't tell.

29
Getting safely out of there

JUNYUR REACHED THE STABLE WITHOUT incident, but inside was chaos. Unbridled horses roamed from open stall to open stall stealing each other's grain and kicking out in defense of their right to take it. The stallion in the back had cornered a mare in heat and mounted her while the two Chinese girls kept taking peeks and giggling behind their fans. Then they noticed Junyur watching them and scurried away.

It looked like the girls had initially tried catching suitable horses to saddle and ride, but they hadn't succeeded in corralling any. At least two horses were wandering around partially bridled. One kept tripping on the reins.

Junyur put his fingers to his lips and whistled as loud as he could.

The girls froze. As if by command, the horses milling around aimlessly in the open areas immediately headed for their stalls. The horses already in their stalls ignored him, as did the stallion and the mare. Junyur whistled again. Junyur grimaced as the stallion continued rutting. That pair had other things on their minds. Then he shrugged. He didn't want a stallion anyhow. Or a mare in heat.

Junyur eyed the horses who'd been eating the grain and hadn't stopped when he came in. They had survival instincts, he decided. It was those horses that they'd take.

"You," he commanded, pointing to the tallest of the girls. "You in the yellow shirt. Yes, you. Come over here and help me with this horse. This is going to be your horse if you can handle her. Come on!"

Reluctantly, the young woman approached, looking as if she'd flee the moment the horse looked up from the feeding pail, but at least she was making her way to them. Junyur caught the girl by the sleeve as she tiptoed into the stall and gently pushed her toward the horse.

The girl braced herself, her feet strongly dug into the straw-strewn dirt, but finally ended up at the horse's flank with her hands on the mare's side. Junyur winced, expecting some sort of tantrum, from the horse, from the girl, or maybe both at once. What happened instead surprised him.

The horse whinnied, then left the feed to nuzzle the girl's outstretched palm. The girl and the horse gazed into each other's eyes and, God help him, Junyur swore later that they fell in love or something.

"Put the bridle on her," he said. "Before she bolts."

A soft chuckle escaped the young woman's throat. Then she astonished him all over again. Used to May Ling's pidgin talk, he wasn't prepared for any of her girls to speak proper English.

"She won't bolt?" the girl asked excitedly, bouncing up on her toes beside the horse.

"She's my horse now, isn't she?" she declared, with a possessive hand placed delicately on the beast's flank.

And then with a beautiful smile tossed Junyur's way, she cooed, "Isn't she a beauty!" And on and on and on with the endearments until Junyur himself slipped the bridle onto the horse's head, then the saddle on the horse's back, then boosted the besotted girl onto the horse and told her to ride back to the whorehouse and wait. She waited for the other girl instead.

The other young woman stared agape, maybe jealous. It didn't take Junyur long, though, to realize it was the horse that had her lustful attention and, thank heavens, not him. He didn't need that sort of thing right now, but it got him thinking.

The girls seemed horse crazy. Would what had worked on one horse work on two more? Or even six more? Six would be just right. It would be greedy to take more than that.

So he paired the girl known as Xi Chang with a gelding who accepted the bridle and saddle with no fight whatsoever. He let the girl called Sara Beth stay with the horse she'd fallen in love with, a mare who tried biting his hand off but acted especially gentle with the girl. Love at first sight for the four of them.

Breaking their reverie, Junyur directed the young women. "Both of you, meet over at the whorehouse. Wait for me there, and keep those horses quiet."

Junyur nodded approval as the girls gingerly rode the horses out of the stable like he'd told them to. Soon they were out of his sight. He returned to the stalls to let the rest of the horses loose. All except for the two extra horses he'd need for May Ling and himself.

A palomino that caught Junyur's eye proved easy to catch, difficult to bridle, and impossible to saddle. Junyur finally gave up, settling for an inferior horse to ride and taking the palomino along as a pack animal.

Maybe after a hundred miles of tandem riding with the palomino carrying most of the load it would change its mind and become a more tractable animal.

With the girls gone back to the whorehouse with their horses, and May Ling packing up at Miss Adelaide's, Junyur was almost happy with his own horse situation. That only left Richard and Squash Blossom to think about.

It was only when Junyur heard the unabashedly carnal squeal of the stallion back in the big stall that it dawned on him—Jai Li and his brother Marcus were missing.

"Gone already," May Ling told him when he got himself, the two Chinese girls, and all the horses he could manage back to Miss Adelaide's.

"Gone? They couldn't have left, surely!" he protested.

"Gone," May Ling said a second time. "I followed. Your brother had horses. Around corner near cage. They rode off. Together."

"Marcus wouldn't do that," Junyur cried. But he could see it in his head just as clearly as if it was just now happening. He coughed to control the itchy, tingling, ready-to-burst-out-crying feeling he felt coming on. The loss of his big brother Marcus struck him in the gut.

The Marcus *he* knew planned things out. The Marcus that was *his* oldest brother never did anything without calculation. The Marcus *he* loved would never have left him behind, or would never have left without saying goodbye.

And yet he'd just done each and every one of those things. What had changed?

Junyur snorted. Why fool himself. Junyur knew what had changed. Junyur himself had changed—once he'd confronted the enigma that was May Ling.

Yet he'd never have expected it of level-headed Marcus. Evidently, Marcus had been felled like an ox by the creature currently calling herself Jai Li. God help him, he thought. Junyur would take a whore any day over the likes of Jai Li.

"We go now." May Ling shook his arm. Then she looked out the window.

When Junyur turned his attention to follow her gaze, it took him a moment to understand what he was seeing. These were all the girls who had chosen to follow the soldiers, or marry the townsmen, gathered in front of Miss Adelaide's with their meager possessions in tow. There were so many! Was it only Sara Beth and Xi Chang who were joining him and May Ling? Seemed so.

No one was coming out from any of the surrounding businesses to see the girls off. Or to stop them. It made the hair on the back of Junyur's neck stir, though, picturing the sort of men who were certainly watching them from concealment.

The Cimarron Bride

No one accosted Junyur as he went about the task of adjusting the horses' girths, estimating the stirrup lengths for each of the girls, and making sure each horse had a drink, but not too much, of water.

The girls from Miss Adelaide's marched quietly on their way out of town, headed for their own sort of adventure. No one said goodbye. From now on, they could take care of themselves. Junyur and his bunch were on their own, too.

That realization led to Junyur's next dilemma.

Wouldn't it be better for everyone concerned if he just took May Ling and her two companions to Oklahoma City, hire some reliable gunslinger to keep them safe, and get back in the land race like he'd intended?

They'd be fine, he figured. He was the one who'd probably break his neck when his horse stepped into a gopher hole and fell on him. Or the Indians would get him. Or he'd choke in one of those dust storms he'd been hearing about. Oklahoma sure had its share of possible calamities.

It took a lot of back and forth arguing with his conscience, but at last, Junyur decided to go with his gut. It was with some regret, and a lot of butterflies in his stomach, but finally Junyur had it straight in his head. Oklahoma City for May Ling, Xi Chang, and Sara Beth. And the Oklahoma land race for him. It was what May Ling had wanted for him. Or so she'd said.

No changing his mind this time. Nope. Not going to be diverted by pretty faces and helpless women into giving up his dream again, not that May Ling was helpless. The guilty turmoil racing through Junyur's head would go away soon enough. After all, he'd be getting all the women to safety before he left. And May Ling would wait for him to get back.

To Junyur's surprise, when he raised his head from altering saddle girths, May Ling and other girls were waiting on him to notice them. Good that he already had a speech ready. Decided to keep it to himself after looking down at the traumatized ladies in his care.

"Riders up," he told them instead, with May Ling looking uncertainly into his face.

Maybe she hadn't understood *riders up*.

"Ladies, get onto the horses and let's go," he said, trying really hard not to bark at them. Had he used small enough words? He guessed not, because no one had moved.

Suddenly angry with the whole bunch of them, but really feeling guilty, Junyur tied his own painted horse to the rail outside the whorehouse, and was at Xi Chang's side before she could squeal a protest.

"Have you ever ridden a horse any farther than from that barn over there?"

She shook her head, and he took it to mean *no*.

Xi Chang must have weighed about seventy pounds soaking wet. Junyur picked her up in his arms and tossed her to the back of the horse. He was surprised she didn't simply fly over the other side, but she caught the saddle horn in her hands and straddled the saddle like she was supposed to.

"Just hold onto it the whole time," he said. "I'll lead your horse until you get used to it."

The girl straightened up and gave him a blindingly happy smile that surprised him. Mischievously, he wondered if she'd be half as excited the next day when she wouldn't be able to walk straight due to saddle sores and the rigors of gripping the saddle so long.

30
Chinese women riding horses

THE OTHER CHINESE GIRL, THE one called Sara Beth, seemed more knowledgeable around horses. Junyur saw her offer her mount a sugar cube from her hands. While he was nodding in approval at her use of a bribe to keep the animal still, she'd boosted herself into the saddle and gathered the reins into her hands.

"Go help Xi Chang," Junyur told her. "Maybe you can teach her something."

Sara Beth snorted, which was a very unladylike noise coming from the delicate beauty atop the horse, but seemed to indicate negative feelings toward the other girl and her ability to learn horsemanship. Junyur felt she was right.

"Xi Chang," he yelled. "Always keep one of your hands gripping the saddle horn. Don't ever let go."

Unless you're falling off, he added to himself, hoping she'd have the good sense not to let herself get dragged under a horse. From what he'd seen of May Ling on a horse, she was in the same predicament. Didn't know one end of the animal from the other.

All of a sudden, Junyur was tired of all the drama. God damn it! He'd made up his mind to take them to Oklahoma City! Why did the thought of abandoning the women right here in Guthrie and proceeding on his own even cross his mind? That was cowardly. He'd do better forgetting about his ambitions to join the land race, and leisurely lead these ladies of the night into a safer environment down along the Texas border.

He'd often heard the phrase *have your cake and eat it too* from his oldest brother Marcus without ever understanding it. Just then he realized that the plan he was embarking on with the women, the one where he took them from Guthrie to Oklahoma City, tried to keep them safe but still left them there to join in the land race, was trying to *have his cake and eat it too.*

There was no way the ladies could win and he could also win at the same time. Something had to give. The women could be made safe, but he wouldn't be able to race. Or he could race and win the property he'd always dreamed of, and the women might be abused or killed while he tried.

Damn Marcus and that horrible witch Jai Li. Marcus could have guarded the ladies. Hell, Jai Li could have kept her former companions safe. Junyur hoped Marcus and his new wife were having a horrible time of it, and that Jai Li would make Marcus's life miserable from now on.

Obviously, Junyur wasn't going to leave his ladies in Guthrie. They were already on their way out of town. He'd have a little more time with them before he had to choose between Oklahoma City and the Texas border.

After a short time on the road, May Ling succeeded in surprising him with her horsemanship. She bounced hilariously in the saddle and had a heavy hand, but she also stayed in the saddle, even at a trot.

Junyur didn't allow a gallop until they'd passed clear out of sight of anyone in Guthrie. He talked to the girls as they rode, unsure they understood him, but it was better than talking to himself.

"May Ling, you need to unclench your hands. Hold them like you hold a, like a flower. You don't want to crush that flower in your hands, do you? Be more gentle."

She followed his instructions for a little while, then gradually reverted to her death grip. Finally, what he expected to happen, happened. She rode one of his former horses that he'd left for the whorehouse ladies the first time he was there. After enduring May Ling's rough handling for the first stage of their escape, Junyur's former horse finally had enough.

The mare stopped dead in her tracks, lowered her head all the way to the ground despite May Ling's desperate sawing, and tipped the girl right off. And then calmly walked away.

May Ling twisted on her way down and landed flat on her back. Junyur was sure she was just winded. He instructed the other two girls to take their horses and keep going for a moment. May Ling's mount followed.

To May Ling, Junyur said, "Learn your lesson there? Go gentle on a horse's mouth. And never think you've really got control. It'll hurt a horse to fight you off it, but the horse will always win if it puts its mind to it."

May Ling turned red in the face and scrambled to her feet.

"Come on," Junyur said, extending his arm. "Get on the back with me. We'll catch up, and you can apologize properly to the horse."

He'd expected her to laugh, or to object, or to scream at his suggestion, but she simply nodded and let him pull her up to ride behind him on his newly acquired horse. When they caught up to the other two, May Ling pulled at his sleeve until he eased her down to the ground.

Although she wore western clothes designed for young boys, she walked toward his former horse with the grace of a great lady. Junyur watched her stop in front of the horse and give it a short bow. Then she said a few things in Chinese and bowed again. She kept her head down and remained in place for more than five minutes before Junyur figured out she was waiting for some sort of response from the horse. She'd never get it, he thought.

May Ling seemed to come to the same conclusion for she reached out to take possession of the reins dangling down the horse's neck. The horse stayed still, but Junyur figured it was only tolerating the girl, and he kept waiting for the explosion he was sure would come. His bet was that May Ling would be able to get back on the horse, but that she'd get bucked right back off. Had happened to him plenty of times.

She surprised him, though. And the horse, too. It behaved like a well-trained riding horse, the first time Junyur had ever seen it do so.

May Ling managed to get herself back in the saddle without help from him. She looked so proud of herself Junyur didn't have the heart to scold her for her careless handling of the reins. It was as bad for the horse and rider relationship to handle the reins too gently as it was to handle them roughly. May Ling would learn, by and by, he thought.

After a few more moments, Junyur let Sara Beth and her horse take the lead, Xi Chang and her horse behind her. May Ling followed them. Junyur brought up the rear where he could keep an eye on his troupe. All through that first day, Junyur kept a steady but slow pace with plenty of rest stops for the horses and the women. The terrain was easy to cross. It was easy on the eyes as well.

As far as he could tell, no one followed them. And the further they rode, the closer the three women bunched together. Junyur could hear them talking among themselves, and sometimes their laughter floated back to him. May Ling seemed to be instructing the girls in some way, but whenever he got close enough to understand what she was saying, she either switched to Chinese or stopped talking.

Eventually, Junyur gave up trying to figure out what she was up to and let May Ling control her former employees. He kept a lookout for possible problems and made sure the horses weren't overworked.

While watching the charming and moderately arousing view of those three derrieres bouncing up and down and sometimes sideways in the saddles on the horses in front of him, Junyur felt his role change from daredevil adventurer to some sort of protector and surrogate family man. Even though it was whores and horses he was embracing with that term.

All plans to abandon his responsibilities vanished.

Junyur regretted losing his ambition, letting go of the land dream, and wondered what the hell he was going to do with three whores on his hands, but for the first time in months, he felt good about himself. The weather was pleasant and calming, the scenery soothed his soul, and getting the women and the horses to safety gave him an honorable purpose.

They rode and they ate and they slept and they talked. Then they were there. Purcell, Oklahoma. He'd diverted them from Oklahoma City without telling them.

Purcell was supposed to be their last resting place before encountering the Texas border. The sight that met their eyes as they topped the rise leading to town stopped them cold.

They were in a hell of a lot of trouble.

31

Land race fever and chaos

JUNYUR WASN'T LOOKING AT PURCELL proper. The town itself lay beyond the masses. As a backdrop. He was seeing the beginnings of the race crowd. At the outskirts of the small town, individuals and families camped in relative sanity on the side of the road, many more clustered far out in the fields. In some cases, they looked like tame picnickers. In others, a wild party. Closer to the settlement, it was as if giant ants swarmed a piece of meat.

Chaos.

Leaving the three women behind where a small rise hid them from sight, Junyur prodded his horse closer. Then closer. Then he stopped.

Even from a distance, Junyur saw hot-blooded and ambitious bullies shoving their inferiors to the side for a spot in whatever line had just formed. Women dressed as men pushed right back and got clobbered without mercy. And when some people were sneaking away from the town and walking out into the wilderness, their peers threw bottles and screamed at them for cheating.

This wasn't at all what Junyur had imagined for the Oklahoma Territory Land Run of 1895. Which he continued to call the land *race*.

Immediately sorry he'd kept them headed for Purcell, Junyur planned to rein in his group and begin turning them around. They needed to get out of the way before the race began. If they didn't, they'd be run down in the stampede and killed.

Junyur trotted his two horses away from the town violence post-haste. As soon as he'd crested back over the small hill, a sea of desperate people laden with possessions surged around him. This wasn't where he'd left his ladies.

Covered wagons, thoroughbred horses, mules, pup tents, packs of dogs, children, pigs, chickens, bison, and a few Indians, among other oddities. But overwhelming everything else, the stink of cooking. Junyur gagged, then rolled his eyes. "God help us," he whispered.

Junyur soon oriented himself. He'd raced down from the other direction. Within a few minutes, he was back with his charges.

He didn't feel he had time to explain himself. He expected May Ling and her ladies to follow his lead. With a slap on each horse's rump, Junyur got everyone in motion. Going back the way they'd come. Then he raced forward to check the route. Junyur didn't want another unpleasant surprise like what he'd run into while fleeing the town.

But turning around, giving up and running away—that was too easy. Junyur knew it from the hollow ache in his belly and the heaviness of his heart. They'd come too far to just quit. Right now, though, he saw no alternatives, so he prodded his horse on. After he'd ridden a ways back the way they'd come, he couldn't hear his companions clopping along behind him. Junyur turned to look.

May Ling and the two young women with her had not followed him. They'd remained at the ridge, watching the scene at the settlement that had scared him so much. The anger swelling up in Junyur's chest dissipated when he caught sight of Xi Chang. She sat in the saddle like a born rider, and chatted amicably with Sara Beth, as if nothing was amiss.

May Ling noticed Junyur watching them, and pointed

down at the town. She yelled back at him loudly enough for him to hear.

"Starting line!"

"Yeah, I see it, too." Junyur sidled up on her left side. "Let's go. There's too many people down there. I want you all to turn around and follow me."

Again, Junyur about-faced his horse. Again, Junyur took it for granted that the three women with him would follow his orders. He didn't feel he needed to monitor their movements. Only the truly desperate or the outright greedy would participate in that circus down there, and Junyur didn't figure that described any of his folks. Though if he really thought about it, he didn't know any of these people very well. Including May Ling.

Junyur got that squeamish feeling in his belly again. And he was right. For the second time, none of the women followed him. Junyur turned back, kicked his horse into a canter, and caught up to them. May Ling had actually started her group down to the settlement. Without him.

Junyur ran his horse into May Ling's and grabbed the reins away from her.

"Don't you understand? I want you all to come back. It's not safe down there."

May Ling pointed and repeated herself. "Starting line."

"Damn it! I know it's the starting line. What in the world is going on in your head? I can't run the race and keep you safe. I'd die if anything happened to you because of me. Pay attention, damn it."

Junyur thought if she said *starting line* one more time he'd grab that fan she was so adept at using as a weapon and bop her on top of the head with it. He knew it was the starting line. He'd dreamed of almost nothing else the past few years. Until he'd found May Ling.

May Ling looked put-upon, but she halted her horse and bleakly looked Junyur in the eyes. That's the only description he could come up with for the weary expression on her face.

It was as if she had the whole weight of the world on her shoulders. It scared him. May Ling belonged in a palace. Alongside someone who loved her.

"Pay attention." May Ling pointed all around them before saying, "This land yours if you race. We want you race. I keep safe. Maybe we run race, too."

"Oh, God, no!" Junyur cried.

He could just imagine May Ling and the others when the starting pistol went off. They'd likely be flung from their horses and trampled to death under their hooves. Or dragged back into captivity by opportunist whoremongers seeing they had no protection.

"By God, you won't," he yelled.

For a second, May Ling cringed before his voice. Then she straightened and put on the mask-like expression that meant she heard you but she wasn't going to pay any attention to your very good advice, your orders, or your prayers to God. Other than tie her up and hide her and her two girls somewhere for the duration of the race, there wasn't much he could do to stop her.

And for a second Junyur contemplated doing just that. But while thrashing it around in his mind, Junyur had to admit he wasn't in charge of these women. If May Ling and the others felt their fates lay down there in Purcell, while his lay in running the land race, it wasn't his role to deny them.

He'd just find another way to protect everyone.

May Ling misread the decision she saw in Junyur's face and started her companions into the throng barring their way into Purcell. Junyur followed, resigned to letting them go, but also keeping a close look-out for obvious villains, knowing full well that it was the innocent-seeming people that stabbed you in the back.

"Make way! Make way!" he hollered when the crowd surged into their path. And they drew back just enough to let May Ling and the rest pass before staring menacingly at their retreating backs.

Junyur twisted around the first time he felt animosity-laced eyes watching him. What he'd seen in that woman's face kept him from turning around the next time it happened. Naked hate, greed, envy, and mischief all radiated from the stranger's eyes. And caution, which he was glad to see.

Caution was good.

Seemed like lots of people didn't want any more people joining in the land race.

Once down in the streets of Purcell, Junyur felt he'd stepped into one of the Arabian nights stories Marcus had read to him as a boy. A Byzantine bazaar magically transported to the Oklahoma prairies met his eyes. The aroma of cooking meat filled his nostrils, as did the reek of human waste, animal dung, body odor, and cloyingly sweet perfumes meant to mask most of the rest of the scents. Men sat at tables selling everything you could imagine. Doors opened into buildings offering rooms for rent, baths for a price, sex, love, marriage ceremonies, coffins, burial services, and dog walking.

May Ling appeared unimpressed, which impressed Junyur.

Had she really seen it all, and at such a young age? Or did she just hide her reactions better than anyone he'd ever met?

Sara Beth reacted just the opposite. She touched everything within her reach from horseback and smelled what she could grab.

"That's licorice," Junyur told her just as the seller managed to get most of it back from her.

"Rish?" she queried. And before Junyur could correct her, she'd grabbed onto something else equally tasty. First an orange she'd plucked from a basket, smelled, and then threw back. Then an apple that she ate.

Junyur rode close into her and stopped her from stealing any more. "Against the law," he told her. "Must purchase. Buy. Give money for."

May Ling cut through all the communication problems

by swatting Sara Beth's hands with her damned fan. "Not now!" she told her.

Junyur wouldn't have taken that approach, but he had to admit it worked. He fished around in his pockets for the appropriate change and paid for each of the items Sara Beth had taken for her own. May Ling seemed to disapprove, however. She scowled at him and flicked the dreaded fan in his general direction.

Once past the market, they were on top of the starting line May Ling had seen from the hill. Junyur wanted to walk his horse over it. That would be the closest he'd get to participating in the land race, no matter what May Ling had assumed. He wanted that for himself, at least. It wasn't too much to ask.

A watchman guarding the line stopped him. "You'll get your turn. Stop messing up the chalk. And get those girls away from here. You want to start a riot?"

Junyur was tempted to cross the line, re-cross the line, double cross the line, step on the line until you couldn't see it even was a line, and even pull out his gun and shoot holes in the line. May Ling stood a little behind the watchman, observing him with sad eyes. Of course, it would be May Ling who understood him better than any other person alive.

Junyur sighed and gave it up. "Sorry, mister," he told the man eyeing him suspiciously. "You're right. I'll get my turn later."

May Ling gestured for him to follow her. Sara Beth led Xi Chang and her horse to Junyur, and forming a line abreast from one side of the street to the other, they calmly rode at a walk away from the starting line. Soon they were again overwhelmed by the chaos of the race entrants milling about for something to do.

Dust rose in the air from too many shoes scuffing the dirt. May Ling pulled a handkerchief up to cover her mouth and nose. Seeing that, Junyur did the same. He noticed right away that it cut the smell, too.

Soon they had more than bad smells bothering them.

Not that it did any good, but Junyur wished he'd never heard of the Oklahoma land race, and that May Ling had simply taken a slow boat from China, disembarked in Galveston, Texas, and—well, he wasn't going to let her marry Marcus, that was for sure.

Too bad they had the reality of the land race as their fate.

Brutal. Common. And hopeless.

It was only supposed to be Junyur here.

32
The safe haven of the Odessa Bath Club

JUNYUR WISHED HE COULD BLINDFOLD his women and spare them the sight of people defecating in the dark corners of the street. Of women baring their breasts in an effort to earn the money it would take to keep their families alive one more day in this place. And of both men and women whipping their mules and horses bloody because the poor animals couldn't walk one step more.

People cried out in humiliation, begged for the mercy of compassion, and screamed in anger at their stubborn animals. If Junyur and his women hadn't seen it, they'd have heard it anyway. He glanced at May Ling to see how she was holding up. She rode her horse through the crowd without looking to the left or right. Junyur noticed the two girls were emulating her the best they could, despite the jostling.

Junyur knew May Ling was right. They might be able to stop and help one or maybe two of these people, but there were thousands standing behind them they couldn't help. If he could just keep May Ling, Sara Beth, and Xi Chang safe ... If he could just get the horses fed and watered and bedded down comfortably ... If he could just forgive himself for putting them all in danger by bringing them into this heart of villainy built around the land race ...

Xi Chang's lips were stretched thin with a tight smile, as if she expected the worst of everyone. Sara Beth all but held her nose. May Ling pulled Junyur over into a side street behind the oddly-named Odessa Bath Club establishment advertising hot water for fifty cents a pail on a sign nailed on its front door.

"You," May Ling addressed Xi Chang. "And you, Sara Beth. Come here."

She soon had them bunched in a corner hidden from prying eyes. Xi Chang and Sara Beth slumped over their horses like tired and discouraged cowpokes who've reached the end of the trail and found themselves cheated out of their wages. Junyur didn't feel much better, but he was curious about May Ling and her plans. He sure hadn't come up with anything brilliant.

May Ling got the girls to be quiet, and then the three of them all turned to Junyur as if he had the answer to all their problems. May Ling seemed torn between amusement and despair. Junyur sighed heavily at the burden they'd apparently placed on him and took a good look at where they were.

In front of them stood the oddest building. In the shape of a wedge, it occupied a tiny space between a vacant plot covered from one end to the other with tents, and a hastily thrown-together banking facility. Tacked onto the door was a business card that said *Odessa Bath Club, members only*. Plus, the hastily scrawled advertisement for hot water.

What the hell was the Odessa Bath Club? Junyur had certainly paid for baths when he was away from home and needed one badly enough. But he'd never seen a club just for bathing.

He had the money. They certainly needed to get out of the way. If the place would only take in their horses as well, Junyur felt he'd rent them rooms or bathtubs or bathing pools, whatever it was the Odessa Bath Club offered, just to get them off the streets and away from the God-awful crush of people.

Junyur didn't dare leave the ladies outside and unattended, or the horses either. Surely, no one would willingly let him lead a horse into a business establishment that wasn't a stable, but Junyur was going to do it anyhow. To hell with the *members only* stipulation. He'd introduce the manager to Mr. Smith & Wesson if need be. The horses had to come inside.

When May Ling saw what he intended to do, she jumped down to the ground and pushed past him, stepping into the just-opened doorway first. She led her horse in behind her, even though it got skittish and neighed nervously and tried to back out on her. Junyur slapped it on the flanks hard enough for the others to hear the clap of flesh on flesh. The horse jumped forward and skidded on an elegant floor polished to within an inch of its life. Xi Chang and Sara Beth followed with caution. And brought their horses inside with them.

On entering with his own horse, Junyur didn't see any baths, or pools of water. As Sara Beth and Xi Chang and their horses crowded further into the establishment in front of him, Junyur stopped to gape at his surroundings. Right then a dapper man old enough to be his grandfather appeared. He took expert hold of May Ling's horse and calmed it down with his hands on its muzzle.

May Ling protested.

"Let me take care of him, my dear," the man said, refusing to let go.

Junyur saw his eyes wander over May Ling's form as if she were something for sale, but maybe he was just assessing her, he thought, since the man continued a respectful conversation.

"We've got room in the back gardens for your mounts, my friends. Let me get them settled for you, then we'll discuss the arrangements. No, my dear," he suddenly told Sara Beth, who'd taken a cup off a table and was sniffing its contents. "Put it back. Right now."

Sara Beth coughed, looked to Junyur for guidance and seeing none, relinquished the tea-cup. "Good tea," she said, as if that explained her attempted thievery. May Ling hid a nervous smile behind her fan, Xi Chang tittered nervously, and as May Ling looked poised to lecture the bunch of them on etiquette, Junyur stepped front and forward to prevent it.

"Sir," Junyur addressed the proprietor, if indeed this was he. "The crowds outside have frightened my small group of travelers. We came in," and here Junyur stopped, unsure if he'd offend the proprietor with his ignorance or not. "Sir, what's a bath club?"

The older man had stood patiently throughout Sara Beth's improprieties and now Junyur's explanation and questions, but now he stirred. He held up a hand to stop Junyur from continuing. "Thank you, young man," he said. "Ladies. Gentleman. As I said before, if you will give me time to care for your horses, then I'll return and make arrangements for you. Will you allow this?"

Junyur knew they might lose their horses to this stranger.

He felt more than a pang of anxiety about that possibility. The man looked a bit strange in his formal clothes, and sounded sinister with his clipped voice. But his eyes had been kind.

Junyur decided to take a chance on that account, and placed his horse's reins in the man's hands. May Ling followed his example; the two girls followed hers. Together they cautiously watched as the old man led the horses out of their sight.

They had a lot of time to ponder the folly of letting a stranger whisk their valuable horses away. The overdressed employee of the bathhouse did not return for quite a while.

By then the silence of the place combined with the unexpected heat had put the bunch of them to sleep. Junyur awoke first to find the man who'd welcomed them bending over May Ling like a vulture over its meal. Junyur immediately thought, *Valentin!*

But, of course, Valentin was dead.

To his further consternation, when Junyur yelled at him, his voice came out as a squeak. Junyur tried to cry "Stop!"

in a booming and authoritative manner, but what came out would have put a mouse to shame. It worked, though.

"We hope this little nap has refreshed your group," the old man said as he straightened from May Ling. To Junyur, it looked as if he'd been trying to steal her breath like a cat does with a baby. As if it was a perfectly normal human activity.

Junyur decided not to ignore the itch between his shoulder blades that told him something was very wrong here. No matter what the chaos was outside, this so called *bath club* had begun to feel like an oven to him. Like one of the witch's ovens in the fairy tales his mother used to read to him.

"May Ling," he called. "Wake up and get up. You, too, Xi Chang. Sara Beth! Get up!"

Then to the proprietor of the place, or its caretaker, Junyur barked, "We'd like our horses returned to us, please. It's time for us to leave. If we have time later, we'll take you up on that bath, but not this time."

May Ling didn't quibble. She saw what Junyur saw and acted. Out came her pistol in one hand and her famous little fan in the other, and she clapped the man on both of his ears with her impromptu weapons to great effect.

The old man howled. He fell to the floor holding his hands to his damaged ears, and continued squalling in such pain Junyur began to feel sorry about what he'd instigated.

After all, he hadn't done anything to them.

Yet.

This was the time to leave if they were going to leave. If they abandoned the horses, there'd be no trouble getting out of the bathhouse.

But then, while Junyur stood thinking through their options, the strange old man grabbed Junyur's ankles. It felt as if a skeleton had taken hold of him. He couldn't help himself. He looked down.

The man he saw hanging onto him stared piteously at Junyur, almost begging him for something. Like a dog expecting a kick. Feeling ashamed of himself, Junyur decided he owed it to the guy to listen to him.

The man at his feet began to laugh. "We've gotten off on the wrong foot, young man," he said, his voice a strident croak. "Miss. Help me up. I want to show you this place. Tomorrow the whole town is going to erupt in racing fever. You won't be safe anywhere. Except here. It's my job to offer such haven as I can."

33

Race. No race. What you want?

"DON'T TRUST HIM," XI CHANG advised with a breathy urgency, throwing out her hand to point directly to the stranger in their midst. And since she had never said much to Junyur before, he paid attention, pulling the injured proprietor of the place to his feet and giving his limp body a hearty shake. "He's not natural," she complained.

Before Junyur could ask her what she meant, the "unnatural" man snapped, abandoning his opossum's trick of playing dead, his voice taking on a bit of Xi Chang's feminine accent in his fury. "I'm just as natural as you are, honey. All that paint on your face! What's it hiding, I wonder."

Twin spots of red flared on Xi Chang's formerly pallid face. That really was some sort of paint on her cheeks and lips, Junyur realized. He'd wondered, but wasn't going to be crass enough to ask about it. May Ling resolved the problem with her fan. With it she slapped Xi Chang's shoulder and directed her to move more than an arm's length away.

"Tell more about race," May Ling ordered the livid man who beckoned them to move further inside. Junyur hurriedly took his own hands off him. What the owner of this place had intimated about the whole town going wild with the start of the race worried Junyur more than he wanted to let on. The spark of sexual interest he saw in the man's eyes worried him, too. But at least it was directed at him, and not one of the girls.

Junyur had originally pictured the land race as starting with everyone arranged equitably on a line. Advantage to none. Junyur had even seen the line. All of them had. He'd imagined that next some official would shoot a gun in the air and everyone in the race would spur their horses out into the wilderness to claim their land.

Junyur could see how accidents might happen, a wagon wheel falling off, a horse stumbling in a snake hole, but that's about as far as his imagination took him. Junyur really didn't appreciate the picture their new acquaintance seemed bound and determined to plant in their heads.

"They will pull you from your horse and shoot you," the little man told them. "They will steal your women from you, rape them in the middle of the street, and then trample them to death on their way out of town."

Turning his head to stare straight into Junyur's eyes, he continued his warning. "The whole populace left behind will go mad with bloodlust, shooting at riders as they pass under their windows, rounding up the stragglers and lynching them. I saw it last time. It's building up to a head as we speak. I can feel it in the air."

Sounded like something out of a fairy tale to May Ling. What she felt in the air was dust getting into the bathhouse from open windows somewhere.

May Ling tried not to show it, but Junyur's reaction to the man's description had her rattled. Could it be her casual dismissal of the proprietor's warnings was a mistake? She'd seen a mob in action once. Maybe it would be prudent to accept this strange man's offer of shelter, at least for a day or two until after the race.

May Ling tried to get Junyur's attention, but he seemed wrapped up in some memories of his own. Finally, his eyes sought hers. May Ling tried to look as unflappable and tranquil as possible. Maybe that would add to the calm.

She knew Junyur thought her impassive, and unreadable. That he'd never know what she felt about anything. That she'd remain a mystery to him no matter how intimate they became.

Often, that was advantageous to her, but it was an act.

It was admirable, too, how Xi Chang and Sara Beth had made a valiant effort to emulate her. Especially now. Only the trembling of their lips gave away their true emotional state.

They were scared to death. As was Junyur. As was May Ling herself. There were too many people in this too-small town of Purcell. It was a tinderbox waiting to be lit.

By now Junyur had backed completely away from the proprietor of this place. He took another look around. It was time to think about money. Junyur figured this hidey-hole would cost them all they had. It was certain that the bathhouse manager, or owner, whatever he was, would saddle them with an enormous bill when they decided to leave. But Junyur saw no safe alternative. Now that they were here, he'd not willingly return his ladies to the streets.

They'd just deal with the cost when it came due.

Junyur raised his voice so all of them could hear. "Then that's that," he said. "Mister, we will accept your offer. And I sure hope you have something other than bath-tubs and soaking pools in this place. I'd give a lot for a good mattress." To lighten the mood, Junyur manufactured a normal-enough chuckle. And grinned.

A subtle change came over the little man in the formal clothes. He straightened himself, he brushed his jacket and trousers clean, and then he nodded formally at each one of them in turn.

"Your safety is my only concern, my dears. And that of your horses," he added. Then peering angrily at the front door, he said, "I never want to see another of these races in my life. I'll do my best to arrange that you not be subjected to this one. There's no way to move the Club away from the starting line, but the walls are thick enough in places to keep the noise out."

While May Ling seemed to be gearing up to make some sort of statement, Junyur let his mouth drop open at the sinister implications of the strange man's promise that he'd *arrange that you not be subjected to this one.*

It almost sounded like a threat. Had the man just subtly warned him that he'd lock them all up? Out of earshot from the outside turmoil. Maybe Junyur was just worn out and imagining problems where there were none.

May Ling interrupted the proprietor's speech, and Junyur's sinister suspicions. "Stop," she ordered. "All of you. Mr. Wilde makes decision here." Then she raised her voice and looked straight at Junyur. "Race, no race. What you want?"

Junyur was amazed at her. And even angry. He'd made his choice already. Was giving up his dream to keep her safe.

Now May Ling was dangling the race back in his face, having realized, as he just had, that this *was* his opportunity to race. The women would be as safe as they could possibly be in this establishment.

With him or without him.

Junyur felt himself waffling. And he didn't want to waffle.

Yes, he wanted his own land. Wanted to get away from his brother's control, to own something he'd won for himself, to marry a woman not hand-picked by his family.

And here was that very woman, May Ling, saying, *Go!*

Once he'd successfully won his property, surely she'd still be here. She'd be here waiting for him, wouldn't she?

But just a little while back, there was that other time she'd told him *Go!* When he'd taken Jai Li away from the whorehouse instead of May Ling.

And see how that turned out!

Oh, hell! Waffle might as well be his middle name.

Make a decision and keep to it, Junyur ordered himself.

But wasn't there something wrong about plowing ahead in the middle of a mistake?

Waffle, waffle, waffle. Junyur hated that word with a passion. Marcus had saddled him with it long ago, having watched Junyur grow up. Having watched Junyur change his mind this way and back again as opportunities arose and circumstances changed.

Junyur wanted to hit someone.

He'd made his decision back out on the street by the starting line, and he meant to keep to it. The women needed his protection, and he needed the safety of the Odessa Bath Club. No more changing horses in mid-stream. This was it. No race. No leaving these people behind. And no hitting anyone. Not even the irritating proprietor of this strange place.

Junyur thought he'd faint, his heart raced so hard. He opened his eyes wide with a snap. Temptation was beginning to annoy him.

This particular race held no allure, not weighed against May Ling.

Let someone else claim the land.

Let the Chinese empress dowager throw her net wide with all those soldiers and hardworking young women she'd conscripted for her scheme.

Let them have the land Junyur would have claimed.

Thinking about that stupid "invasion" made Junyur grin. Wouldn't succeed. Not in a million years. Not in this country. Foreigners owning the land!

Looking into May Ling's eyes, "No race," Junyur told her. "We'll wait it out here where we're safe."

He couldn't tell if she was pleased or sad. But for himself, it was as if a particularly onerous burden had dropped from his shoulders.

Sara Beth burst into tears. "Then my horse won't have to die!" she said between sobs. "Horse safe, too."

What in the world did she think he was going to do to the horses, Junyur wondered. Eat them? Then he remembered

Big Jim's threateningly prophetic statements about him running his horses to death just to get the land.

"Horses safe, too," he reassured the girl. He heard Xi Chang stifle what sounded like soft crying over where she stood. The proprietor looked affronted and May Ling stoical.

Junyur tried to explain himself to the strange man. "The girls thought the race would kill the horses."

The proprietor interrupted with a snort. "Of course, it would. What sane man would think otherwise?"

Junyur's throat filled with a tight ache of guilt. He had never given it a thought. Even experienced enough with horses to know their limits, he'd never figured they'd die under him. He'd never considered the cut-throat nature of the race until Big Jim had thrown it into his face.

"That's settled then," the proprietor said. "Let me get you moved in. We don't want to be up front after it gets dark. I don't want anyone knowing you're here."

Again, May Ling stepped forward to do what was right, and again it left Junyur with that ache of guilt. "What your name?" she asked the strange man in the formal clothes.

Junyur thought the man stood straighter, almost perked up at evidence of May Ling's interest.

"My name is Michael Post," he told her. Then he looked at each of the rest of them in turn and repeated himself. "Michael Post. And I'm at your service."

"Kind of you ..." Junyur said before May Ling cut him off.

"Not kind. Smart. He only one here. Needs us to protect building. Show everything, Mr. Post." And then she took off into the recesses of the place without waiting to see if they'd follow.

Junyur watched Post as the man tried to decide what to say and what to do in the face of May Ling's accurate but stark judgment. Junyur gave him a few minutes to digest his new reality, then he finally shrugged at the man.

"Follow her," Junyur advised. "Makes it easier if you just do what she wants."

Xi Chang and Sara Beth both broke out into giggles, and then they skipped after May Ling as if they had no concerns at all for their safety. Junyur guessed allaying their fears about the horses might have falsely given them the impression that all would be well.

Post's stories about the previous land race frightened Junyur more than he wanted to admit.

Scared didn't even begin to describe what he was starting to feel about what was coming.

34
The secret of the pool

J UNYUR JUMPED A DAMNED FOOT in the air when Mr. Post clapped him on the shoulder in what Junyur belatedly interpreted as an attempt at male reassurance. It made his skin crawl.

But Post only wanted to begin his tour of the bathhouse.

This was no bathhouse. It was as if the dining room of an ornate mansion had been plucked up and dropped unharmed into the middle of a warehouse. With not a bath anywhere.

Already the amount of furniture pushed out of place and stacked waist-high near the entry made Junyur nervous. Looked like someone was getting ready for a siege. There had to be a back way out of here, but Junyur couldn't see it. The lighting was dim, and flickered. Gaslight? He sniffed the musty air. Yes, there was just the smallest scent of gas.

"Miss May Ling!" Post called out. "Wait up. Let us catch up to you."

Junyur snapped to attention. While he'd ruminated on the oddness of their refuge, May Ling had slipped past him and now was nowhere to be seen. Junyur heard her musical laughter coming from somewhere below, in the bowels of the building.

For a second or two, Junyur stood in wonder, unable to keep the smile off his face. The acoustics of this place were phenomenal. Junyur could hear the clock ticking on the wall opposite him, and Mr. Post's labored breathing at his neck, as well as May Ling's breathless giggles, but not the many panicked horses just outside the walls that he knew were there. He was about to ask about May Ling when their mysterious benefactor cut him off.

"Oh, dear," Post cried. "She's down at the pool," he announced in an excited voice. "Not the safest place to be. Let's get down there before she falls in."

Junyur figured that the area below stairs represented the bathhouse portion of this edifice and wondered how to get down there. He hadn't seen any stairs. Mr. Post walked away from Junyur to corral the other two girls just now returned from their own exploring, and soon had them bunched up near the front door. He gestured at Junyur to join them. Junyur ambled over while looking all around him in awe.

This "living room" was a bigger room than could reasonably be expected. In some societies, it could have doubled as a ballroom. Junyur could easily see fancily-dressed young women whirling around to the sound of a piano. And that was a piano right in front of him. Blocking his way, and right next to an inappropriately placed bed.

Junyur wondered if someone had abandoned both pieces of furniture in a futile effort to place them next to the wall with the rest of the tables and chairs and other junk. He gave Mr. Post a surreptitious glance. Surely, Post hadn't moved all those cabinets and bookcases and the desk all by himself. So where was the rest of his staff?

And was that horse dung on the floor, or something worse? Junyur bent down to investigate. One pinch of the gunk between his fingers answered all his questions. Definitely horse shit, and smelling to high heaven when brought to within inches of his nose.

After shaking it off him as best he could, Junyur looked way across the room for a back way out, expecting that was where their horses had gotten off to. He was just getting ready to ask about it when someone began pounding on the front door. A few seconds later, they'd resorted to a battering ram.

Three times they slammed it against the door with a mighty shrieking *wham*. The tortured hinges whined from the stress. It wouldn't be long before they gave way.

Mr. Post shrugged as if it were an everyday occurrence, having your door battered into kindling. Then trotted away without looking to see if anyone followed him. Indeed, he vanished so quickly, Junyur doubted his eyesight. One minute he was there, the next he was not.

Junyur didn't follow right away. The pounding on the door continued for several more minutes. Then someone took an axe to the heavy wood. The hinges did more than whine under this assault. They surrendered, clattering to the floor like discarded jewelry.

To Junyur's surprise, no one entered.

He didn't push his luck.

Junyur quickly changed his mind about how dangerous following Mr. Post would be. But he trod carefully. He found Mr. Post quite quickly. Or at least he heard him. In the middle of the floor—appearing abruptly as a broad span of steps going down, down, down—was a damned staircase. Junyur peered down over the rail and couldn't see the bottom to the stairs. Sara Beth and Xi Chang crowded behind Junyur and fluttered.

Junyur raised his voice so Post could hear. "Someone's broken down your door," he yelled down the staircase into the dark.

"Won't do them any good," Post cryptically called back up at him, not explaining a thing. "Come on down. Let's catch up to Miss May Ling before she gets too far away."

By the time Post finished talking, Junyur could tell he'd walked away from the stairwell.

Junyur eyed the steep staircase with suspicion. Who would put such a disfiguring structure in the middle of such a well-appointed room? Junyur could have easily fallen down it if he'd not been paying attention. He took a few steps down, then stopped. Xi Chang and Sara Beth bunched up behind him.

From far below, Mr. Post's chuckles spoke volumes about his frame of mind. Mad. Delusional. And probably their only hope of surviving the night.

Junyur feared falling down the stairs until Xi Chang pointed out the iron handrails. Between the sturdy support of the handrails and the two girls constantly tugging on his shirttails, Junyur descended. This was a very strange place. It was as if the ground floor and the basement belonged to two different buildings. Aboveground for the wealthy. Belowground for the rest of them.

The rest of them.

He had to laugh. Junyur was one of the wealthy himself. But he felt more at home with the whores and the shopkeepers. Always had.

When an alluring play of turquoise light caught Junyur's eye, he recognized it as the reflection from a pool, and hesitated no more. Maybe this really was a bathhouse. The peeling paint from the railings cut into his hands as he leveraged his way along.

Halfway down, when Junyur could still see into the ground floor room above his head, he stopped his descent and listened for the would-be intruders. All was still quiet. They obviously hadn't gotten in, and the person who mattered most to him was already below. He even heard splashing, which brought him the wildly inappropriate image of a naked May Ling floating face upward in a heated pool. Waiting for him.

Xi Chang and Sara Beth both pushed past. Junyur clung fiercely to the railings. By the time the girls got most of the way down the steps, Junyur had regained his balance. Mr. Post came back into view, looking embarrassed, and exasperated. Sara Beth went to the left of him and Xi Chang to the right.

Yep. Mr. Post was as mad as a wet hen.

"It's not my fault!" Junyur called down at him.

He hurriedly clambered down after the girls, careful not to trip over his own feet. To get his mind off his fantasy of a naked May Ling, Junyur concentrated on the disapproving proprietor of this place glaring up at him. Once Junyur stepped clear of the stairs, he let the impatient Mr. Post walk him to the edge of the pool where both of them peered down into its depths.

Their bizarre tour continued.

Junyur saw several areas in the pool where bubbles had formed and were floating to the surface. An underground spring fed this pool. For a moment he envisioned the whole room filling with water, but the place looked old. And there were no water marks on the walls. The spring must have another outlet. One that made this room safe for bathers.

This was the bathhouse area of this place all right. The doors Junyur spied along the sides must lead to dressing rooms and the like.

He turned around to find Post studying him. Evidently, he'd telegraphed his caution about the safety of the room to its owner.

"Yes," the old man told him. "The spring follows another course outside the boundaries of the building. But there's a way to divert it into here, if it ever came to that."

Junyur shivered. Just knowing it was possible to flood this room was scary. His blood ran cold. Drowning, especially drowning in an enclosed space and in the dark? It was a horrible fate. And not one he'd like for himself. Give him a good, clean bullet through the heart any day.

Post sidled up to Junyur and directed his attention to a more pleasant prospect. But evidently not to Mr. Post. The three women sheltering here with Junyur seemed mesmerized by the sight of the turquoise water and leaned dangerously out over the edge of the pool.

"It's a beautiful sight, Mr. Wilde, but we have more to

explore while we have the leisure. Would you ask them to come over here, please?"

And then Post squatted all the way down and cupped water from the pool in his hand, letting it slide out when he wiggled his fingers. "The color is remarkable, isn't it?" he commented. "Mr. Wilde. Please. Call the girls over."

Junyur felt like asking him why the hurry, but the sound upstairs of people milling around answered that question.

"God damn it, we're trapped down here!" Junyur balled his fists.

"I expected it, Mr. Wilde. Do not worry yourself," Post chided him. "We have a secret way out down here. The interlopers upstairs will most likely content themselves with the main room. Even if they come down to the pool, there's nothing to worry about. Very few members know about these hidden areas. We should be safe to move around, but get the women settled. Please."

Mr. Post looked like he'd had enough of Junyur's hesitation already, and given their circumstances, Junyur didn't blame him. From the corner of his eye, he could see the three women studying the walls, then the water in the pool. He turned his attention to the bathhouse proprietor.

"The people up there who have broken in? Is there any safe way to see what they've done?" Junyur asked.

"Safe enough," Post replied. "If you leave the women down here," and at May Ling's sudden glare, he added, "at least the two younger ones. But we have to be quiet, and we have to be careful."

"I both," May Ling declared, separating herself from her companions. "Come. I go with you."

"Not there, my dear," Post told May Ling who'd started back up the way they'd come.

She stopped at his command, turned, and stepped back to the pool's edge. Post spread his arms wide as if to say, *there it is*. To Junyur's surprise, May Ling ran her gaze over the wall opposite from where he'd told them to sit, and then quickly skipped past them to disappear into thin air. Junyur stepped back a pace and then peered worriedly after May Ling.

"It's a hidden door, my dear."

Post was talking to Junyur. Junyur didn't like the "my dear." He also didn't like that he couldn't find the exit when clearly it had been easy for May Ling.

Mr. Post looked condescending, but Junyur figured he deserved the man's contempt. After all, May Ling clearly had seen what was what, and Junyur hadn't.

As Mr. Post continued to smirk most annoyingly, Junyur followed May Ling's lead. He could barely see the door's impression, but she'd gone right to it. So, he prepared to join her.

Junyur sensed Mr. Post come up behind him, then felt his breath on the back of his neck. Hearing May Ling's feet cross a larger area of stone and then her trotting back to them was all that kept Junyur from smashing his fist into him.

Xi Chang had been right. Clearly, Mr. Post was unnatural. Junyur would have to be careful about being alone with the man from now on, but at least he was sure that Post would never lay a hand on any of the girls. Junyur hoped the rest of the male employees at this place shared Mr. Post's preferences. If indeed Post wasn't alone here like May Ling thought.

May Ling pattered back across the landing with a light step that made Junyur's soul sing. It was as if a lovely butterfly had taken human form and rushed to welcome them. "Come," she said. "You see this!"

And then, while Junyur savored his butterfly fantasy, a loud crash from above him made him jump. He almost stomped on May Ling's foot as they were violently thrown together.

Mr. Post pulled the both of them away from the hidden door and shut it behind him. "No time," he explained.

Quickly, he had both himself and Junyur at the bottom of the broad staircase leading to the main floor.

May Ling remained behind and in the shadows. Sara Beth and Xi Chang hugged the wall.

As Post and Junyur looked up, a stranger appeared at the head of the stairs, holding a lamp and demanding in a loud voice strongly laced with a Southern accent, "Who the hell are you bunch?"

Before anyone thought to answer, the lamp the stranger held in his hand flared up, momentarily blinding those looking directly at it. Junyur thought the man was going to throw it down the stairwell at them, so he raised his pistol to shoot the guy.

He stopped himself just in time to prevent an unforgivable tragedy.

35
Saving everyone else

"STOP RIGHT WHERE YOU ARE!" Junyur commanded the stranger at the top of the landing. And to his surprise, the man froze just as he'd told him to, probably never realizing how close to death he'd come.

All fear of falling forgotten, Junyur bounded up the steps. He pushed Mr. Post to one side, sparing a glance back down the staircase where May Ling had disappeared into the shadows.

Good girl. He hoped she had that pistol of hers at the ready. And would protect Sara Beth and Xi Chang.

"Give me the lamp," Junyur called out to the stranger, ascending the stairs once more. "That's right. Nice and slow."

Junyur relieved the interloper of the light and held it up so everyone could see him clearly. The man blinked repeatedly behind eyeglasses so thick they could have come from a medicine bottle. Junyur bet he couldn't see worth a lick without them.

"What gives you the right to break in? This is private property," Junyur demanded. His voice rang out louder than he'd intended and bounced off the walls of the stairwell like an echo.

The trespassing stranger collapsed to his knees, holding his arms out in supplication. Junyur retreated down a couple of steps. He didn't want the man touching him. Whether by accident or design, one push from him would send Junyur head first down the staircase.

"Please, mister," the man cried. "They stole our horses off our wagon. They dragged me and my wife and my two girls into the streets and took our provisions. And when the race started? Oh my God! Oh my God! They ran us over."

Junyur flinched. He could picture the scene all too well. But the man wasn't finished talking.

"My wife, she's hurt bad. Someone told us there was a doctor here. Are you a sawbones, mister? Please help. My family, they're back near the entrance to this place in some sort of reception room."

May Ling materialized quietly behind Junyur, joining him on the upper level. "I doctor," she announced.

Junyur's mouth dropped open in shock. She was no more a doctor than he was. She couldn't be. But as she climbed past him, he got a good look at her face. May Ling seemed totally serious.

"Show me the wife," she ordered. "You!" she commanded, "Mr. Wilde! Make the bath man bring clean towels. Sheets. Cloth."

Junyur didn't have a chance to reply. Mr. Post had finally reached the top level, coming out of his crouch halfway up the stairs to stumble the rest of the way. When he got to the stranger, Post stepped to one side of him and completed his ascent. In a trice, he disappeared from sight, hopefully going for the supplies May Ling requested.

May Ling bit her lip. She regretted not exploring the ground floor rooms earlier when she had the chance. She needed an infirmary, or at least a kitchen. And lots of willing hands.

From down by the pool, Sara Beth and Xi Chang called to her. "Coming up now, mistress. We help. Coming up!"

Shaking his head, Junyur attempted to interfere. He wanted *someone* to be safe. To stay in a safe place where he wouldn't have to worry about them. If it wasn't going to be May Ling, then it needed to be her two girls. He prepared to rush down a level and prevent them from risking their lives.

But as Junyur turned, stubbornly intent on getting his way, May Ling pulled him to a standstill by grabbing hold of his sleeve.

"No," she said.

And it stopped him dead.

He wondered why.

But it wasn't only him. Everyone was taking May Ling's orders.

Junyur didn't know why, but this slip of a girl commanded more respect from her people, and even from total strangers, than Junyur had ever gotten from the cowboys who worked his brother's ranch.

Even he found himself looking to her for answers.

And was letting her boss him around like they were married or something.

As Junyur watched, May Ling reached down to the distraught man on the landing and took his hand in both of hers.

"Be at peace," she quietly told him. "Mr. Wilde protects us. All will be well. We fix wife."

Junyur heard her every word and started to choke. From the back of his head to the tips of his toes his body exploded with electrical fireworks. Never before in his life had he been so overcome by emotion as this. In his mind's eye, purple and orange and red flowering water images succeeded each other at a dizzying speed.

If he hadn't been leaning on the railings, Junyur would have fallen to his knees, fainting like an overwhelmed girl. He managed one long gaze into May Ling's eyes before an unmanly groan of desperation escaped his lips.

She'd told everybody he'd keep them safe. That Junyur Wilde would save their lives. There was nothing to worry about as long as he was there.

Did she believe that herself, or was she simply pacifying her charges? And did it matter? He'd do what he could. May Ling wanted to get to the man's wife. Junyur could do that for her.

Junyur didn't want to touch the man, but it was easier getting him off the landing if he manhandled him out, than wooing him to safety with words. He used words, too.

"May Ling will help your wife," Junyur told him, plucking at his sleeve. "It's safe in this building." And he hoped that was true. "We'll get you and your family fixed up. Help me get them moved. Come on. Your wife needs help."

Sara Beth and Xi Chang proved themselves very useful in getting their unwelcome guest out of the stairwell and then back to the vestibule where everyone was most vulnerable to attack.

One look at the woman writhing on the floor told Junyur they'd have to stay here with her whether they wanted to or not. Moving her would kill her. She had broken bones sticking out of her skin. And a thin pool of blood underneath her.

Junyur gave scant attention to the open door, other than noting that someone had been irresponsibly lax at not blockading it. The noise from just outside irritated him. Mr. Post reappeared with some of his employees just as Junyur began to worry about anyone else forcing entry.

Mr. Post hadn't been quite alone in the bathhouse. Four well-muscled young men followed him to the door.

Junyur didn't believe the injured could be safely moved. And they needed to be moved.

Everyone passing from outside could see them. Anyone in need would surely stumble their way inside.

There were only so many people May Ling could help.

Post finally understood Junyur's concern about the door. He and his staff spent the next half hour trying to reinforce it. At last they gave up, taking guard duty positions and rigorously preventing anyone trying to enter.

The husband stopped his whimpering when May Ling squatted at his wife's head and smoothed her trembling brow. Junyur left off wondering about Mr. Post and what other surprises this "bathhouse" had in store for them when he heard May Ling singing to the injured woman as she applied a makeshift tourniquet.

One more surprise up her sleeve. She could sing like an angel.

"That's a compound fracture," Junyur told her. Immediately he wished he'd kept quiet, but he just had to blurt out his fear or start blubbering.

"I know," May Ling told him. "Get splints. Over there. Get splints."

Junyur's stomach roiled at the thought of setting that woman's broken bones. He'd seen it done once. He shuddered, remembering the carnage, and then found May Ling quietly watching him. Splints. He was supposed to cobble together something they could use as splints.

Junyur twisted his head before turning his body, suddenly seeing something that might be useful. An easel stood in the corner of the room displaying a portrait. If he could break it into pieces, May Ling might get the splints she needed.

The woman's husband followed his gaze, understood what Junyur had found, and leapt up. He ran across the room to the easel and pulled it apart by kicking and tearing it. Junyur watched as animal desperation convulsed the man's face and then slowly dissipated with his success.

"Over here, man," Junyur yelled. "Good job. Bring it over here so we can get to work on her."

Then, because he did have a smidgen of experience splinting compound fractures, Junyur took it on himself to push the screaming woman's leg as straight as it would go, repositioning the broken bone where it belonged. Going on to the other injury, Junyur breathed a prayer of thanks that the woman had fainted.

May Ling beamed her approval. Junyur had applied the correct leverage, and the woman's legs were as straight as they'd ever been.

"Make her drink," May Ling told him, coming up behind Junyur with a steaming cup of vile-smelling liquid that Sara

Beth had brought. Only briefly did he wonder where she got it. This place was proving itself a treasure trove of useful items. "Will control bleeding," May Ling explained. "From Mr. Post. Medicine cabinet," she added.

Sure, he told himself. Sure, it was. If the man could materialize a squad of helpers out of thin air, he probably had a well-stocked room full of medicines. Probably had a cooking stove, an ice box, and maybe one of those new-fangled devices called telephones as well.

Junyur kept his mind off the many oddities of the building they'd sought shelter in. And the man who ran it. Exasperated by May Ling's closeness to him, and his drifting concentration, Junyur snapped, "She's out like a campfire, May Ling. How do you expect me to get her to drink anything?"

"Use brain," she replied. Then she shoved a towel and the cup of tea at him. "Another patient at door," she said.

"Who?" he asked, agitated at the idea of even more people to care for. If Richard had still been with them, and Big Jim had still been alive, they'd have kept the hordes at bay. Junyur only had the girls Xi Chang and Sara Beth. He didn't think between the three of them, they could even brace the door shut. Not that it was much of a door by now.

"Who?" he repeated.

"More family. Victim of land race." May Ling gave Junyur a stern look and gnashed her teeth at him. He'd been about to reach out and touch the lock of her hair that had come loose. He snatched his hand away, afraid she'd really bite him. The teacup full of the medicine he was supposed to pour down the unconscious woman's throat trembled in his other hand.

"Right," he said. "I'll figure it out. Go and save someone else. Save the whole world while you're at it. We'll be safe enough."

He was talking to the air. May Ling evidently took him at his word and had left without further discussion. Junyur sighed. He had a rag in one hand and a teacup in the other. He wondered if the unconscious woman would suck on the rag if it tasted good. It seemed a logical leap of faith.

This bathhouse was more like a hotel than otherwise. And it was to their benefit that it was. There had to be a kitchen here somewhere. And in a kitchen, there had to be sugar.

Or maple syrup.

Or honey.

Turned out it was honey.

36
General May Ling

"Honey?" Sara Beth asked. She stood erect in front of Junyur with her arms piled high with towels. Behind her crowded Xi Chang with what looked like sheets hanging over her shoulders. "Sugar?" Sara Beth inquired.

Junyur shut his eyes in exhausted defeat. He really needed Mr. Post, whose place this was. He'd know the location of the kitchen and might even be familiar with the provisions. But Junyur hadn't seen hide nor hair of the man since May Ling had ordered him to procure sheets and towels and he'd come back to barricade the door instead.

Xi Chang was watching Junyur with a worried expression in her eyes. He shook himself alert. He was the one who was supposed to be protecting everyone here. If he let on how downtrodden he felt, how overwhelmed, he figured the gates would fall and the barbarians would raze the bathhouse.

Junyur never expected sixteen-year-old girls turned whores to take charge instead, to settle him gently in a chair and bring him blankets, to fix him tea while attending to the needs of the gravely injured woman May Ling had left in his care. He found himself shivering uncontrollably while gulping hot tea as if it were ambrosia. It hit his empty stomach with a gurgle that reverberated all the way up to his trembling lips.

"Not so fast," Xi Chang chided him while taking the cup

away and replacing it with another, equally hot. "Sip," she said. "Need my help?"

Junyur had tilted the cup straight back, aiming for his mouth and mostly succeeding in gulping half of it down before Xi Chang caught the lip of the cup and held it for him. "Slowly," she said, making him slurp the rest out of the saucer. "Slowly."

When Junyur next looked around him, Sara Beth had knelt by the man's injured wife and begun wrapping her like a cocoon. Or a mummy. Junyur strained forward, needing to reassure himself that his patient still breathed. Xi Chang pulled Junyur back and threw another blanket over him. Sara Beth nodded gravely to him and said, "To keep warm."

Delirious, Junyur thought she meant him. She was right, he thought, surprised. He was finally getting warm. It felt so good. He wanted to just close his eyes and drift off into dreams of May Ling. It took all his concentration to remember the injured woman Sara Beth had just mummified.

"Her?" he croaked. "Did she die?"

May Ling slid into his sight, walking slowly toward him, stopping every second or two to issue orders to the girls, to the woman's husband that Junyur hadn't even realized was in the room with them, and then to the injured woman herself who answered back.

"Not dead," Junyur whispered into the wool-lined blanket pillowing his cheek against his shoulder. The woman wasn't dead, thank God.

"Not dead," May Ling asserted as she crouched down to his level and looked him in the eyes. "Whiskey," she told him.

Junyur had no idea what she was talking about. Drifting off, finally feeling safe in the knowledge that May Ling was coordinating things for him, he jumped when she poked him in the chest.

"Use whiskey on towel with medicine. Trickle onto lips. Then trick them to swallow medicine." May Ling calmly checked off each of her fingers as she illustrated her instructions. Junyur still didn't know what was going on, but he could listen to her talk softly in his ear until the cows came home.

May Ling snorted, then laughed in his face. "Cows come home?" she said. "Horses, maybe. All safe. No worry. Horses safe. Girls safe. Strange man safe. Patients safe."

Damn. He'd said that aloud.

Junyur fell asleep with May Ling whispering about safes in his ear. He dreamed of robbing banks. When he awoke, he was no longer in the chair nor in the large room with the rest of the refugees. He sank into the soft mattress of a too-short bed that was half occupied by someone else.

When that someone else reached over to touch the waistband of his pants, he smelled the flowery perfume May Ling preferred and knew it was she who shared his bed. Sinking back into the warm covers, he let her do what she wanted with him. Couldn't have stopped her if he wanted, and he certainly didn't want to. The only thing he'd have asked for differently was enough light to see his partner.

He knew in his heart that this was May Ling. She had the curves the other girls lacked. She smelled of May Ling's perfume. She eschewed talking, and May Ling rarely chattered. But finally, after she'd fingered him and rubbed him and sucked on his fingers, on his lips, on his tongue, and then had taken him inside her, Junyur knew for sure. It was May Ling. Probably by light she'd be gone.

After exploding with more pleasure than any man had a right to, Junyur fell back into his woman's arms hoping to sleep with dreams of even more wonderful encounters. But May Ling unexpectedly dissolved into tears and broke his heart. Faint light from the emerging sunrise crept into the room from a window above them.

"I didn't mean to hurt you," he cautiously apologized.

Junyur planned to apologize some more, but now she was laughing! Then back to crying! May Ling turned her tear-stained face away from him, suddenly chortling into her hands, her shoulders heaving. Laughing again!

Bemused and helpless, not knowing what was going on, Junyur decided to enjoy the view. He'd gotten his wish at last: a naked May Ling in private with enough light he could actually see her. Like Jai Li, she had tattoos along the shoulder area. Unlike Jai Li, May Ling was shaped like a woman. Her breasts overfilled his hands when he cupped them, her waist invited his embrace, and the mysterious place between her legs just begged to be pummeled.

But she'd cried. Junyur took back the hand he'd been inching toward her inner thighs and pulled her into his arms for a hug instead. He half expected May Ling to continue her sexual explorations. She'd done it each time they'd been in bed together before. But this time she seemed content in being held.

Junyur fought back the disappointment he felt. She needed him in another way right now. He smoothed her hair out of her face and kissed her eyelids. Something disquieting surged through him at her sigh. He wished the bed were bigger. Then he'd have room to turn her around and cuddle her properly. They'd just have to make do with one of his legs thrown across hers, his arms circling her torso, and his chin poking into her shoulder blades.

May Ling murmured something, but Junyur couldn't understand it. She rose up on her elbows and projected her voice back at him. "Prepare for worse," she said. "Tonight. More patients tonight."

"All right," he said. "We'll get ready for them. But just a little more sleep. Just another hour ..."

They didn't get another hour. Junyur awoke to loud voices demanding help from out in the corridors and two girls separating him forcefully from May Ling in the bed.

"Mistress needed," Xi Chang explained as she lightly flicked water in May Ling's face. "Wake up. They want doctor. Wake up."

Sara Beth worked on getting Junyur dressed. Muzzy from too little sleep, Junyur passively allowed it. May Ling regained her alertness before he did. He watched with an air of proprietorship as the lush curves and hidden recesses of her body vanished into a shield of the boy's clothing she'd left Guthrie in.

Day two of their siege had just begun. Junyur needed to be out there on the ramparts. Post's four strongmen couldn't possibly keep everyone out.

Thank God, May Ling had left him with enough beautiful memories to last him the rest of his life.

But both of their lives would be long. This day would not be their last.

He'd make sure of it.

37
A decision made

Day two of their siege proved to be the last of it, as well.

Mr. Post reappeared dragging a pallet with every towel in the establishment hanging off it. May Ling immediately directed him to get her something else and then marched away to heal and comfort the many lost souls the bathhouse had accumulated in her absence.

Of course, she left Junyur behind to figure out a way to protect them all, to feed them all, to get everyone to safety before the madness of the race turned into the madness of disappointed participants returning with nothing to show for it.

When Junyur reappeared down in the vestibule where the newest refugees had bunched together, he noticed that the rioting seemed to have stopped outside.

May Ling busied herself holding hands, singing soft tunes to children, and replacing bloodied bandages for clean ones. Xi Chang followed May Ling around with scissors, thread, strips of sheeting, pails of water, and seemed content with her lot.

Junyur found Sara Beth making the rounds with food. His stomach growled. He hadn't yet eaten, but it was more important to check the streets for mayhem.

With no men the likes of Richard or the Patton father and son team to stop him, to help him, or to advise him, Junyur walked through the clumps of May Ling's refugees

The Cimarron Bride

to get to the front door. He opened it and stepped through its battered planks to the outside where he heard nothing to disquiet him.

Piles of broken furniture littered the storefronts. Junyur smelled the stink of whiskey and vomit and blood permeating the air like a miasma. The men he saw cleaning up the debris all had a certain hangdog look to them that made him figure they'd been responsible for some of the violence. That they also were repairing the damage gave him hope.

Junyur stepped back inside the bathhouse and began a count. He assumed that the people huddled together were family members, or friends, or at least had some attachment to each other.

Ten such clumps of frightened humanity slumbered or crouched along the walls and tumbled into the middle of the main room right near the front door. These were the last to have come into their haven. The ones from last night.

Junyur lost count three times, his mind back on the street and what might be happening there, and finally he just guessed that there might be seventy-five people in front of him.

The man, injured woman, and their children who had been their initial refugees remained close to the door. Just a little less than a hundred people congregated in a building Junyur suspected had to be much bigger than it seemed. Maybe after they'd rested and eaten and calmed down, he could persuade most of them to leave.

When he suggested this a short time later to May Ling, who was bracketed by Sara Beth on one side and Xi Chang on the other while making a vile-smelling herbal tea in a large pot on the stove, she whacked him with the spoon.

"They like you," she said. "Nowhere to go."

Everybody had to have come from somewhere. Just as Junyur had traveled up to Guthrie from Texas, everybody else here had worked their way into Oklahoma from somewhere else. If he could return home, though he didn't really want to, then they could, too.

But Junyur wasn't interested in returning home. May Ling might not take to the plainness of his brother's ranch, or to the ordinariness of that sort of life, and he'd decided once and for all that wherever May Ling went, he went. She just didn't know that yet.

Junyur's mind ran riot with all sorts of possibilities. If they did return to his brother's ranch, there'd be room for Xi Chang and for Sara Beth.

The girls would have to work, at least for a while, but he'd bet before long they'd be married and pregnant and happily keeping house for one of the many, many single men who had gravitated to the Texas-Oklahoma border in search of riches the past few years.

No one had to know they'd been whores. Or, if they did, Junyur already knew a handful of men who wouldn't care. And there was even one of them who'd probably think it was an asset.

If he took May Ling home with him, they'd have a safe and comfortable future working the ranch for his brother.

They might even be able to take in one of the families currently sheltering with them. Marcus was always complaining about the quality of cooks he'd hired and then fired and hired and fired. They needed horse wranglers who'd stay around for more than one season, too. The house could use an experienced gardener. No one had kept up the garden since their mother had died, but even so, Junyur relished the occasional lettuce leaf that struggled to the surface.

A whole world of possibilities opened up in Junyur's mind as he aided in May Ling's care and feeding of their refugees. But would she come with him when it was all over? And would she be happy so far away from luxuries? Did May Ling care for him at all? Or was it all simply a case of being thrown together during a crisis?

Junyur asked himself these and countless more fruitless

questions, fully aware he'd probably never know the answers. What would happen would happen.

Suddenly everything changed.

The remains of the bathhouse front door banged open as a horse shouldered its way inside, scattering the refugees who'd been closest.

"Greetings and felicitations, my people," cried the turncoat. The troublemaker. The renegade Princess Jai Li.

Jai Li perched jauntily astride the sweaty and exhausted mount she'd stolen from Junyur back at the Guthrie livery stable and addressed him specifically. "Mr. Wilde!" she yelled, meeting Junyur's eye just beyond the closest refugees clogging the entrance. "I've brought you your heart's desire!"

Junyur didn't care one bit what Jai Li might have brought him. He wanted to push his way to her and grab the horse's reins, but he had to be careful of the injured people all around. Jai Li had no right at all coming back into their lives spouting nonsense at him in stupid, stilted, flowery, British-sounding English!

At last he got close enough to spring at her. It was a miracle, but so far the horse hadn't injured anyone. Junyur whistled at it. The horse stopped and stood still like he'd trained it to.

Jai Li evaded his reach. Jumped to safety on the other side of the horse. "Whoa!" she cried, tripping her way from one bunch of the sick and injured to the other, holding a stick with a flag or something dangling at its top.

That flag-topped stick irritated Junyur so badly he wanted to take it and beat her with it. But his old horse nickered right then, and Junyur turned toward it instead.

Behind him, he heard Jai Li continue to flounder from one group of damaged people to the other. Junyur heard her yelling at him, but his attention was only for the horse now. This wheezing and ruined animal had been one of the horses he'd taken from Marcus to meet May Ling for the first time.

Junyur felt like crying. He remembered the warning he'd

gotten from Big Jim that if he took his horses into the land race he'd run them to death. It looked like Jai Li had done it for him. This horse was on its last legs.

Junyur had never put a horse down, and he couldn't do it now. There were children in this room who shouldn't be subjected to even more tragedy and violence. Junyur blocked out whatever Jai Li was screaming at him and began to lead the horse toward the back, where Mr. Post had said he'd sheltered the rest of the horses they'd come with.

Maybe a good mouth of hay, a long drink of water, and lots of rest could save this horse.

The miraculous Mr. Post came back from his duties for May Ling and stopped Junyur before he'd gotten halfway out of the room.

"Give the horse to me," Post said. Then, not waiting for compliance, the bathhouse owner deftly slid the reins from Junyur's hands and pulled the horse away from him. For a second, Junyur had the horrible premonition that Post would take the horse away and he'd never see it again. He tried grabbing the reins back, his eyes wild with deserved guilt. May Ling stopped him this time. He hadn't noticed her leave her patients.

"Horse has chance if you let go," she told him. "Let go."

Common sense told Junyur he needed an explanation, that he shouldn't trust her. What did a whore know about horses?

Suddenly Jai Li marched back over into their little circle and distracted him with her stick and flag.

May Ling distanced herself, and circumspectly took the horse with her.

Junyur saw her go as he rushed at Jai Li, intent on tackling her to the floor. But the princess easily evaded him. *Junyur* sprawled on the floor in a jumbled heap as Jai Li carelessly stood with her hands on her hips, looking at Junyur like a snake eyeing its next meal.

The horse, May Ling, and Mr. Post had all quietly left.

Junyur wanted to say something scathing. Or murderously clever and mean. He sure hadn't expected to see Jai Li again. Or at least, not so soon.

There were dozens of pain-wracked families huddled around him. As he stood back up to face her, Junyur's mind continued searching for the memorable thing to say.

But his mouth said, "Welcome home."

38

What the hell does that flag on a stick have to do with anything?

Jai Li faced down Junyur like the hellion she was, eyes ablaze with self-righteous anger. Junyur was lucky she only held a stick in her hands.

"What the hell do you think this is, you cretin!" she demanded of him, waving the damned stick back and forth in front of his face. "Look at me. Tell me! What's going on here?"

One by one, the battered inhabitants of the bathhouse scrambled away from Jai Li and her strident voice. Junyur suspected the children would follow Mr. Post as he and May Ling dragged his poor horse to its fate, if they hurried. Maybe if he just paid attention to Jai Li like she demanded he could get her straightened out and get back to what was important. Like figuring out how to survive!

Why the hell did she keep waving that little flag in his face?

Junyur held up his hands. "I see you," he told her, and then he decided to walk closer. After all, he could only die once. "What's that you're holding?"

Jai Li gave the stick a little shake, as if she was finally bored with it. Junyur glared daggers at her. Why didn't she just answer him and stop playing this game?

"How did you find us?" Junyur asked, deciding the stick wasn't that important after all. "And why are you back here? I thought you'd run off with my brother."

Marcus, Junyur suddenly thought. Where was Marcus? Had Jai Li abandoned his brother out in the wilderness? It would be just like her.

Junyur suddenly reached out to grab her, but she slipped away easily.

"Oh ye of little faith," she said, dancing from his grasp. Then she held the stick and began to lecture him. "This is a placement marker. A placement marker," she repeated, enunciating all three words very slowly as if he were deaf. Or stupid. "It belongs to the tract of land you now own in the Cimarron Strip. If you get it to the assayer's office in time and fill out the proper paperwork. You can thank us later."

Junyur dizzily tried to understand what she'd told him, giving up almost immediately. She had to be insane. Jai Li must have slipped into a delusional state. Or it was heat stroke. Junyur hadn't entered the land race. He'd chosen to stay behind with May Ling. He'd been protecting the people who'd gravitated to the bathhouse for safety. That placement marker didn't belong to him, so why was she teasing him with it?

Junyur shook his head to clear it of the fog rising up to confuse him. And what did she mean, *we?* "You mean Marcus?" he cried. "My brother is still with you?"

Jai Li laughed right up into his face, her sparkling black eyes lighting up her face. She almost looked beautiful, all animated as she was. "Marcus married me, you dolt," she reminded him, jumping back a pace at Junyur's annoyed expression, as if she expected a blow.

"You're going to have to start calling me Mrs. Wilde, my new brother-in-law."

Junyur's anger flared. That stupid scheme of hers! Marrying his brother to get the empress dowager of China off her back. Junyur set his jaw by grinding his teeth, and prepared to denounce Jai Li as the charlatan she was, but she surprised him once again.

"Whoa! Don't be so angry. Marcus is outside making sure no one sneaks up on you," she cried.

Junyur only heard the last statement. He took his hands off Jai Li's shoulders, and she fell back from him. All at once the puzzle clicked into place. Jai Li and Marcus had run the very last of the Oklahoma land races. His big brother Marcus *hadn't* abandoned him.

And from what Jai Li had said, as impossible as it sounded, Marcus and Jai Li had gone in Junyur's stead to claim land for *him*.

And now Marcus patrolled outside the bathhouse to keep Junyur and his group safe. Junyur twisted away from Jai Li and started for the door.

Jai Li sped after him and knocked his legs out from under him with one well-placed kick. He fell to all fours with a thump that caught everyone's attention.

"Will you please listen to me?" Jai Li yelled at him. "If you want the land we got for you, you're going to have to act before everyone else starts crawling back. Make up your damned mind. We thought you wanted the land!"

Christ, he was so tired. It would probably take a week of sound sleep before he could clear the cobwebs out of his head. Junyur thought it was to his credit that he didn't rise to the bait. He kept his mouth shut.

In a bit Junyur managed to stagger away from Jai Li, tripping over one sad bundle of someone's possessions before he came to a halt and took stock of himself. He stayed perfectly still and thought long and hard about the gift Jai Li and Marcus had just offered him.

Junyur was twenty-two and the youngest brother in the Wilde clan, owning nothing and lusting after the sort of life his brother Marcus had.

Wife, child, home, respect, and affluence.

Junyur's reality was dreaming about those things. He had little adventures on the side, but had never made any serious attempt at family life.

Of course, Junyur wanted the land they offered him. But at what cost? He hadn't won it for himself, she had. The princess had.

And if he'd learned anything about Jai Li in their short time together, it was that you could trust her as far as you could throw her. She'd betray anyone. She'd ride a horse into the ground to get what she wanted.

And Junyur no longer wanted to be a man who'd ride a horse to death.

Junyur wanted to be a man willing to save a building full of broken human beings. Someone worthy of a woman like May Ling.

The damaged and ill-repaired door in front of them opened with a clang and a cooling gust of wind that spread through the room. Junyur knew it was Marcus without even looking. Jai Li's excited shriek told him that, but the hair on the back of his neck bristled as well. And that had always been one of the warning signs that Marcus was going to slap him on the back of the neck and laugh his huge laugh. And Junyur was right about that just one more time.

Big brother Marcus Wilde strode through what remained of the Odessa Bath Club entrance acting like the hero of a penny-dreadful come to save the day, rescue the maiden, and punish the villain. But for once Junyur didn't see him that way.

Junyur had been the one to rescue the maiden. Richard and Squash Blossom had been the ones to punish the villain. And Mr. Post and May Ling, Xi Chang, Sara Beth, and Junyur himself had been the ones who'd saved the day.

The strangers sitting in relative safety on the floor and leaning against the walls watching the end of the story play out in front of them already had their heroes. Marcus Wilde and Jai Li were like the chorus in one of those Greek plays they made everyone watch once a year when the actors came around. The chorus that made everything clear to the audience so they could go home satisfied they'd understood the story.

Junyur flung his hand behind his neck too late. Again, Marcus slapped him familiarly on the same spot he always hit and then roared with laughter at Junyur's recoil.

"You've got to learn how to roll with the punches, boy," Marcus said. "And my God, who are all these people?"

The woman with the compound fracture who lay on a blanket farthest from the crowd was the first to respond. "We're his people, good sir."

Junyur twisted away from Marcus to look at the woman who'd spoken. She'd already fallen back onto the blanket, and her husband busied himself tucking her back into immobility. Junyur felt a slow fire building in his stomach that threatened to rise. He didn't know if it was a medical problem or his ego inflating. The pair thought of themselves as *his people*, did they?

Junyur sort of remembered that the man said he worked as a carpenter before the lure of the land race brought him and his family into Oklahoma. And the wife was a seamstress.

They had need of such people back on the family ranch along the Texas and Oklahoma border. Many a half-finished project waited for someone who knew how to hammer a nail properly. And clothes always needed mending, needed refitting.

The virgin territory in the Cimarron Strip where Marcus and Jai Li had grabbed this new land wouldn't support the injured woman and her husband.

But Marcus at his family ranch could.

The quiet rustling sound of pant legs against pant legs advanced toward Junyur. He knew without looking that May Ling had just re-entered the room. His soul sang. It was proving more and more difficult to hide his reaction to her. Both Marcus and Jai Li had their eyes riveted on him. Jai Li interpreted his flushed face response to May Ling correctly and snorted her amusement.

To Junyur's surprise, Marcus reined her in. He drew the five-foot-two hellion close in to him and shook his head in negation before bending down to kiss her gently and way too slowly for Junyur's comfort, and right on the mouth, too, out where everybody could see them.

She'd said they'd gotten married. Junyur guessed that they had.

Jai Li, his sister-in-law.

Junyur wasn't sure there was anything at all she liked about him.

And he'd sure liked her a hell of a lot better when she was a cowed, quiet, and mysterious girl whose only vice seemed to be gambling.

39
Making love in the pool

SEEING HIS BIG BROTHER AND the bane of his recent life, Jai Li, play kissy face in public embarrassed the hell out of Junyur Wilde, though he knew it shouldn't have. He didn't dare step back from them for fear of looking like a prune-faced prude, but he sure wanted to. Carefully, Junyur cast his eyes around for help, and found it instantly in May Ling.

Looking as demure as a debutante, so innocent and cool that butter wouldn't melt in her mouth, May Ling stepped forward to stand between Junyur and the objects of his discomfort. Secretly, she was amused at her lover's disgust, and a tiny bit put out at Jai Li's triumphant return. May Ling had spent the last two days saving people's lives. Jai Li had come back to them waving a little flag.

And showing off a new husband.

May Ling coughed softly to get their attention. Then repeated it more loudly when the couple ignored her. Junyur opened his mouth to object to her spitting on the floor to make her point (from experience he knew that was what she'd do next), but rolled his eyes upward as if to heaven. May Ling had a hard time repressing a grin. She changed her mind about spitting. But she wanted to.

Her grin abruptly became a belly laugh. Marcus and Jai Li sprang apart in surprise. The women bowed to one another, very formal and correct, as if they hadn't both just come out of a whorehouse, and then May Ling bowed to Marcus. Jai

Li did not bow to Junyur, and May Ling noticed him starting to work up a lather over the insult.

"Over here, brother," Marcus said, distancing himself even farther from Jai Li. "Tell me what's going on here. My bride seems to think you don't need our little present. How'd you get into such a mess?"

Junyur paid no attention to him. He kept his attention on May Ling. He saw tears on her cheeks. Momentarily confused, Junyur eventually understood. If Junyur went over to Marcus, May Ling thought she'd lose him to the land race one last time.

Willfully unconcerned with his brother's scrutiny, Junyur thought back on everything he'd recently learned about May Ling. Everything was starting to make sense. From the first time he'd met May Ling to this very moment, she'd been surrounded by some sort of made-up family she'd cobbled together. Most of them total strangers in some sort of distress.

Finally, he began to understand her.

She was a nurse.

She was a mother.

She was a general. The head of the family.

She needed people around her who relied on her. And no matter how much he worshipped her and wanted her for his own, and even if she married him, she'd always be happiest with a group around her.

And here was her group, ready-made by fate.

"Marcus," he said, sounding befuddled even to himself. Junyur stumbled away from his brother and toward May Ling, taking a few moments to fashion a speech. Marcus wanted to know what was going on. He'd tell him as much as he could, but Junyur was going to leave out some of the hard stuff, like May Ling being a prostitute, and just how horrible Jai Li actually was.

"Oh, hell," Junyur said, looking Marcus straight in the eyes and without a bit of apology in either his tone of voice or demeanor. "I changed my mind about the land race. When we got into town, our only goal was to stay out of everyone's way until it was over. All these people," he continued, waving his hands at the refugees huddled by the walls watching them and probably barely daring to breathe, "they didn't get out of the way in time. We're helping them. And I'm thinking of bringing them back to our ranch in Texas. All of them."

Marcus looked blankly at him. "Is that it?" he asked finally when Junyur had been staring aggressively back at him for several minutes. "Jai Li tells a different story. It's why we raced in your place and flagged the land for you."

A curse escaped Junyur's lips, but he wouldn't admit to any dismay or uncertainty over his new choice in life. He shrugged as if to say, *Believe me or believe her, I don't give a damn.*

Marcus returned shrug for shrug. He narrowed his eyes. "How about we register the claim for you anyhow?" he suggested. "In case you find out communal living doesn't suit you."

Junyur felt insulted. He didn't need an insurance policy to give him false security, he needed to gamble everything he had on May Ling.

If she'd accept him.

Junyur shot a glance her way. She smiled shyly back, giving nothing away.

Marcus slapped Junyur, on the back this time, instead of on the neck. Junyur saw it as a promotion into adult status.

"All right," Marcus told him. "We'll let someone else claim the land and start making alternate plans."

Marcus used his chin to point May Ling's way, then commented, "She's quite the little general, isn't she?"

"Yep," Junyur admitted. "Wouldn't have suited you at all."

Marcus chuckled. "No, she wouldn't. You're surprised I married the little one, aren't you?"

Junyur swallowed hard and tried to come up with a lie, but couldn't. "Marcus, she jumped off a moving train! She stole our only means of transportation and left us out in the wilderness. She's been nothing but trouble from the very beginning."

"She'll calm down with experience, Junyur. She's just so different from my boy's mother. My first wife. I need a woman that will keep me jumpin'. Someone exciting. Someone to tame."

Junyur couldn't help it, but at least he kept his immediate comment to himself. *So get another wild horse*, he thought. *Or a bobcat or something.*

"Show me around, Junyur. If we're going to take all these people back home with us, I need to know what they're going to need." But at an overloud sigh from May Ling, he changed his plan. "Ah, I guess we'll do it later. That's your woman telling you to come over. I'll just wait at the back for you."

May Ling rose from the middle of the supplicants at her feet, gestured in a gentle manner that dispersed most of them, and then waved Junyur over. To his surprise, she then took his hand and led him out of everyone's sight and into the stairwell that led to the pool.

"Down," she ordered him.

Junyur worried about someone walking over him, but if she wanted him down on his knees in front of her, he'd comply.

"No, down to pool," she told him as he steadied himself by grabbing the leather belt that was keeping her blue jeans from slipping off her hips.

Junyur really needed to talk with her, but if she wanted a swim, he'd swim with her. Or more accurately, wade in the water, since he didn't know how to swim.

But they really needed to talk about stuff. Did she know what he had planned for them? Would she agree to live with his family? Would she even want to marry him now?

All those questions raced through Junyur's mind as he descended one step and then another down to the deserted pool in the Odessa Bath Club. His head buzzed with pleasurable pulses that almost made him miss the last step. The slow swaying movements of May Ling's various curvy places had totally mesmerized him.

Junyur barely caught himself from falling. To prove his fervor, he impulsively gathered May Ling into his arms at the landing and ran with her to edge of the pool.

There he didn't dare let go of her, and May Ling didn't try to escape. With one hand always on her arm, Junyur slowly peeled the coarse cotton men's shirt from May Ling, leaving it on the tiles looking like a butterfly's discarded cocoon. Then he pulled her jeans from her legs.

"Yes," she said.

Oh, yes. Junyur hadn't looked at her thighs and the place between her thighs yet, but he ached to put his hands all over her. She stopped him with her lips at his chest.

"Marry you, yes," she said, opening his pants and leading him to the steps that went down into the pool. "And move injured peoples near your ranch, with jobs."

Had he actually asked her to marry him right then?

Junyur didn't remember. He couldn't concentrate, and he didn't know how *she* could while exploring him with her hands the way she was. For a split second the words *marry you* and *whore* crossed his mind at the same time, but the advice of his neighbor who had actually married an ex-prostitute surfaced and calmed his anxieties.

"Yes," Junyur told her, hoping May Ling realized he was both answering her about marriage, taking these people back to the Wilde ranch with them, and his mounting excitement about what she was doing with his private parts.

And then suddenly they were in the pool, in the water, and he had pushed her back to the edge where the water came up to his waist, and they happily did what they'd come down there to do.

May Ling scared him by fainting in his arms at one point, and while he apologized and apologized and promised to be gentler next time, she laughed and said, "No, harder. Harder."

40

Richard and Big Jim make great girl's names

THEY'D MADE LOVE.

Again.

It was when May Ling cried afterwards in his arms over the plight of the people drawn to their haven, that Junyur realized this was lovemaking and not merely lust. The curvy beauty floating at his side in the pool, this most remarkable woman he'd found for himself, this most beautiful woman in the world ...

Well, he loved her.

He didn't just lust after her, he loved her. And bit by bit he gathered his courage to show her just how much. Haltingly, he told her his plan.

"Marcus agrees this?" she asked, gazing brightly up at him.

"It's always been his greatest ambition, having all his family under one roof at the ranch," Junyur admitted ruefully, not willing to muddy the waters by telling her again about his own ambitions for himself. She'd heard it before, of course. Junyur sort of hoped she'd forgotten. Though with the evidence of the land race literally all around them, she'd be a nitwit not to remember his original plan.

May Ling absolutely noticed, but didn't let it show. She was both appalled at his willingness to go back home and live under an older brother's rule and blissfully happy that he'd understood her character and was adapting accordingly, as a good husband must.

She'd make it up to him. Maybe with lots of children.

The couple lounged around in the hot spring-warmed pool until their hands turned pruney, and still neither made an effort to leave. Junyur cradled May Ling carefully against the warmth of his torso, mightily in awe of the future they were projecting for themselves.

Not one, but two Chinese brides for the Wilde brothers.

No longer the lonely existence of three brothers and Marcus's motherless children struggling to make do on the Texas border. They were going to build a small town out of their ranch land.

And once the injured were made well and the strangers became friends, Junyur could see all sorts of relationships developing. Some of the girls who'd gone off with the soldiers and the men from the town might wander back their way—

"They saved your horse," May Ling whispered into his ear.

Junyur's mouth dropped open. He'd thought for sure Jai Li had murdered the steed. This was nothing less than a miracle, and if he had any say in Jai Li's activities once back in Texas, she'd never touch a horse again as long as she lived.

"You saved Jai Li, you know," he whispered, thinking that Jai Li, who'd started all this, would have been May Ling's primary concern.

"Yes," she responded. "But not others."

Junyur knew she meant the girls Valentin had put in the cages over the past year. And Big Jim.

"You saved about a hundred people upstairs," Junyur said, pointing up to the ground floor. "And Squash Blossom. Sara Beth. It wasn't your fault the soldiers arrived with their grand scheme to grab Oklahoma land for themselves. Those girls they took are probably all right."

"Couldn't save Big Jim."

"He gave his life to save yours, May Ling. Just like your job was to protect Jai Li, his was to protect you. And he succeeded. And Richard did you a big favor taking Valentin out. He'll be okay where he is."

"Say names again," May Ling demanded. It sounded to Junyur like she was crying, so he complied.

"Yes, their names were Richard and Big Jim," he replied.

"Name babies Richard, Big Jim."

It took a minute.

Talk about being nonplussed. But Junyur finally understood.

She meant *their* children. His and hers together. May Ling wanted to honor the men who'd cared for her by naming her sons Richard and Big Jim.

Junyur tried his best, but he couldn't suppress a chortle at the thought of one of his children being called Big Jim.

But he agreed without discussion.

"Do you have any girl names?" he asked. Then he didn't pay too much attention. It was time to get both of them out of the pool, find towels to dry off with and clothes to redress themselves in. He almost missed her reply.

"Richard. Big Jim," she said. Then before he could correct her, she added, "Girls Richard and Big Jim too."

It took a really big effort to keep from laughing, and they needed to get dressed before he got distracted again by her nakedness and decided they had the time for one more tryst in the pool, so he agreed with her.

"We'll name the girls Richard and Big Jim, too," he promised.

The odds were really slight that with three brothers in his family and no sisters at all there'd be any daughters for May Ling and him. Junyur couldn't let it bother him. Not right now. And not in the future, either.

There were hundreds of things to coordinate upstairs before they could begin the trek into Texas.

For one thing, they needed to know everyone's names and relationships. They needed horses and wagons and food and as many supplies as they could carry.

And they needed an understanding.

May Ling, Xi Chang, Sara Beth, and Jai Li were to be

acknowledged by the others as respectable women, and not as whores.

Marcus had to make himself known and tell everyone about the ranch and the area of Texas they were headed to.

And there was more. If they did everything Junyur had racing around in his head, and they really should, it would be weeks before anyone left this place.

But Junyur bet they'd just leave, and that it would be some time tonight, under cover of darkness and before any more race rejects stumbled into town.

When he said so to May Ling, she smiled her tired smile at him and agreed. There was such a thing as too many people.

"Come," she told him, leading him not back to the pool but into that recessed room she'd disappeared into when they'd first been shown the pool. A pile of towels and sheets in the corner made a comfortable place to settle for a moment or two of privacy.

"We marry now," May Ling said, slipping down into the nested softness of the sheets and towels he was nudging with his boots.

"Uh," he said. "Not exactly. Need preacher."

"No, we marry now. Ceremony later."

Who was he to argue with this woman, this nurse, this general, his everything?

With Marcus upstairs, everything would be safe.

With Jai Li upstairs with him, she wouldn't be down here bothering them.

If May Ling wanted to marry with him once more this night, (and how cute she called lovemaking marrying) or twice, or even three more times, Junyur was game to try.

The Wilde brothers had gotten a Cimarron bride apiece, that was for sure, but Junyur wagered Marcus had no idea what type of woman he'd lassoed.

Maybe he'd gift him a copy of Shakespeare's *The Taming of the Shrew* as a wedding present. Junyur remembered it having lots of helpful hints.

EPILOGUE
What happened to everyone else

MAY LING WAS SURPRISED ABOUT five years later to receive a letter from a man she'd never even met—Mike Shale. Seemed he wanted to catch her up on his circumstances.

Snug and happy in the Texas ranch near Sherman where she'd settled with Junyur Wilde as his wife, May Ling was intrigued.

Junyur had told her that Shale had been the first to try to claim the bounty on Jai Li's head. His action might have been the fallen domino that knocked all the rest out of order. If that was so, May Ling owed everything she now had to Mr. Shale's interference.

Shale wrote that he'd turned back from leaving Guthrie the very day Junyur and May Ling rode away, to ask the waitress at the Chinaman's teahouse to be his wife. May Ling remembered the girl. She'd been very pretty. Shale had convinced her to accompany him back to his place where they joined his sister and her family raising the huge horses Jai Li had told her about.

May Ling wanted one of those horses. Or better yet, two. She'd tell Junyur to get them some.

Seemed that Sheriff Patton and Deputy Patton had settled most honorably into their jobs once Valentin had been deposed. Shale wrote that Squash Blossom sang nothing but praise concerning the pair.

About Squash Blossom, Shale waxed poetic. He told May

Ling that Squash Blossom and May Ling's former bodyguard Richard had become partners. *In more ways than one*, he'd slyly added in the postscript. Squash Blossom had gone back to wearing women's clothes, Shale wrote.

May Ling's former bodyguard Richard had helped clean up Guthrie of the worst of Valentin's hired help, and between Squash Blossom and him, they'd turned Valentin's criminal empire into a legitimate and successful chain of pharmacies, among other businesses. They'd finally begun selling a new sort of drink called Coca-Cola® and were making a fortune off it, Shale added.

And strangely enough, Shale even knew what had happened after May Ling's godmother Miss Berrigan had disappeared.

After following May Ling and Jai Li from Peking to Oxford, and then to New York City, and then to Guthrie, Oklahoma, Miss Berrigan finally admitted to herself she had the soul of an explorer. After becoming besotted with the tales of another woman explorer, Gertrude Bell, she decided to emulate her.

When last Shale had heard from her, Miss Berrigan was traipsing around the Norwegian fjords with a young man named Amundsen.

May Ling answered Shale's letter with news of her own.

Sara Beth and Xi Chang had married and set up households of their own nearby. The strange man from the Odessa Bath Club had turned up unexpectedly after everyone had made homes for themselves. He didn't try opening another bathhouse, however. He was in charge of all the horses.

May Ling made another note to ask Junyur about getting some of Shale's horses for their stock.

And finally, she wrote him, just as she'd vowed, May Ling and Junyur had named their first two children Big Jim and Richard.

The older of their girls objected, eventually, and the

compromise of Jaime, which Junyur assured everyone was a variation of Jim, was accepted.

The younger girl still answered to Richard, for the time being. May Ling didn't appreciate Jai Li's suggestions, which had been *Coeur de Lion, Simba, Sabor* and all manner of other nonsense, and told her in no uncertain terms to stop agitating her daughter about her perfectly good name. She'd let Richard pick another name for herself by and by.

May Ling didn't want to go into Jai Li and Marcus's problems with Mr. Shale, so she only wrote that they were doing well, and that Jai Li had started a school teaching kung fu.

What she left out was that Marcus and Jai Li fought like cats and dogs, and that at one point the princess had run off with an itinerant old Shaolin priest and master of kung fu who had wandered into Texas.

Jai Li had quickly returned, much chastened by her adventures, and after Marcus set her up as a kung fu instructor, seemed quite happy with her life.

THE END

AUTHOR'S NOTE:

Don't expect to find a wedge-shaped, historic old bathhouse in Purcell, Oklahoma. Or mention of an 1895 whorehouse in Guthrie populated by young Chinese women.

The Oklahoma land races of the late 1800's were real. Oklahoma City, Guthrie, and Purcell are real towns, and were at the time of *The Cimarron Bride*. And there really was a empress dowager of China ruling in this time period. How I depicted them is fiction, just like it's stated in the disclaimer at the beginning of the book.

I made it all up. The details, the settings, the characters, the various nefarious plots, and the chalk line. I wanted a chalk line, so I put one in.

I took another liberty in changing the historic Oklahoma Land Run (or Land Rush) into the Land Race. It made a lot more sense in both the narrative and dialog for Junyur to *race* rather than *run*.

Hope you enjoyed *The Cimarron Bride*.

ABOUT THE AUTHOR

Genre writer Gretchen Rix was born in North Carolina many, many years ago, but got to Texas as soon as she could. She now resides in Lockhart, a small town near Austin that is the official BBQ capital of Texas. Her current wish list is for a Schlotzsky's or Taco Cabana to set up shop in town. (News flash—we just got a Schlotzsky's).

At one time her favorite books were TARZAN OF THE APES and THE BLACK STALLION. By now, all the books by Terry Pratchett and Dick Francis have joined the list. Plus a lot more. She still loves STAR TREK.

She's been writing since she was ten (inspired by Jo of LITTLE WOMEN), and has been publishing since 2010. Her books range from the sweet, romantic comedy of THE COWBOY'S BABY series to the humorous mystery series beginning with TALKING TO THE DEAD GUYS, and even to the action-adventure of THE SAFARI BRIDE, ARROYO, and THE GOODALL MUTINY.

She loves reading series books. She loves writing them too.

Although she has seldom written poetry, she does write short stories from time to time. She loves movies and television, has vowed she'll never write a screenplay, and enjoys long walks through the neighborhood with the dog. (And without the dog.) The cats weren't so easy to walk, so they stay inside at home.

OTHER BOOKS BY THIS AUTHOR

THE SAFARI BRIDE
THE COWBOY'S BABY
THE COWBOY'S BABY GOES TO HEAVEN

TALKING TO THE DEAD GUYS
TEA WITH A DEAD GAL
BABY SINGS THE BOOS

ARROYO

TWISTED RIXTER
ILL MET BY MOONLIGHT

THE GOODALL MUTINY
THE GOODALL MANIFEST
THE GOODALL MARAUDERS